CASTLE GARAC

The son of a distinguished surgeon, Nicholas Monsarrat was born in Liverpool in 1910 and was educated at Winchester and Trinity College, Cambridge. His first book to attract attention was the largely autobiographical *This Is the Schoolroom*, published in 1939. On the outbreak of war he joined the RNVR, serving mainly with corvettes: his wartime experiences are vividly described in *The Three Corvettes* and *Depends What You Mean by Love*. In 1946 he became a director of the UK Information Service in Johannesburg and subsequently in Ottawa. His most famous book, *The Cruel Sea*, published in 1951, is one of the most successful stories of all time and was made into a film starring Jack Hawkins. Other famous novels include: *The Tribe that Lost its Head* and its sequel, *Richer than All his Tribe*, *The Story of Esther Costello*, *The White Rajah* and *The Pillow Fight*. Monsarrat lives with his wife, Ann, in Malta.

CASTLE GARAC

NICHOLAS MONSARRAT

UNABRIDGED

PAN BOOKS LTD : LONDON

First published 1955 by Alfred A. Knopf, Inc., New York.
First British edition published 1968 by Pan Books Ltd.,
33 Tothill Street, London, SW1

ISBN 0 330 02001 3

2nd Printing 1973

Printed in Great Britain by
Cox & Wyman Ltd., London, Reading and Fakenham

As Thomas Welles approached the newspaper kiosk, he slowed down to a saunter. He was not buying a paper today, but he would walk slowly enough to read the headlines as he passed by.

VISHINSKY DEAD. What difference would that make, if any? he wondered. A smart man, Vishinsky, and clever. If he had only been a hundred-per-cent American, now, or an Englishman with an old school tie, the diplomatic history of the last few years might have been rather different.

The beady-eyed old woman huddled behind her newspapers stared at him coldly, a scarf around her head and knotted under her chin so tightly it almost seemed as though it were for the purpose of attaching her lower jaw to her gnarled, weather-beaten old face. It was obvious that she resented this rather seedily dressed young American who loitered in front of her kiosk every morning filching news from the papers, the sale of which provided her with a living.

MARILYN. She seemed to have recovered completely from her recent operation, and Joe DiMaggio was reported to be more or less on hand, friendly like. Tom Welles chuckled to himself. That was baseball for you.

He wandered down the narrow street, skirting the crowds of vociferous housewives doing their morning shopping, dodging coveys of bicycles as he had to step off the pavement into the street itself, until he reached the post office.

There was a queue in front of the Poste-Restante wicket. An old man with a long, drooping grey moustache, obviously a fisherman up from the harbour. A swarthy hulk of a French sailor so restless that his feet seemed to be almost dancing, with the bright, gay pom-pom on his cap dancing too. A rouged street girl, white and haggard, with a shawl thrown over her flimsy evening gown; she was obviously on her way home after a hard night's work.

The sailor standing first in line was handed a letter and two cards. The old man and the girl left empty-handed. At the grilled wicket Tom felt the tension growing just as it always had every week-day morning for the last two weeks.

'Thomas Welles,' he said slowly and clearly. He pronounced the *Thomas* as the French did, *Tomas*. The old clerk turned to the pigeonholes behind him and withdrew a handful of letters. Even with his thick glasses he seemed to be having trouble with the names and addresses. Tom waited there impatiently. It was almost as though the clerk were reading not only names but addresses. Finally he was through.

'*Rien aujourd'hui, monsieur.*'

'Jam yesterday, jam tomorrow, but never jam today!'

Tom shrugged. He made his way out into the clear, crisp morning air. It would be hours before it would warm up even under the hot Mediterranean sun.

He stood there irresolutely. If he went into one of the little bistros in the city he could save ten francs or better on his morning coffee. On the other hand, if he walked down to the café on the Promenade des Anglais he would be able to drink the coffee, and there would probably be a newspaper lying about that he could read. In his mind he tossed a coin and called heads. The coin came heads. That was the advantage of tossing a coin with your mind instead of with your hand. It always landed as you wanted it to land. He would breakfast on the Promenade des Anglais. He sauntered on – winding his way through the business section, down toward the harbour and the beach.

At this hour of the morning the Promenade des Anglais was almost deserted except for a few children under the supervision of their black-garbed nurses and the usual collection of elderly men exercising their wives' dogs. Ahead of him loomed the glistening white Negresco, but Tom stopped before he reached the sector of the *Grands Hôtels Européens* and entered a relatively modest café.

There was only one table occupied. Tom stared. He did not know the man seated there alone. What interested him was the table, bearing not only its steaming coffee, but a basket of crisp, round croissants, the sweet sugar bun resting regally on its own plate, and the curled wafers of pale-yellow fresh butter, the jar of honey, and even hothouse grapes.

God, he was hungry!

Almost automatically Tom seated himself at a table close by where he would be able at least to sniff at his neighbour's breakfast. And when the waiter appeared he ordered a *café crème* in a grim voice, his eyes never leaving the near-by table.

Something of a puzzle, this young American, the waiter thought as he shuffled away to fill Tom's order. A good face, the American had, with alert eyes. The tweed suit was well cut, but it was old and threadbare. He had noticed the American before. His shirts were clean but not well laundered, almost as though he had washed them himself. And he kept pulling down the sleeves of his coat as though trying to conceal the fact that the cuffs of his shirt had no cuff links, and were fastened with safety pins. That would be the result of a visit to the Mont-de-Piété. The first few times the American had come to the café he had smoked, but recently no. And of late he had ordered only coffee, never a roll or a croissant or an egg. Down on his luck, no doubt, but Nice was no place for even an American down on his luck. If one lost everything gambling at the Casino, one should go away, decently. It was too bad that this one frequented the café. Shabby clothes like that were not good for business. The Promenade des Anglais was for the prosperous and the rich, and, besides, this young American's recent tips were not as generous as they had been a few weeks ago. Well, one could not throw him out as long as he paid, so one might as well serve the coffee. There would be only two lumps of sugar with the coffee today. The American was given to extravagance with the sugar.

With the return of the waiter to his table, Tom reluctantly drew his eyes away from where they had been feasting. Silently the waiter filled one third of his cup with the almost black chicory coffee. Then the pot of milk hovered over the cup and a stream of steaming white milk transformed what seemed to be a deadly brew into a fragrant, almost golden-brown concoction.

'Thank you.'

'*Service, monsieur.*'

'Have you an American or an English paper?' Tom asked. 'Perhaps a *Paris Herald-Tribune*?'

'*Je ne comprends pas,*' the waiter muttered.

The devil you don't, Tom thought grimly. You probably speak better English than I do. Perhaps we're becoming *persona non grata* in this joint.

Absently he dropped the two lumps of sugar into his coffee and began to stir. His eyes crept back to the food on the near-by table and then he looked at the man. He was eating slowly, rather indifferently, as he studied the local paper. He had the air of one accustomed to good living and plenty of money. His clothes had been cut either in London or in Rome, and they had cost a pretty penny at that. He was perhaps forty – sleek, sophisticated, with a face in which boldness, intelligence, and a kind of amused cynicism were equally mingled.

Why didn't the bastard eat, with all that food there in front of him? Wasn't he hungry? He was just licking at things! Had he ever known what it was to be hungry? Certainly not, or he wouldn't be behaving so outrageously. That big brown roll, for instance. It didn't look as appetizing as the croissants, but it was bigger and would be more filling – probably 150 or 200 calories in that roll – perhaps more. He had never thought much about calories until recently, but now he was becoming acutely aware of calories. *Petits pains,* they called those rolls. *Petit,* indeed! It was enormous! Just one of those rolls would do him nicely for a few hours.

His neighbour took out a gold cigarette case and selected an expensive cigarette. He examined it carefully. Apparently there was some slight imperfection, for he tossed the cigarette on the table casually and took another from the case. He lit the cigarette, and the fragrant, rich aroma of an expensive Turkish blend drifted over to Tom's twitching nostrils.

With a sigh Tom Welles turned back to his own coffee and slowly began spooning it out of the cup. One did not *drink* the coffee nowadays. One spooned it out slowly. That way it lasted longer.

Somewhere from the back of the café he heard the shrill ring of a telephone, and then the waiter's voice: '*Ne coupez pas, madame.*' A moment later he was shuffling over to the man at the near-by table.

'Monsieur Ehrenhardt?' the waiter asked.

'*Oui.*'

'*Le téléphone, monsieur.*'

The man dropped his paper and rose. He followed the waiter to the back of the café and around a corner.

Tom was alone. As if under a spell, he stared at the deserted food on the next table. He would be able to reach that beautiful brown roll by hardly rising from his chair. Those rolls and croissants had been carefully counted, of course, but that spendthrift, who was now chatting on the telephone, undoubtedly with his young, beautiful, red-haired, green-eyed mistress, was not the sort who would notice that he had been charged for an extra roll when he paid his bill. The cigarette he had discarded so carelessly was still lying there on the table, too.

Hastily Tom looked around. Yes, he was alone. He could still hear the man at the telephone, and the waiter had not reappeared. The temptation seemed irresistible. Should he or shouldn't he? He felt his heart beating as though he were contemplating a serious crime, such as robbing a bank or holding up a train. He would have to make up his mind quickly. In a moment the man would return or the waiter would appear and it would be too late.

Quickly he arose from his chair, seized the *petit pain*, and shoved it down deep into the side pocket of his tweed jacket. His hand hovered for an instant over the Turkish cigarette. He snatched that up too, and then he was back at his own table slowly spooning out his coffee.

God, he was just in time! Behind him, he could hear that bloke walking slowly back across the floor towards his table.

Tom's neighbour seated himself slowly. He did not pick up his newspaper again. Without raising his eyes, Tom knew instinctively that the man was studying him. There wasn't a sound. Apparently he was not even eating. Tom felt himself shifting nervously in his chair. Had he been too late? Had he been seen filching that damn roll?

9

Finally he could stand it no longer. Tom raised his eyes and looked at his neighbour. There was a curious expression on the man's face. Tom had been right. The man was studying him. There was an alert interest in his eyes. There may even have been a twinkle. Tom wasn't sure of that, nor could he tell whether or not that twitching at the corners of the mouth meant that he was trying to control a smile. The cigarette drooped down from his lips, a thin spiral of blue smoke drifting up in the still air. It was as though the man had lost all interest in the cigarette and had completely forgotten that it was there. His hands, resting lightly on the table, were motionless.

It was a still tableau, one frame of a motion picture held on the screen, both immobile, staring at each other, each trying to read the other's mind.

Then something snapped, and the reel began turning again. The man relaxed, took a long pull on the cigarette he had forgotten, then carefully placed it in an ashtray on the table. He removed a gold-cornered alligator-skin wallet from the inside pocket of his coat and extracted a small white card. His eyes raised and seemed to be searching for the waiter.

'*Garçon!*' It was a rich, strong voice.

When the waiter appeared the man handed him the card and gave him directions in swift colloquial French which Tom did not follow. The waiter looked mildly astonished, scratched his head, and then deliberately and unnecessarily circled the tables and with a flourish presented the card to Tom. There followed a voluble explanation which in his confusion Tom missed completely.

The card was engraved simply: 'Mr Paul Ehrenhardt.' Tom was nonplussed. Had he been spotted? If so, did this Ehrenhardt feel that he had been insulted and was this a challenge to a duel?

'I don't understand,' he muttered.

The waiter looked down at him contemptuously. 'Coffee!' he growled. 'That gentleman!' And he motioned towards Tom's neighbour.

Slowly Tom looked up at Ehrenhardt. The man was smiling now and his head inclined towards Tom in a ceremonious gesture.

'I'm sorry,' Tom said quietly, 'my French isn't all it might be. I don't understand what this chap was saying.'

'Just that I was wondering if you would do me the honour of taking a cup of coffee with me,' Ehrenhardt explained smoothly.

Tom's stomach muscles relaxed. His spirit lifted. The affair of the *petit pain* had not been noticed. Such an invitation was most surprising, but at least he was in the clear. Relieved, he looked again at Ehrenhardt's card and rose.

'That's very kind of you, I'm sure.' He glanced at the card a third time and then at Ehrenhardt. 'I don't have a card, Mr Ehrenhardt,' he admitted, as he dropped into a chair at Ehrenhardt's table, 'but my name is Thomas Welles.'

'And I should say you were an American.' Ehrenhardt smiled.

'Yes. I suppose it sticks out all over me.'

Ehrenhardt turned to the hovering waiter and ordered fresh coffee.

'You have undoubtedly had breakfast, Mr Welles,' he said with a smile, 'but I find the croissants here more delicious than in the average restaurant. Perhaps you would try one. The *petits pains* are – well, just *petits pains*, nourishing, no doubt, and useful in their way, but they do not appeal to me. This patisserie, here, I find rather too sweet for so early in the day, but perhaps your tastes differ from mine.'

With difficulty Tom restrained himself until his coffee arrived. Then deliberately he selected his croissant, broke it, and applied a large dab of butter.

Ehrenhardt watched him quizzically for a moment, then summoned the waiter. 'Monsieur will require more butter, I believe.'

Tom grinned. 'You're being very hospitable,' he said.

'Not at all!' Ehrenhardt gestured with his mobile hands. 'I have always found meeting any American a rewarding experience. You have been in Nice long?'

'About four months.'

'Ah, then you have many friends here. You must like Provence. Most visitors do not stay in Nice for so long.'

'As a matter of fact, I know no one in Nice,' Tom admitted. 'The only friends I had left some time ago.'

Ehrenhardt frowned. He seemed puzzled. 'But there are many Americans here, and certainly in four months you must have made at least some English and French friends.'

Tom shook his head. 'I have been finishing a novel,' he explained. 'Working all the time, and I have been avoiding everything and everybody that might interfere with my work.'

'You take this writing very seriously,' hazarded the other man. 'You are most severe with yourself.'

'I have had no alternative. I had just a little money, enough to carry me through for a certain period of time, and I had to finish my book before my money ran out.'

'And have you finished your novel?'

Tom had switched to the *petits pains* in spite of Ehrenhardt's lack of enthusiasm about them. 'This is very, very good,' he said thoughtfully. Then he looked up at his companion. This man was asking a lot of personal questions, but he really seemed to be interested. It would be discourteous not to respond, particularly as he was enjoying Ehrenhardt's hospitality. 'Three weeks ago,' he said.

'And then?'

'Then I sent it off to my agent in New York.'

'And I hope you have had good news?'

'I have had no news. My agent is an admirable character and he knows his business, but he is not given to unnecessary correspondence.'

'And so you wait and wait and wait,' Ehrenhardt observed thoughtfully. 'You writers must have to develop the virtue of patience. I do not think I should take up writing. I would find it very difficult to develop patience. . . . And before you started on your novels?'

'I was a journalist, and, like every other newspaperman, felt I had to write a novel. Probably a great mistake.' Tom was eyeing the sugared bun appraisingly.

Ehrenhardt summoned the waiter again. 'Monsieur will have more coffee,' he said. Then he smiled at Tom. 'Mr Welles, perhaps you *should* try that patisserie. As I said, it is rather sweet, but really excellent.'

Tom put down his cup. 'See here, Mr Ehrenhardt, did you

see me take that roll from your table when you went out to answer that telephone call?'

Ehrenhardt's expression was bland. 'Did you take a roll from my table?' he asked.

'You *did* see me?'

Embarrassed, Tom dug the *petit pain* out of his pocket and dropped it on the table. Ehrenhardt looked at it as though he had never seen it before, but the corners of his mouth were twitching again.

'When is a roll not a roll?' he murmured. Then he looked up at Tom. 'Mr Welles, the unexpected and surprising appearance of that roll on the table perhaps justifies my asking you a most impertinent question. Might one assume that while you have waited to hear news about your novel, your resources have been seriously depleted?'

'They have,' Tom admitted.

'And perhaps you do not have enough money for your return passage to New York?'

Tom Welles shook his head.

'And you might be living under the roof in some *pension* in the cheap part of the town? Perhaps you may even be behind with your rent?'

'Not very much, only two weeks.'

'Could you not get help from the American Consul here?'

'Perhaps, but I've been expecting to hear something from New York day by day.'

'Mr Welles, how much money do you think this novel of yours might earn for you?'

Tom shrugged. 'God only knows. If anyone buys it, I could probably get enough of an advance to pay for a passage home on a cheap ship – perhaps a little more. After that—' He shook his head. 'When it is published, the book might never even earn its advance, or it might make a lot of money. There's always the possibility of a magazine or a picture sale, but those are long shots.'

'Possibilities! Possibilities! No, I'm quite sure that I would not care to be an author. Will you have a cigarette, Mr Welles?'

'I took one of your cigarettes, too,' Tom blurted out.

Ehrenhardt smiled. 'The paper of that cigarette was torn, and by now the cigarette itself is undoubtedly crumpled. Have a fresh one?'

'I haven't smoked in three weeks,' Tom admitted as he took a cigarette from Ehrenhardt's case.

'Perhaps you should not start again. It is unquestionably a vice. And recently all this talk in the papers! I found myself becoming very worried by reading what smoking cigarettes might do to me – so I gave up reading.'

After Tom's laugh, there were a few moments of silence at the table. Ehrenhardt seemed to be thinking over some problem. Finally he addressed Tom abruptly.

'Mr Welles, under the circumstances, would you be interested in a temporary employment which would alleviate your present difficulties?'

'Anything short of murder!' Tom grinned. 'And if I could be persuaded that it was justifiable homicide I might even be persuaded to take that on. What sort of job have you got in mind?'

'I'm not quite sure,' said Ehrenhardt, his eyes narrowing as he thought it over. 'Perhaps a sort of secretary, a confidential secretary.' Then he smiled. 'If, for example, I wished you to find me a girl—'

Tom shook his head. 'I don't think I'd make a very good pimp,' he said bluntly.

'Mr Welles, you misunderstand me. If I wanted a girl to sleep with, I could find her by myself, but I assure you that I am a most respectable person. At the moment I am staying here at Nice quietly with my wife, and any thought of amorous dalliance is far from my mind. When you interrupted me, I was about to tell you that I am, in a way, a sort of impresario. It is quite possible, let us say, that I might need a certain type of girl to play a certain part in a production that I am thinking about, and that if you were working for me, one of your duties might be to act as – think in America you call it a "scout".'

'Sorry. I misunderstood you.'

'If you were acting as my confidential secretary, your duties

14

might be very varied. I really don't know what they would be,' Ehrenhardt admitted vaguely. 'Why don't you think it over? But of course it would be a purely temporary position.'

'Well, I'm for hire,' Tom said.

'I must think this over a little more carefully,' Ehrenhardt said, 'and I would like to have my wife meet you. She is a very good judge of character.'

There was a pause. Then Ehrenhardt motioned to the waiter and called for his bill.

'I must go now, Mr Welles, but would it be convenient to come to the Negresco at three o'clock this afternoon? Here, give me that card. I'll write the number of our suite, and then you will not be bothered by having to make inquiries at the reception desk.'

'I'm quite certain that I have no engagement at three o'clock this afternoon, Mr Ehrenhardt. I will be at the Negresco at three. How may I express my thanks for one of the most delicious and one of the most needed breakfasts I've ever eaten?'

Ehrenhardt bowed politely and smilingly. 'Not at all! As I said before, I have always found meeting any American most worthwhile.'

2

AT THREE o'clock that afternoon Tom Welles walked confidently past all the gold braid at the entrance of the Negresco, strolled through the ornate lobby and into an elevator. There had been the definite suggestion from Ehrenhardt that he should not stop at the reception desk, and he took the hint.

A few moments later he knocked on the door bearing the number that he had been given. He stood there for perhaps half a minute, then the door opened.

The woman confronting him had one hand on the edge of the door above her head. The other hung relaxed by her side.

She had startling black hair that swept down over her shoulders, and her oval eyes were very dark – almost black. It was a sculptured face, with wide cheekbones and a slightly Oriental cast. She was tall – nearly as tall as Tom. She wore a long green hostess gown of velvet that modelled every curve of her body from her neck to a line below her hips, then flared out into a flowing skirt. Her bare white arms and the deep white slash from the shoulders narrowing to a point far below her breasts were in startling contrast to the emerald costume and her jet-black hair.

She stood there absolutely silent, her eyes studying Tom's face. Then, as though she had made up her mind to something, her red lips parted in an inviting smile, and with her smile the whole character of her face changed. It became alive, animated, provocative.

'You must be Mr Welles,' she decided. It was a good voice, cultured, trained, but with the same slight foreign accent as Paul Ehrenhardt's that Tom could not quite identify.

'Come in,' she said. 'I am Anna Ehrenhardt. My husband is late, I'm afraid. He thought he might be, and asked me to entertain you if you arrived before he returned.'

Turning, she led the way into a richly but impersonally furnished hotel salon.

'Won't you sit down?' she invited, as she sank down on to a chaise longue herself.

'Thank you,' Tom said.

About twenty-eight, perhaps thirty years old, he was thinking. A Continental, but what nationality he did not know. Very much a woman of the world. Beautiful, but sleek like her husband, perhaps a little too sleek, patently a man's woman, with an elusive quality which was either alluring or slightly repulsive. Tom couldn't decide which.

'Tell me about yourself, Mr Welles. All my husband told me is that you are a writer and that you and he were discussing the possibility of your temporarily becoming his confidential secretary.'

'Mr Ehrenhardt did not even ask me whether I could take dictation or type. I didn't realize it until afterwards, but since

I can't take dictation and can only type with one finger, Mr Ehrenhardt is probably going to be very disappointed.'

Anna Ehrenhardt dismissed that with a gesture. 'That's the last sort of a secretary Paul needs,' she assured him.

'What sort of a secretary does he need?'

'Someone he can trust, someone who will do what he is asked to do, and someone who is, above all, discreet. My husband, I'm afraid, is a lazy man. He thoroughly enjoys having someone else do his work for him.'

'That's just being human,' Tom grinned.

'You're here alone in Nice? No wife? No family? No sweetheart?'

'No nothing. . . . Did your husband tell you about the roll?'

She frowned. Tom could not make up his mind whether her perplexity was real or assumed.

'No, what roll? Roll of what?'

'He had better tell you himself,' Tom decided.

There was a silence which seemed to Tom to last a very long time. Anna Ehrenhardt's eyes were still on him, objective now, appraising, but as impersonal as though she were studying a portrait in a gallery.

'I think I would like to have Paul engage you,' she announced deliberately. 'I think if I came to know you well I would like you.'

'Thank you,' Tom said. He felt as though he were a puppy, being selected from a litter of twelve.

She rose from the chaise longue. In some strange way, it was almost as though it were an act carefully rehearsed to arouse the interest of the spectator. Her slow movements had a sinuous rhythm, and they seemed to be arrested for just a fraction of an instant at certain fixed moments of the rite.

Tom rose to his feet as she did and stood there silently. She crossed the room to what seemed to be the door to a bedroom and opened it.

'If you will excuse me, Mr Welles, I must change. I'm sure my husband won't be long. You do not mind waiting alone, do you?'

'Not at all, Mrs Ehrenhardt.'

She started through the door and then turned back. She was frowning again.

'My husband said you had been here in Nice about four months, but had no friends. Four months without a *petite amie*? You do not seem to be the type to be in Nice without a mistress.'

Tom laughed. 'Mrs Ehrenhardt, regardless of type, a mistress requires a certain amount of time and a certain amount of money. I've had neither to spare.'

'*Quel dommage,*' she murmured, and disappeared into the bedroom.

Five minutes passed before Tom heard a key in the door. It swung open, and Paul Ehrenhardt entered briskly.

'Mr Welles, a thousand pardons for my tardiness. It was unexpected but unavoidable. Where is my wife?'

Following Ehrenhardt into the room was a short, stocky man with bristling white hair, broad in the cheeks, with a square chin and a livid scar which ran from the top of his right ear to the corner of his mouth. He was conservatively dressed in dark grey. He might have been sixty years old.

Ehrenhardt flung his cane and his gloves on the sofa and faced Tom. 'Where is my wife?' he demanded again.

'Mrs Ehrenhardt excused herself. She said she had to change her dress.'

'Ah, yes, that cocktail party with the Baron. I'd forgotten. Would you excuse me for just a moment? I would like to speak to her.' At the door to the bedroom he paused and knocked. 'Anna, may I come in?'

There was a muffled assent beyond the door and he entered, closing the door after him.

Tom faced Ehrenhardt's companion doubtfully.

There was a crooked smile on the old man's face, distorted probably by the drawn scar across his cheek.

'Paul forgot to introduce us, yes? My name is Hugo Forchet. I am a friend of Paul's. Perhaps you might even call me an associate.'

'I'm Tom Welles.'

'Yes, I know. Paul has been telling me of you and your novel. Are you going to work for Paul?'

'I haven't the slightest idea. He hasn't asked me yet.'

Forchet chuckled. 'Anna will tell him whether or not to offer you the job.' He made an expressive gesture with his hands and his shoulders. 'She's telling him now whether you'll do.'

'Mrs Ehrenhardt seems very charming,' Tom observed carefully.

Forchet nodded. 'An understatement,' he said. 'Anna owns us all, body and soul.'

The door opened and Paul Ehrenhardt reappeared. 'Sit down, Mr Welles. May I order you a drink?'

'I would love a drink,' Tom confessed.

'Scotch? Brandy? What you will.'

'Scotch, please.'

'And you, Hugo?'

'Some brandy to settle my stomach.'

Ehrenhardt rang for the floor waiter. He arrived so promptly that it was as though he had been waiting outside the door.

'Now, Mr Welles. What about it? Do you think you would like to work for me? What was the man called in *Robinson Crusoe*? Man Friday! Yes, that was it, Man Friday. Do you think you would like to be my Man Friday and confidential secretary?'

'I told Mrs Ehrenhardt that I couldn't even take dictation, and I am a bad typist.'

'Perfect. I hate writing letters; I write very few letters. Your lack of experience will encourage me to write none.'

'Are you offering me a job?'

'Of course. My wife agrees with me that you could be very useful to us.'

'To us?'

'My wife's and my interests – our projects – are the same.'

'I told you this morning, Mr Ehrenhardt, that I would take almost anything as a temporary job.'

'Good! Then it is settled. Hugo, let the waiter in. We need those drinks. . . . Here, Tom, I ordered a double Scotch for you. The French single portion of Scotch isn't worth drinking. Now that you're working for me, I shall call you Tom and you shall call me Paul.'

'May I asked what I'm supposed to *do*, working for you – Paul?'

'All in good time. All in good time.' Ehrenhardt frowned. 'Your salary is a problem. I haven't the slightest idea what to pay you.' He looked over at Tom critically, and then turned to Forchet. 'Hugo, it will cost a small fortune to dress the man. He must have some decent clothes.' And he swung back to Tom. 'You've probably even pawned your dinner jacket, haven't you?' he demanded amiably.

'I didn't even bring one over with me,' Tom admitted.

'There isn't time to have one made. You'll have to do the best you can with a ready-made dinner jacket. Hugo, it will take the best part of a hundred and fifty thousand francs to outfit Tom.'

From his pocket he took a thick stack of bank notes pinned together, looked at them casually to check their value, and tossed them over to Tom.

'You know how to dress. Fit yourself out with whatever you need for a few weeks. That is the most important thing to do first. I have to think about your salary, but I promise you it will be generous.'

Ehrenhardt faced Tom. The smile had left his face. It was serious, almost stern. 'There is one condition to this employment, Tom. While you are working for me, you will ask no questions. You will do exactly what you are told to do just as you are told to do it. While you are working for me, and afterwards, you will keep your mouth sealed, and forget every detail of your employment and your work. Any indiscretion on your part would have most unfortunate consequences for me – *and for you*.' The last words were almost menacing. 'Will you accept those conditions?'

'Yes,' Tom said quietly. 'But, I reserve the right to quit if you put me on to anything which I think is too raw.'

'You will not be asked to do anything which will get you into trouble.'

'Am I to go on living where I'm living?'

'Yes, but give me your address.'

'When do you want me to start?'

Ehrenhardt was again his normal suave self. 'Perhaps you would join Anna and me for breakfast here tomorrow morning at ten o'clock,' he suggested. Then he chuckled. 'I will have a very good breakfast waiting for you, Tom, including a basket of *petits pains*! Now go about your business and get yourself some presentable clothes. And don't forget to get your cuff links out of pawn! *Au revoir!*'

Thomas Welles was not one to do things by halves. Ever since the English discovered the Riviera, Nice has been a cosmopolitan city. If one looks, one finds any type of shop, and although the male is not catered to quite as elaborately as is the female, it did not take Tom long to find an outfitter who might have been a little out of his class on Saville Row, but who would have run well on Oxford Street.

For the first time in his life Tom had the experience – and delightful it was – of spending someone else's money, knowing that he was not going to have to render a meticulous expense account.

Happily, he had one of those figures that can drop into an already tailored suit without alterations being really necessary, and that evening as he surveyed the display that almost covered the old red quilt on his bed, he shook his head as though to clear his thoughts.

'Is this you, Welles?' he muttered out loud. Two suits, a dinner jacket, shoes, socks, shirts, not to speak of underclothes and handkerchiefs. 'Paul Ehrenhardt, where have you been all my life?' And if Anna was partly responsible for this good fortune, God bless her, too. After this, if she wanted his body and soul too, she could have it.

And only then did Tom realize that he had forgotten to make his afternoon call at the post office, and now the post office was closed.

He counted the francs he had left in his pocket, and found that the big pile of bank notes had dwindled alarmingly. He wondered if Paul Ehrenhardt planned to feed him as well as dress him in his job, and then promptly decided that a hungry secretary would be of no use to anyone and that he owed it to his employer to find the biggest, best dinner that Nice could provide.

Going down the stairs, he wondered how old Anna Ehren- hardt really was. Certainly not more than thirty, he decided, and thirty was only two more than twenty-eight.

What Tom did not know was that at the moment when he was reflecting about Anna, he himself was the subject of a dis- cussion between Anna and Paul Ehrenhardt.

'Of course, he is absolutely up against it and desperate. Therefore he will do as he's told, probably without asking – even of himself – questions that might be troublesome if they were answered,' Ehrendhardt admitted. 'Nevertheless, Anna, these Americans are a scrupulous lot – full of ideals and prin- ciples, and, as you well know, ideals and principles are often embarrassing.'

'Leave young Tom Welles to me, Paul.' Anna's voice was almost a purr. 'Ideals and principles require an object. I think I would rather enjoy being the object of Tom Welles' ideals and principles. He's quite attractive, you know, and rather different. In spite of the fact that he stole your roll and a cigarette, I think he's essentially honest.'

'That's what worries me,' Paul muttered.

'It doesn't worry me in the slightest,' Anna said calmly. 'He obviously has been leading a monastic life, and he might even fall in love with me.'

'You be careful, Anna.'

'And when have you known me not to be careful, my stupid one?' There was a lilt of affection in her voice. 'Just arrange things, Paul, so that I have some time with our young friend Tom Welles, and it will turn out, I think, to be a very happy arrangement – for everyone. I think you've bought yourself a very perfect stalking-horse. . . . You might let me have his address, Paul. I might need it some time.'

3

THE NEXT morning Tom went through the routine of calling for letters at the Poste-Restante – with the usual result.

At ten o'clock he knocked at the door of the Ehrenhardt suite at the Negresco. The door opened, and this morning Anna's costume at the door was a shockingly diaphanous boudoir robe.

Her eyes greeted him, but she inspected his clothes silently and critically.

'Very, very beautiful,' she announced finally. 'I wouldn't have dreamed that you could do so well without a tailor.'

'Thanks be to your husband.' Tom grinned.

Then he noticed the breakfast table set for two and felt an automatic twinge of disappointment. 'Aren't you breakfasting with us?' he asked.

'You are breakfasting with me,' Anna announced. She made a careless gesture. 'Paul is out somewhere with Hugo. They had business. Paul, as you will learn, is unpredictable. When he plans ahead, the purpose seems to be to have a plan that he can change for something else.'

'Perhaps you'd rather I left now,' suggested Tom awkwardly, 'and came back later when Paul was here.'

Anna was standing quite close to him, and she looked up into his face with wide-eyed innocence.

'Why? Wouldn't you like to have breakfast with me? Aren't you hungry?'

Tom grinned. 'I want to have breakfast with you. I am very hungry, and so far I'd say this was the most delightful job anyone has ever had.'

'Then sit down, Tom. I suppose we do call each other by our first names, since you and Paul seem to have reached that point.'

He pushed her chair in and took his own place.

Anna surveyed the covered metal platters, warm over their

spirit lamps, and then her eyes wandered over the rest of the table.

'Orange juice, of course, for any American, and having heard about American breakfasts, I ordered you lamb cutlets, coffee, croissants, honey – and of course *petits pains*.'

'So Paul did tell you about how we met.'

'Paul tells me everything.'

'And do you tell Paul everything?'

'Certainly not. That's the difference between a woman and a man. I'm devoted to my husband, but my personal life is my own.'

They ate silently for a few minutes, and then Anna asked him whether there was anything else that she could order for him.

'Good heavens, no. . . . Do you and your husband expect to be here long?' he asked impersonally.

'We don't know. We were discussing that last night. We're a little tired of Nice itself. We thought it might be fun if we could find one of those picturesque châteaux or old castles up in the mountains somewhere which we could rent for a few months. We're both tired and need a rest. Do you know that hill country up towards Grasse and to the south?'

'Only as seen from an autobus,' Tom admitted.

'We may not seem it, but Paul and I both are rather primitive people and like to be alone. And the Maritime Alps are so beautiful, especially just this side or the other side of the Italian border.'

'Yes, they're magnificent – what I've seen of them,' Tom agreed.

'Paul was talking last night of the possibility of sending you up there to scout around to see what sort of place you could find for us.'

'Yes?'

'Yes. We'd have to rent a car, of course. It's the only way to get around in those mountains. I don't suppose you have an international driver's licence, have you?'

'No.'

'But you do drive a car, of course.'

'Oh, yes.'

'Well, it's very easy to get an international driver's licence. . . . Paul may have made up his mind about his plans overnight. I didn't see him this morning. He simply left a note for me and said to give you breakfast and ask you to wait for his return.'

Try as he would, it had been impossible for Tom to keep his eyes away from the unashamedly immodest figure across the table from him. Anna caught his covert glances with some amusement and smiled. Then she looked down at herself appraisingly.

'I suppose this is a rather dashing costume to wear to breakfast with a comparative stranger, isn't it?' she admitted.

'I'm sorry if I seem to have been staring,' Tom blurted out.

'I really haven't minded at all, but I'm sorry if you have been distracted from your breakfast,' Anna murmured demurely. 'Perhaps I *should* put something else on, however, before Paul returns.'

She rose and passed slowly in front of the window towards the door, and then turned back to Tom. 'You will wait, won't you?'

'Yes, I'll wait,' said Tom with certainty in his voice.

Three days later Thomas Welles found himself piloting a rental-agency Simca up the road from Nice to the Grand Corniche.

The three days that had passed were almost like a fairy-tale. He had not accustomed himself yet to this new life – apparently the life of a young American millionaire on the Riviera, pleasure-bent with no responsibilities.

Tucked in a big manila envelope by his side – his pockets couldn't hold them – were road maps, lists from real-estate agencies (although they had a queer name for them here), literature from the Tourisme Office, and an English-French dictionary.

'Now, Tom,' Paul Ehrenhardt had told him when he eventually returned to the hotel room that morning three days before, 'perhaps Anna's told you we have decided to try and find a retreat up in the mountains. We both love solitude. Nice, Cannes, Antibes, Monte Carlo— Bah! Magnets for tourists and visitors. It is up in the mountains that one finds the real Provence. Things there, of course, are primitive. One has to make compromises, but I have a production ahead of me that requires thought and concentration and rest, and I need the atmosphere of an old château or perhaps a castle.' And he waved his hands expressively. 'I need perhaps towers, battlements, and stone ramparts. I must withdraw into a bygone age in order to re-create the mood necessary to reproduce this – well, call it spectacle, call it play, call it opera, call it what you will.

'You must find us such a place. If Anna and I went searching for it, all my enthusiasm would die before we found the right spot. You must find us the place we need, and make the arrangements, and then we will go there with anticipation, readily receptive.'

'You know without my telling you that my French isn't so hot,' Tom observed.

'That does not matter in the slightest. One does not need French to find what I'm looking for. A refuge where I can imagine myself living a hundred and fifty or two hundred years ago, before the days of automobiles, before the days of airplanes, before the days of radio and television, and, God help us, before the days of atom bombs. I need the atmosphere of the eighteenth century or the early nineteenth century, with preferably a fifteenth- or sixteenth-century background behind that. After all, in the seventeen-hundreds in this part of the world, people still lived much as they did hundreds of years before. The conveniences of modern civilization did not really appear until a hundred years ago.'

'You mean there is to be no plumbing and there is to be an outhouse, rather than a toilet and things like that?' Tom asked politely.

'Not necessarily, but perhaps it will be so. I don't know. It is the atmosphere that I want, and, as I said, stone walls and towers, if possible. I don't imagine there are moats down in this part of the country. I don't think they used them. No water, I suppose. Too bad! A moat would be most helpful.' Paul Ehrenhardt was obviously enjoying himself, but shook his head gloomily. 'It is not easy to project yourself spiritually

26

and emotionally into the past. With modern surroundings, one needs help!'

While this conversation was going on, Anna was lounging there on the sofa in the big salon, smoking a cigarette in a long amber holder, saying not a word, watching her husband with speculative, interested eyes. Occasionally her glance would shift to Tom, and her expression seemed to say: 'You and I understand each other. He is putting on a good show. Give him his chance.'

'So, Tom, my wife and I shall wait here in Nice for you to find us the proper retreat. Today I'll arrange for a car for you to drive, and we shall have to get you an international driver's permit. Get yourself a list of people here and in Cannes and probably in Monte Carlo who sell and lease property in this part of the country, and then start exploring.'

'And how will I know when I've found the right place for you?' Tom asked Ehrenhardt.

'Oh, you'll come back here every two or three days or so and tell us about what you have seen and what you have found. I shall lend you a camera, and you will have pictures. We can then judge for ourselves.'

'And if I do find something that you're interested in, you'll want to lease it for how long?'

'Oh, certainly for not less than two months, but if necessary longer than that if you find just the right place. A few thousand francs here or there doesn't matter, and we can always leave when we want to.'

'And you don't care how primitive it is?'

'It *would* be nice to have a bathroom,' murmured Anna.

'Very well, don't let a bathroom dissuade you, but if necessary we can do without it.'

'And what about servants in this castle or château?'

'Don't worry about that. Hugo Forchet will take care of that end when the time comes. He'll be going up there with us, and any additional help we need he can find. This is his part of the country, and he knows people. Just you find us our retreat.'

Tom wondered why it would not have been better to have Hugo Forchet, a native of the country, head up this search, but

27

that was Paul Ehrenhardt's business, and, after all, wandering around in the Alpes Maritimes for a few days in a car by himself was not an unpleasant prospect.

'And when you move up to your castle in the mountains, am I to go with you?' Tom asked.

'Possibly. Possibly not. But I can assure you, Tom, that as soon as you've found what we're looking for, I have another very important mission for you to execute. By the way, we have not discussed your salary. If we just forget the expense of your outfit, would you be satisfied with a salary of thirty-five thousand francs a week?'

'Good God, yes!' Tom blurted out.

'Incidentally, you *did* get a dinner jacket, didn't you?'

'Oh, yes. You told me to.'

'Of course. Good. There is an opera here tonight that Anna is anxious to see, and I have a business engagement. Perhaps you could accompany her to the opera?'

'I would be delighted.'

'Have you enough money left for your daily expenses?'

'I have twenty thousand francs left,' Tom said.

'That should do for the moment. Be off with you. I shall attend to the rental of the car. You get your *permit de conduire*. Get your house-agency list and—' Paul turned to his wife. 'Anna, will Tom be taking you to dinner or will you meet him before the opera?'

Anna raised her head, and her eyes were inscrutable. 'I should like to have dinner with Tom – if he has no other engagement.'

'Of course – Anna.'

'Good,' Paul said briskly. 'It will have to be early, if you are to be on time for the opera.'

Then that evening with Anna! Tom had called for her at the hotel at six thirty.

It seemed that it was always to be Anna who opened the door to him at the Ehrenhardts' suite. To his surprise, she was not dressed in an elaborately formal evening gown, but one that would have been suitable for a cocktail party or an informal dinner.

'Good evening,' Tom said.

'Good evening – Tom.'

He followed her into the apartment. She crossed the room to the buffet that stood against the wall. She said: 'I ordered very, very dry martinis. Isn't that right for an American?'

'Very right,' Tom agreed.

'With English gin.'

'Thank God! French gin is awful.'

There was a silence.

'I don't particularly want to go to the opera,' Anna observed.

'No?'

'No.'

There was another silence.

'Do you mind?'

'No. Personally, I never cared much for the opera. I'm one of the uncultured Americans, I suppose.'

'I don't suppose you have your driving-permit yet,' she asked, as she slowly stirred the ice in the tall glass cocktail-shaker.

'Yes, as a matter of fact, I have. I took my test this afternoon and passed brilliantly. I've got a perfectly beautiful pamphlet in my pocket filled up with empty pages until you almost reach the end, and on the last pages you discover that Thomas Welles, American, resident of New York City, has an international permit to drive a car almost anywhere in the world except a few little holes in the wall like Russia and—'

'The car Paul rented is downstairs,' she interrupted casually.

'All right, we have four pieces to our jigsaw puzzle – a *permit de conduire* and an automobile and a woman who doesn't want to go to the opera and a man who doesn't care whether he goes to the opera or not but would a little prefer not to. What does that make?'

'Do you like gambling?'

'Anna, that's a silly question to ask me. I suppose anyone should like gambling, but to gamble you have to have lots of money, and I've never had any money. So therefore I don't gamble, and because I don't gamble I don't know whether I like to gamble.'

'*I* like gambling,' Anna announced. 'It excites me. You know, Tom, I think if you gambled you'd probably be very lucky.'

'If I gambled,' Tom grinned, 'I'd *have* to be very lucky.'

'Paul has flown to Marseilles,' Anna observed.

'Marseilles? What for?'

'Business. Business as usual, I think you Americans say. Paul has many irons in the fire.'

'All right,' Tom agreed, 'we have another piece to fit into our puzzle. Paul has flown to Marseilles.'

Anna turned with the martinis, one in each hand. She held the right one out to Tom, then raised her glass. 'To *Monsieur l'Américain.*'

Tom Welles faced her gravely and raised his glass. 'To *Madame la*— I couldn't finish that toast. I haven't the slightest idea what nationality you are,' he explained.

'Tom, *chéri*, I don't wonder. I haven't the slightest idea of what I really am either. There's French and there's Belgian and there's Hungarian and some Russian, a little Turkish, and, for all I know, probably some Greek and Egyptian. What will you have?'

Tom raised his glass again. 'To *Madame l'Internationale.*'

'Do you know La Bonne Auberge?' Anna demanded.

'No, I never heard of it.'

'It's on the road to Cannes, near Antibes.'

'Expensive, no doubt,' he commented.

'Well, reasonably expensive,' Anna admitted. 'The flowers are beautiful, though, and the hors d'oeuvres are perfect, and the rest of the dinner is always in the best tradition.'

'It sounds possible,' Tom admitted.

'And from La Bonne Auberge—' her voice was tentative '—we could drive to Cannes or perhaps even Monte Carlo, and we could gamble with Edward VII.'

'He's dead, Your Highness. He died long before you and I were born.'

'Nonsense. That's just an English superstition. King Edward VII is still living. He has a small but beautiful château near Monte Carlo. He is driven down to the Casino almost every night. There's never been a night that I haven't felt him there at the Casino.'

'Have you seen him?' Tom asked politely.

'Oh, no, of course I've never *seen* him, but he's there, gambling away, usually at the big baccarat table. One can't get near that, of course, it's always too crowded, but there are the *chemin-de-fer* tables near by, and even at those tables one senses the presence of King Edward. Besides, he wanders about frequently. He keeps his eyes open, Edward does, and when he sees a very beautiful woman that he has not noticed before—'

'This is getting a bit fanciful for an American.'

'Nonsense, Tom. It's perfectly impossible to look around the Casino at Monte Carlo without realizing that King Edward is still there. The Sporting Club, of course, is just a modern, vulgar hangout for gamblers of today, but the old Casino gives you something that no other casino in the world has dared preserve. It is a blatant and defiant display of the Victorian dignity and splendour that the modern world has chosen to condemn.'

Tom sipped his martini. It was very good and very dry. 'On the strength of your husband's expense account, could I ask you to dinner at La Bonne Auberge, and after dinner we might go on to the Casino at Monte Carlo?'

Anna smiled. 'Tom, you have read my mind. How *could* you have guessed what I really wanted to do tonight?'

'I have a highly developed extrasensory perception,' Tom told her dryly.

'One more martini and we go.'

'Are you sure Paul will approve of this?' Tom asked. 'After all, I'm working for him. I'm his man, so to speak.'

'You Americans with your scruples! I told you that I do not tell Paul everything. The opera I can discuss in detail. I've seen it a dozen times. And he won't ask *you* embarrassing questions.'

'Don't forget we do need another martini,' Tom said.

'You mix it, Tom. I shall get a coat.'

As he stirred the martinis Tom Welles shook his head. This was going to be a most unpredictable job, he decided. Pleasant, no doubt. Well paid. But one's duties and responsibilities and obligations were confused and not very clearly defined.

Dinner at La Bonne Auberge had been superb, and as they drove into Monte Carlo, Anna opened her purse and pulled out a sheaf of bank notes. 'You'll need this,' she observed.

'What for?' demanded Tom.

'Well, in the first place, it would be a little better if you rather than I paid for your card of admission – I have mine – and then you will need something to gamble with.'

'Anna, I'm not gambling. I have no money to gamble with.'

'I told you I felt you were going to be lucky tonight. You'll be playing for me – I mean half for me and half for yourself. I have a strong feeling about your luck tonight. If you win, half of your winnings will be yours.'

'And if I lose?'

'Then my premonition was wrong. I live by my premonitions.'

'Heads I win, tails you lose,' Tom muttered.

'You're not going to lose,' Anna announced calmly.

'No, I am not going to play with your money, Anna.'

'You will spoil my evening if you don't! *Please*, Tom.'

'And you,' Tom demanded, 'you're going to play?'

'Of course.'

'Will you win or lose?'

'I haven't the slightest idea. I shall either lose a little or win a lot. That is the way I play.'

At the Casino, Anna had led Tom straight through the public halls to the Salle Privée and found a place at a high-stake *chemin-de-fer* table. She settled down. 'You must choose your game and find your own place,' she told him. 'It is luckier that way.'

Tom, never having been in the Casino before, wandered around curiously. There was one table for dice in the outer room with a rather desultory, synthetic pair of table men aping the technique of Las Vegas and Reno. There were tables with a strange game of *rouge-et-noir* of which he had always heard but which he could not understand. In the corner of the big gambling-room was the baccarat table with the brass rail protecting the regular players, and a barrier for *hoi polloi*. There were roulette tables everywhere. Tom did not pause at the roulette tables. He knew the game and its principles, but never having played the game himself, it seemed to him that watching a little white ball rolling interminably around the wheel and finally settling into one pocket identical to all the other little pockets except for its number was certainly a boring way to spend an evening. And then there were the *chemin-de-fer* tables. It was a curious game, with cards being dealt out of a long tilted box to just one player and the dealer. The one player apparently played for everyone at the table, all against the dealer. If the dealer won, the individual bets were raked into the pile of chips in front of the croupier. If the dealer lost, each player received chips to match his individual wager.

The rooms themselves were like nothing Tom had ever seen. High, spacious, overly ornate, of course, but colour everywhere and rich with gold. The magnificent ceiling must have cost a fortune. It lived up to Anna's description, and Tom understood why she insisted that Edward VII frequented the place. Certainly if he were not here in the flesh, the Casino was haunted by his ghost.

The bank notes in Tom's pockets had been burning hotly, and he had noticed that men wandered from table to table of *chemin-de-fer*, and had the privilege of betting against the dealer the whole amount of the bank in the centre of the table. The bets by players at the table were insufficient to cover the dealer's stake. The technique was to call 'Banco' in a loud voice.

He also discovered that it was possible to consult the croupier about your cards, and that you could ask him whether to draw a third card to add to your original two. You apparently tried to get a point of eight or nine or as close to eight or nine as possible. It seemed that you did not count face cards and subtracted tens. It was a little like a game of twenty-one or blackjack.

He was standing by a table where the betting seemed lethargic and slow when suddenly, without consciously opening his mouth, he was horrified to hear his own voice calling out the

33

fateful demand 'Banco.' It was so involuntary that it seemed to be someone else who had spoken.

'Banco, monsieur?' the croupier verified.

Tom nodded. It was too late to withdraw now.

A moment later the long thin paddle deposited two cards before him on the green flat table.

There was an enormous pile of chips in the middle of the table. For the first time Tom really noticed them, and his heart dropped into his shoes. He had no idea what that pile of chips amounted to or how much he was betting.

This was appalling. He stood there for a moment stunned, unable to even pick up his cards, the croupier waiting, the players waiting. Then, as the voice of a saviour, he heard Anna whispering to him over his shoulder :

'Pick up your cards, darling, and let me read them.'

Tom leaned forward, picked his two cards off the table, and held them up so that Anna could see them over his shoulder.

'It couldn't be worse,' she groaned. 'Ask for another card.'

'A card,' Tom repeated obediently.

Another card came sliding across the green table.

'Pick it up!' Anna said urgently.

The spots on the three cards seemed to add up to nine, but he wasn't sure. What should he do next? His answer came over his shoulder again: 'Wait – until he draws.'

The dealer took another card from the shoe and his three cards seemed to add up to seven.

'*Sept!*' the dealer declared with satisfaction in his voice.

'Put your cards down!' Anna ordered. 'Face up!'

Tom placed his cards on the table.

'*Neuf!*' announced the croupier, and almost simultaneously his lovely long smooth paddle shoved the huge pile of yellow and blue and red chips towards Tom.

He turned to Anna. 'Are these mine?' he muttered.

'Yes, my infant, those are yours.' Anna was smiling and speaking very quietly. 'Pick them up and go away quickly. I told you that you were going to be lucky tonight.'

'What do I do now?' Tom demanded, still in a state of utter confusion.

Anna was watching him with amusement. 'On the strength of that, Mr Welles, you can take me to the bar and buy me a drink. Then I am going back to my own table, and you will be on your own again.' She eyed the pockets of his dinner jacket, bulging with chips. 'You won a lot on that *coup*,' she said thoughtfully. 'Don't expect that sort of thing to happen too often.'

Realizing that he knew no more about the game than he had before, when Anna left him Tom had wandered from table to table, but either the gods of fortune or his own uncertainty had kept him from repeating his banco bet. When Anna finally rejoined him she said: 'It is time for a *fine*, and then we should go home, Tom. Cash in your chips over there.'

He walked over to the cashier's desk, cashed in his chips, and to his startled surprise came away with 275,000 francs.

When he came up to Anna his face was grave. 'My God, Anna, if I had lost that bet I wouldn't have had enough to pay it. What would have happened?'

'You didn't lose that bet, *chéri*. That is all that matters,' she said lightly. 'I told you that you would have good luck tonight.'

Back in Nice he had escorted Anna up to the Ehrenhardt suite. She handed him the key and he opened the door. She entered and turned. They stood there, she just inside the door, he on the threshold.

'Paul is in Marseilles,' she observed.

'Yes, but it is Paul whom I'm working for,' he said slowly.

There was a long pause.

'Then you are not coming in?' she asked.

'No, I'm not coming in.'

'And if I told you that I wished very much that you would?' she pursued.

'You are Paul's wife,' he pointed out.

'What makes you think that Paul would care?' she demanded.

Tom had thought that one over. 'That isn't a question for me to answer,' he blurted out. 'If I weren't drawing a salary from Paul and working for him – well, I would be coming in.

35

As long as I'm on Paul's payroll, I guess I'll do what he tells me to do and stay away from things he hasn't asked me to take care of.'

Anna regarded him with an expression blended of amusement and irritation. 'You Anglo-Saxons are difficult to understand,' she confided. Then she put her arms slowly around his neck, drew herself to him, raised her face to his, and their lips met and clung.

When her arms released him, she stepped back inside the door.

'Good night, Mr Welles,' she murmured.

And the door closed in his face.

The following day had been spent interviewing information offices and real-estate agents, some of whom spoke English and some of whom did not. Tom's specific definitions of what he was looking for did not discourage the agents at all. Here, obviously, was a rich young American who thought he wanted an antique castle in the mountains, but of course he really didn't know what he wanted himself, they told themselves, so why not rent him a villa on the beach at Juan les Pins or a nice little apartment over that *boulangerie* right in the middle of Cannes, and then what about a fine house at San Remo? True, it was across the Italian border, and Monsieur had specified France, but what was a border between friends, and there was really no difference whatsoever between resorts the other side of the border and those on this side.

Paul Ehrenhardt had spent some time with Tom poring over maps of the mountains and highlands that the Ehrenhardts fancied, and Tom had very specific instructions.

In order to satisfy the Ehrenhardts, this retreat must be in an isolated spot, quiet and immune to intrusion. It must, however, be available by car. Then, an absolute essential was that it must be walled.

'Why in heaven's name does it have to have a wall?' Tom had demanded.

'My dear Tom!' Ehrenhardt began to pace the room. 'Obviously, you have not lived in Provence long enough to recognize

36

what was the real symbol of life in the Middle Ages in this locality. The wall was the essential element of existence until quite recently. Your wall kept your women and your slaves within, and it kept your enemies without. Whether you lived in a town or in your own private castle, there was always the wall. I would think that they built the wall before they built anything else. There would have been no point in starting building anything unless you could protect it. No, we must have a wall, and a good wall. Anything without a wall would reek of the Victorian age. A place without a wall would be as useless to me as a well without water.'

'All right,' Tom had sighed, 'we'll have to find you a wall.'

Then the structure itself had to be really old. A certain amount of modernization was acceptable, but the building itself, château or castle, must be at least one hundred and fifty or two hundred years old, preferably older. And there must be authentic atmosphere.

The furnishings seemed to be relatively unimportant. There was a place in Nice where they could rent silverware and linen and cooking-utensils. Hugo would take care of all that when the time came. That would be his responsibility. Just let there be a few beds and a few habitable rooms that could be aired out, and all would be well.

'Paul, you must not forget the chapel,' Anna had thrown in.

'Oh, yes, Tom, there must of course be a private chapel.'

'A chapel?' demanded Tom.

'Certainly. Every château worth its salt in those days had its private chapel. I would find any place without a chapel quite lacking in the spiritual atmosphere and feeling that was so universal in those times. If one is trying to project oneself back into a bygone age, a chapel is most important.'

'Do you prefer a large chapel or a small chapel?' Tom asked politely.

Paul seemed in doubt, and there was a moment of silence.

Then Hugo Forchet cleared his throat and spoke up in his firm, prosaic voice. 'It is probable that you would find the chapel to be merely one room in the main building,' he observed.

'Yes, of course, that's it,' Paul decided briskly.

And, last but not least, Tom was to understand, and this point was emphasized with gravity, that it was he, Thomas Welles, the rich young American, who required a retreat in the mountains, not the Ehrenhardts. The Ehrenhardts were not to be involved in any way. They wished to disappear from the world. There was to be no trace of their whereabouts. Not only were the negotiations to be conducted in Tom's name, but if a suitable place was found, the lease would be in his name. He, Tom, need have no fear of financial complications resulting therefrom, because he would be given enough to pay the rental for the entire term of the lease when he signed the papers.

And now, Ehrenhardt had announced, he must hurry off because it was time for the pigeon-shooting and was Anna coming to watch today or not?

No, Anna was not going to attend the pigeon-shooting today.

And then Tom had left the Ehrenhardts to commence his search.

Anna and Paul and Hugo Forchet had sat there in the Ehrenhardt salon a few moments in silence, their eyes on the door through which Tom had disappeared. Then Anna sighed and lit a cigarette.

'How long do you think it will take him to find it?'

Hugo shrugged. 'A few days. Not more, surely.'

'Paul, couldn't you have narrowed down the territory a bit to save time?'

'Not without running the risk of there being suspicion aroused later on. There is time, Anna, plenty of time, and this must seem completely fortuitous.'

'It will not take him too long,' grunted Hugo. 'The trail is clearly marked.'

And now Tom was swinging the Simca around the last big turn before the steep straight hill that leads up to the Grand Corniche itself. He had studied the maps and he knew exactly where he had to turn off for his first objective, and his only concern was that there be someone there who spoke English. It would have been much easier if Paul had sent Hugo along with him. He had made the suggestion, but it had been quickly vetoed. Apparently Paul had other plans for Hugo.

Three quarters of an hour later Tom found himself approaching the first place on his list. He drew up along the side of the road and surveyed the building appraisingly. Then he shook his head in disgust. The château itself wasn't bad — grey stone, a good roof line, and there was even a tower. Once there had been a wall, but there was no wall left except a rubble of stones leaving a tracery around the grounds. Obviously everyone was not as enthusiastic about walls as Paul was, and at some time or other it had been pulled down, probably so that the stones could be used for some more utilitarian purpose than medieval defence from hazards that no longer existed.

Tom pulled out his maps, made a careful study of how to reach his next objective, then switched the Simca around in the narrow road and headed back towards the highway.

4

THAT NIGHT, after a number of disappointments and beginning to feel as though he were on a wild-goose chase, Tom drove into the village of Vence and found a room at the little inn there.

Seven possibilities had been crossed off his list. Where he had found a wall, he had found no chapel. Where he had found a chapel, there had been no wall. Towers seemed to be at a premium, too. Obviously, many of those builders dead and gone had shown a shocking disregard of Paul Ehrenhardt's requirements when they made their plans.

After his dinner at the little inn at Vence, however, Tom made one important discovery: *marc*, that pungent but almost acrid heady drink pressed from the refuse of grapes after they had yielded their wine, a concoction made from the dregs and the seeds that some vintner threw away. It was quite unlike anything he had ever tasted before, and he realized very soon that a little *marc* went a long way.

Up in his room Tom found himself restlessly wondering about the black-haired, sloe-eyed, quite enchanting waitress who had been so solicitous of his needs during dinner. Her smile had been warm and her eyes had been inviting. Young American millionaires travelling in Provence apparently were very welcome at the inn.

He wished his French were better. This girl apparently spoke no English. Tom wasn't at all sure how much significance could be given to what seemed very frank advances on her part. As a matter of fact, he wasn't at all sure what his own desires were. Could he have asked her to go for a walk after she finished her work? But what in the world would they have talked about? Perhaps he was being oversubtle about this sort of thing. He remembered Anna's incredulity over his having lived in Nice all those months without a mistress, but aside from the difficulties he had mentioned to Anna, lack of time and money, this language problem was a definite handicap.

In America it was so simple. Doing anything tonight? No? I feel like dancing. Any place around here we could go for a while after you've finished work? That's grand. Where will I meet you? ... And if you were in a strange town, you'd find out if you could get drinks at whatever place you were going to or whether you should bring a bottle with you.

After that, whatever the outcome, things proceeded naturally. You danced, you drank, and you flirted, and then you either went home alone or you did not go home alone. The outcome of the campaign was not decided by either person when the offensive was first opened. It depended altogether on what happened from then on. There was time for investigation and for finesse. But with this damnable problem of language complicating matters, you had to take a high dive into the swimming-pool without knowing whether there was any water in it.

In his small room Tom found himself walking up and down nervously. Anna Ehrenhardt, now. Had she just been amusing herself in leading him on, ready to check him severely if he went too far, or had she been ready to go to bed with him that night after gambling at Monte Carlo? She had lost a lot that night at the tables, she admitted, but did not specify how much. It did not seem to matter to her, and nothing that Tom had been able to say had persuaded her to change her decree that half of Tom's winnings were his to keep. She had accepted her half share, and stopped him there. Well, it felt good to have money in your pocket again that really belonged to you.

But that black-haired girl downstairs. She couldn't have been prettier, and judging by her bare arms, there must have been a ripe, wholly desirable body shrouded in that voluminous peasant costume she wore. Her advances had been almost brazen, and he had not even asked her name.

Thoroughly irritated with himself, he began to undress and prepare for bed. 'Welles,' he told himself sadly, 'you may or may not some day become a man of letters, but you show no signs of developing into a man of the world.'

Half an hour later the black-haired, sloe-eyed girl mounted the steep, narrow stairs of the inn, paused hopefully at the handsome young American's door to ask whether there was anything that Monsieur desired before retiring. Monsieur had been very shy, but perhaps he did not understand. He was a man, however, and now certainly— She knocked softly on the door. There was no response. Then she knocked again, louder.

Finally with a shrug and a sigh she turned away. Monsieur must be *very* tired and very sound asleep.

Two nights later as Tom Welles dropped down to Nice from the Moyenne Corniche he decided that he knew every road in that section of the Maritime Alps – that is, every road that the Simca could manoeuvre.

He had covered every possibility on his list. He had also visited another six or eight spots suggested by the local talent with real-estate interests. To his surprise, he seemed to be learning a little French – quite a lot of French, as a matter of fact, for it had been a question of sinking or swimming.

One day if it were possible he'd have to go back to Vence and start all over again with that pretty black-haired girl. He knew the old theory that the best and easiest way to learn the

French language was to take a French mistress who couldn't speak English, but he had always had definite doubts about the validity of that theory and how it worked out. He always suspected that such a technique might lead to a rather restricted and narrow knowledge of French with a definitely limited vocabulary. Still, that would be better than nothing.

He wondered whether it was too late to get in touch with Paul Ehrenhardt that night. There were six possibilities he had not eliminated from his list, but there was nothing that he felt he could really recommend to the Ehrenhardts as a place to retreat. After the second day, he had had to lower his sights a bit and modify his requirements. Towers and walls and castles were all very well, but if one planned to live in a place it had to have a roof which did not leak too much, and water one could drink. The absence of an icebox one could overlook, but a stove was certainly a necessary, and even Paul had specified there should be beds to sleep in and some furniture to sit on. As for mould and dampness, Tom had come to accept that as inherent in any structure built of stone, and in the Alpes Maritimes there were very few structures not built of stone.

When the Ehrenhardts saw the result of his quest, they probably would change their plans. The idea of a walled château was romantic, a walled castle even more so; but God forbid you should have to live in one. He preferred his own attic room in Nice.

To illustrate his report he had taken innumerable pictures with the camera Paul had given him, and he could get the films developed and printed first thing in the morning. If the Ehrenhardts insisted on renting any of the ruins he had examined without investigating further themselves, which they said they were not going to do, it would be on the basis of seeing what the place was like from a picture and not as a result of his report.

He drove to the Negresco and on the house telephone called the Ehrenhardts' suite. There was no answer. He wondered whether to leave the Simca at the Negresco or find a garage for it in town. He decided to have dinner and then try the Ehrenhardts again. So he drove back to a little bourgeois restaurant near the harbour which specialized in bouillabaisse.

The *marc* that he ordered with his coffee reminded him again of the black-haired girl in Vence. Her perfume had been so fresh, so fragrant, and he remembered the tingle he had felt when she had leaned against his arm as she served him.

Feeling able to cope successfully with the French telephone now, he tried the Ehrenhardts again from the restaurant, but there was still no answer. He drove into the city, garaged the car, and made his way up to his room.

Tom wondered just what Paul Ehrenhardt was up to, what this strange project of his really was. If Paul were a creative writer looking for atmosphere, why didn't he say so? Why the mystery? Perhaps he was an actor or a director. Perhaps Ehrenhardt wasn't his name at all. Well, perhaps he was a motion-picture producer. Wholly impractical, with extravagant ideas, this whole business was no more fantastic than some of the stories he had heard about Hollywood, and it wasn't his business anyway, and first thing in the morning he must go to the post office to see if there was any word from New York about his novel.

Tom took up a position in front of his cracked mirror and studied the reflection of his lips. Haltingly, painfully, he asked himself: '*Mademoiselle – voulez-vous faire une petite promenade ce soir?*'

'Hell, maybe she doesn't *like* to walk,' he muttered as he turned away. Damn Anna Ehrenhardt anyway! Until he met her he had not been having this sort of trouble for a long, long time.

5

'R IEN AUJOURD'HUI, Monsieur,' the postal clerk informed Tom the next morning, so Tom went on his way, and half an hour later Ehrenhardt's voice over the telephone at the Negresco told him to come up to the suite immediately.

Paul greeted him jovially. 'Ah, my Tom, you have found us our castle?'

'For you and Anna's sake, I hope not,' Tom said.

'Anna! Anna!' Paul called. 'Tom is here. Come in and let us see what he has found.'

'I have a lot of pictures to show you,' Tom observed, 'but they won't be printed until late today. Here's your camera, by the way. I worked it overtime.'

'Sit down at the table there, Tom, where you can spread out your map and your papers.'

'I got in last night. I called you twice. You must have been out.'

'Yes, Anna and I were at the Casino in Cannes.' Paul rubbed his hands together. 'And a very good evening we had of it, too. Anna was especially lucky.'

The door opened, and Anna sauntered into the salon. 'Anna is often lucky,' she observed impersonally. 'Welcome back, Tom. Were *you* lucky?'

'Lucky that I don't have to live in any of the places I looked over.' Tom grinned. 'I don't think you and Paul are going to like anything that I have to show. I suppose real-estate people all over the world, regardless of who they are, have to view their properties through rosy-hued glasses in order to overlook every drawback. But I must say these French real-estate agents have less regard for the facts of life than anyone I've ever known. Theirs is a true world of illusion.'

'Oh, come, Tom,' Paul protested, 'you Americans with your central heating and your storm windows and your electrified houses are completely spoiled. In other countries one learns to do without many of your modern conveniences – or rather, we have never known them.'

'Don't you have all those things in your country?' Tom asked artlessly. What nationality was this man Ehrenhardt anyway?

Paul Ehrenhardt shrugged. 'My country! What is my country? I do not know myself. One could start at Turkey and work west. Almost anywhere one stops, I could say *that* is my country, and yet I would not be sure.'

'There are such things as passports,' Tom observed. 'They usually tell you where you live or what nationality you are.'

'Passports! Bah! A relatively modern device without any real significance beyond a stupid legal technicality! A passport merely records where you happened to be residing at some stage of your life. No, I don't trust passports at all. But enough of this. I'm eager to hear what you have found.'

Tom spread out the map on which he had made six small crosses, numbered one to six. Ehrenhardt seated himself on Tom's left, and Anna sank into the chair on his other side. As she looked at the map, her shoulder pressed against his, and the aroma of her perfume beguiled him, but it was much stronger and heavier, he decided, than the fresh scent favoured by the girl in Vence.

'All right, Tom, number one. Begin the story of your odyssey,' Paul commanded.

'Well, number one is a medium-sized stone château on a hill. Rather nice-looking, as a matter of fact. It's not badly furnished, and it's in pretty good shape. There is a caretaker there who lives in a stone cottage by the gate.'

'How old is it?' Anna demanded.

'You might even be comfortable there,' Tom went on.

'How old is it?' Anna repeated.

'Well, it's not terribly old, I suppose,' Tom admitted. 'As far as I could make out from the old man's French, it was built about a hundred years ago.'

'Not old enough,' decided Paul, 'and you haven't said anything about the chapel or the wall.'

'As a matter of fact, there is a small outside chapel.'

'Humph!' Paul grunted. 'What about the wall?'

'The wall happens to be a tall modern steel fence,' Tom admitted. 'Can't you imagine that the fence is a wall, Paul? This is probably the most comfortable place of them all.'

'No, no. It is atmosphere I'm looking for, not comfort. That will not do at all, too modern, and no wall! Now what about number two?'

'Number two is one of the most picturesque places I've ever seen, and it would cost you from fifty to a hundred thousand dollars, I should think, to make it even habitable for one night. Why the real-estate joker put it on the list I don't know. I doubt if anyone has lived in the place for thirty years. I would bet even money that the agent has never even seen it himself. There is not a stick of furniture there, and the only thing to do with the roof would be to pull it all off and start all over again.'

'I'm afraid that won't do,' Anna sighed.

'I've got a fine picture of it,' Tom promised her. 'You can enlarge it and frame it, study it and absorb all the atmosphere you want right here in comfort at the Negresco. But as for living there, you'd do much better to dig a nice big cave in the side of one of those hills and start house-keeping there. Number three and number four were even more modern and more livable than number one. No walls. No chapels. The people who built three and four seem to have had the ridiculous idea that they wanted to be comfortable, and they wasted their money on bathrooms and plumbing instead of building towers and things like that for Paul.'

'Obviously *nouveaux riches*,' Anna murmured.

'Now we come to number five,' Tom announced. 'This is really quite a joint – or, at least, once upon a time it was quite a joint.' He pointed to the map. 'See, it's right up here, only a few kilometres from the Italian border. If you were a multimillionaire and bought the place and were willing to invest a fortune, you might eventually be able to dish it up and make it into a place where you could live.'

'Hmm, this is beginning to sound interesting,' Paul decided. 'Go on, Tom.'

'It's an old, old castle, but the owners must have done a lot of renovating forty or fifty years ago. At the moment it is completely deserted. No one lives there, and from what they told me at the village two or three miles away, it's been empty for about twelve years. Believe it or not, it even has a fine tower and an inside chapel, Paul! And what a wall!'

'Who owns it?' Anna demanded.

'As far as I can make out, the county or the province, or whatever the local authority is, has taken it over. I couldn't get the whole story because my French isn't good enough, but the people who owned it and lived there –' Tom consulted his notes '—were named de Garac. They all died of the plague or vanished

46

up the chimney or something of the sort – I couldn't quite make out – all at the same time. There do not seem to be any family or heirs. No taxes have been paid for years, and the local government has more or less taken over title.'

'This sounds very interesting,' Paul said.

'Is it furnished?' Anna demanded.

'Well, it's partially furnished,' Tom said. 'It must have had a lot more furniture at one time. There are some beds and a table here and there, and random chairs, and an old wood stove which probably would work. If there ever was an icebox, though, it has disappeared.'

'A bathroom?'

'One bathroom, but no running water. The servants apparently had to carry the water by hand, and the outlets from the bathtub are just pipes running through the wall and out.' Tom grinned. 'After you have taken your bath, Anna, Paul could stand down in the courtyard when you pull the plug out. It would save carrying a lot of water!'

'Could you manage with that, Anna?' Paul demanded.

'If I had to,' she murmured.

'The place is pretty damp and musty,' Tom went on, 'but there are a lot of open hearths around, and if you kept big fires burning for a few days I suppose the place would dry out a bit.

'Your wall is really superb! It is crumbling a little in spots, Paul, but, at least from what I could see, it is all standing. You could look at the broken bits and tell yourself it occurred the last time your enemies raided you.'

'Anna,' Paul exclaimed, 'this is the place we have been looking for! It sounds ideal! I cannot wait to see Tom's pictures. You have pictures of this— What is it called, by the way? Has it a name?'

Tom consulted his notes again. 'Ah, yes, Castle Garac. I gather the de Garac family – until the time they disappeared – had lived there since about the time things crawled out of the sea and decided to try things out on dry land. Now we come to number six.'

'I am not interested in this six!' Paul declared firmly. 'It is this Castle Garac that I want. Anna, you agree, of course?'

Anna nodded. 'It seems to be – the sort of spot you've been looking for.'

'Well, that is unfortunate,' Tom said.

'Why?' Paul's voice was sharp.

'Because the Castle Garac is not for rent,' Tom announced.

'Not for rent? It must be for rent, otherwise why were you sent there?'

'I told you that these French real-estate agents lived in a land of illusions. The authorities have been trying to sell the place for years so that they could get their taxes paid, but no one seems to want it because it would be too expensive for modern living.'

Paul rose and began to stride up and down the room. 'But it must be for rent! It has to be for rent!'

'Well, it just isn't,' Tom said calmly. He consulted his notes again. 'Just for the record,' he informed them, 'there's a little item of about 983,000 francs due for back taxes which, my friend the mayor tells me, the authorities would like very much to have. I suppose that includes interest on the unpaid taxes. My impression is that for that amount of money you could become lord of the manor or count of the castle or whatever you'd like to be. They might compromise, but I didn't bring the matter up because I did not think you were interested in buying at any such figure.'

'But if they rented the place, they'd at least get something,' Anna protested.

'I pointed that out to them, but I *believe* that what they said was that this would be strictly illegal and that no one had the right to rent the Castle Garac, only the right to sell it.'

Paul turned on Anna. 'What time did you tell Hugo to be here?' he demanded.

'He should be here now.'

'We must talk to Hugo about this. He was born and brought up here. There must be some way around this difficulty.'

'A little bribery?' asked Anna.

'Possibly, possibly,' Paul muttered.

'And you're sure you don't want to hear about number six?' Tom asked. 'I'll admit that number six is—'

'No. It is Garac or nothing. Where the devil is Hugo?'

48

Fifteen minutes later Hugo Forchet knocked at the door.

'Ah, Hugo, we need you, we need you badly! Tom has found just what we want, the place created for my purpose. It is called the Castle Garac.'

'I have heard of it,' Hugo admitted.

'From what Tom says, it sounds ideal; but he says that it cannot be rented. The state has taken it over for taxes and will only sell. What can we do?'

Hugo took a package of Blues from his pocket and thoughtfully removed one of the black tobacco cigarettes. He lit it and pulled in the acrid smoke with an air of enjoyment.

'Wouldn't a little bribery help?' Anna asked.

Hugo shook his head. 'Probably not. This would be too important a matter, and it could not be concealed.' He thought for a few moments. 'So the law is that you cannot rent under such circumstances,' he muttered. There was silence again.

Tom noticed with interest and curiosity that Paul was really agitated. It was the first time he had seen any loss of self-control. This suave, polished man of the world had been checked, and was grim and hard.

Anna sat there relaxed, her eyes veiled, her face inscrutable, waiting.

Suddenly Hugo snapped his fingers; Tom saw his leathery face crinkle, and the crooked smile.

'Paul, will you please order two double cognacs. I think I have earned it.'

Paul rang for the floor waiter. 'What is it, man, what is it?'

Hugo shook his finger in front of his nose, and there was a sly expression in his eyes. 'You are impatient, Paul. Wait until I get my cognac.'

There was a tense atmosphere in the room, a tension that Tom could not quite justify or explain, based on the situation as he knew it. The Castle Garac seemed to be much more important to Paul Ehrenhardt than it should be. Even the imperturbable Anna seemed to have been drawn into the rip-tide. Hugo seemed the least affected. He stood there with his legs apart and his hands in his pockets, his cigarette drooping from his lips His eyes were narrowed, but he was humming.

His cognac arrived, and he took it from the waiter.

'Yes, I think this would work,' he said quietly. 'Since the Castle Garac cannot be rented legally, it cannot be rented. The local authorities have no authorization to rent – only to sell. The state wishes to recover the unpaid taxes. That is reasonable. And if a property is rented, that could perhaps justifiably be considered a delaying factor in connexion with any possible sale.

'But what would happen, Paul, if a rich young American, our friend Tom here, went to the authorities and said that he was contemplating *purchasing* the Castle Garac? It would be reasonable that he must determine just how much it would cost to restore the castle and make it livable, which of course would take some time, and naturally he does not propose to invest either his time or his money on such an investigation without a definite option to purchase.'

Tom could see Paul Ehrenhardt relaxing a little.

'An option to purchase for the full amount of the delinquent taxes,' Hugo went on. 'It would be say, a four months' option. Such an option would call for a substantial payment. If the option price were large enough, undoubtedly the option could be made to include the right to live in the castle during the time of the option.'

'Hugo, I have underrated you!' Paul exclaimed. 'Would this work?'

'It is not illegal,' Hugo said cautiously. 'One should be able to do anything that is not illegal.'

Paul had completely recovered himself. Once more he was the urbane, confident entrepreneur. He turned to Tom. 'Tom, you will need a lawyer for this. This is a most delicate matter. You will tell the lawyer that you wish to purchase the Castle Garac, but that you will not be in a position to pay for it for some months, and that therefore you must have an option – as cheap as possible, of course – with the provision that you have the exclusive right of occupancy during the period of the option.'

'Is this really as important to you as all that?' Tom asked curiously.

'It is more important to me than all that,' Paul retorted.

'When Paul develops an idea,' Anna drawled, 'it becomes

50

more important than anything in the world.'

'Well, all I ask is that you find me a lawyer who speaks English.'

'That, I am sure, could be very easily arranged,' Hugo said smoothly.

'How long should such arrangements take, Hugo?' Paul demanded.

Hugo shrugged his shoulders. 'If the young American is persistent and impatient, it should not take too long,' he decided. 'It must be put on the basis of a sudden decision which must be immediately decided one way or another. Americans have the reputation of making up their minds suddenly and of requiring immediate action. Such an unreasonable attitude on the part of Mr Welles might even be expected.'

'Good!' Paul rubbed his hands. 'Hugo, you must see that Tom gets into the hands of the right *avocat* – but discreetly, of course. The *avocat* will ask who recommended him, and Tom must have an answer for that. It must not be you.'

'That I understand,' Hugo agreed calmly.

Tom did not understand.

Paul walked swiftly into the bedroom and, a moment later, reappeared with a toppling stack of bank notes.

Tom looked at it and whistled. 'The Bank of France,' he observed.

Paul smiled. 'Not at all, my dear Tom. Merely payment for a few hours of honest work at the Casino at Cannes. I told you that Anna and I had a most successful evening last night.

'Hugo, you and Tom be on your way, and I'm counting on the Castle Garac being available for occupancy five days from today.'

And in five days the Castle Garac was available for occupancy.

With the help of Hugo, Tom established contact with a young lawyer in Nice who was perfectly willing to tolerate American aberrations if a substantial fee were involved, who appreciated the fact that it was important to get things settled at once lest the deal fall through, and who spoke enough English to explain to Tom exactly what was happening day by day.

There were conferences; there were three trips to Latire, the village adjacent to the Castle Garac; there were long telephone conversations with the French authorities. Everyone seemed delighted to aid and abet this rich young American in his folly of acquiring the Castle Garac, and, as Hugo prophesied, the 'permission to inhabit' during the term of the option was quite legal, or at least not illegal, and presented no difficulties. Tom detected an expression of pity occasionally on the faces of some of the officials he was dealing with, but they must have stifled their consciences, for they afforded him complete cooperation. The possibility of recovering twelve years of taxes due to the Castle Garac inspired everyone to a frenzy of activity.

The night of the fourth day Tom entered the Ehrenhardts' suite triumphantly and tossed a thick sheaf of papers on the table.

'The Castle Garac is yours,' he announced.

'Not at all, Tom,' Paul said softly. 'The castle is yours. Let's have no confusion about that point. When we move in, it will be merely as your guests and your friends.'

'Am I to go up there?' Tom demanded.

There was a pause. 'I don't know yet. That we will decide later. I'm pleased, Tom. Very pleased.'

'When are you – or when are we – going to move in?' Tom demanded.

'That I don't know yet, either,' Paul admitted. 'There are one or two things still to do here. Hugo will go up at once, I think, and prepare for our arrival. Certainly we cannot move into the place as it is now.'

'And what do I do now?' Tom demanded.

'Ah, your next commission should be an enjoyable one,' Paul assured him. 'I must leave now, but at ten o'clock tomorrow morning we shall discuss your next responsibility. Good night, Tom, good night.' He paused. 'By the way, Tom, you have heard nothing from New York about your novel, have you?'

'No, nothing, Paul.'

'Ah, too bad. But be patient. One of these days you will have news, and I am sure it will be good news!'

6

'REPORTING FOR orders, Paul,' Tom announced the next morning.

'Good! I have asked Anna to give you the instructions and the data for what you are to do next. Being a woman, perhaps she can be more helpful than I would be.'

Paul went to the door of the bedroom and announced Tom's presence. Then he turned back to Tom. 'You will excuse me, won't you, Tom? Anna will be here in just a moment.'

When she appeared she came across the room until she was standing very close to him.

'I've scarcely seen you for a week,' she said softly .

'No, as you realize, I've been busy.'

'I've missed you, Tom.'

'You're very kind to say so,' Tom responded lightly.

'Paul will be out tonight,' she observed. 'I would rather like to see where you live and how you live. Would you like me to pay you a visit tonight, Tom?'

Tom's heart was pounding. There stood a most desirable, seductive woman frankly offering herself to him. Why? He had no illusions about himself. Certainly there was nothing about Tom Welles to sweep this sophisticated, worldly woman off her feet. Either this was her normal behaviour with any man that came along, or there was some purpose behind her attempts to throw herself into his arms. Suddenly he felt himself on guard. His instinct told him that he was walking on very thin ice, and that this was more than just a case of a beautiful woman bored with her husband seeking excitement elsewhere. He had a sense of foreboding and danger.

'Anna, I think it would be better if you did not come to see me this evening,' Tom said quietly. 'I told you the other night why.'

She walked away from him with a shrug of her shoulders.

'As you will,' she said lightly. And then her manner changed. 'Sit down, Tom, and listen carefully. The next thing Paul wants

53

you to do for him will not be easy, so pay careful attention to everything I say.

'For this project of his, Paul must find a girl who, in order to play her part, must have certain definite qualifications, and each one is essential. Are you listening?'

'Yes.'

'It makes no difference how old she actually is, but she must be able to pass easily for nineteen. She must not only *look* nineteen, but act as a nineteen-year-old girl would act. Next, she must be fair – not with bleached blond hair, but naturally fair. The fairer the better, both as to skin and hair. She does not have to be beautiful, but she must be distinguished-looking. None of your nightclub *poules*. She must have the looks and bearing of the aristocracy.'

'This is a tall order,' Tom said.

'That is only part of it,' Anna admitted. 'Her circumstances must be such that she will be willing, for the sake of a very, very substantial sum of money, to disappear from where she had been living, cut herself off from any friends she may have for perhaps some time, perhaps as long as a year. And she must be free of any attachments, either of family or of a sentimental nature, that would complicate her disappearance and her new life.'

'What in the devil is this all about?' Tom blurted out.

'You shouldn't have asked that,' Anna said. 'One of the terms of your employment was that you would not ask questions which could not be answered. I promise you, however, that what is ahead for such a girl, if you find her, will not be unpleasant and might be very much to her advantage.'

'Let's get this straight,' Tom requested. 'You want a girl who is either nineteen or could be nineteen, preferably without any family or friends, who can act like a lady, looks like an aristocrat, and she has to be a blonde.'

Anna nodded.

'And if there should be such a person alive and I were able to find her, what next?'

'You report to us,' Anna told him. 'There is one other thing: of course she must be French-born, and French must be her native language.'

'Wouldn't it be simpler and save time to advertise for this goddess?' Tom demanded.

'Under the circumstances, that is impossible. It is imperative that no one know that we are even looking for such a person.'

'Let's suppose that I find somebody who seems to look like what you want: how do I find out about her family and friends and the circumstances of her life, as you call them?'

'You will have to make her acquaintance and investigate yourself. If she has close family ties or has a lover or a child – many unmarried women do have children, you know, Tom, whether you realize it or not – she would be of no use to us.'

'This is the damnedest proposal I've ever heard,' Tom broke out. 'Now see here, Anna, I can't possibly do this. How would I go about it? I haven't the slightest idea where to start or what to do. This is like looking for a needle in a haystack.'

'It won't be easy,' Anna admitted, 'but it is not impossible. There are girls everywhere – in Nice, in Cannes, in Monte Carlo and Antibes. You might even try Marseilles. You have your night clubs and your restaurants, and you have your houses that are still operating, although illegally. And then there are the casinos. Understand, we are not interested in her morals or her past as long as she can play the part, as long as she seems to be such a girl as I have described.'

Tom shook his head. 'I can just see myself going up to a beautiful young girl playing roulette and saying: "I beg your pardon, mademoiselle, are you an orphan, have you a lover?"'

Anna laughed with real amusement. 'And, Tom, I swear you probably would do it just in that way. No, my friend, you're going to have to develop a more subtle technique and a safer approach. You must meet her as though you yourself were interested in her. If she does not repulse your advances, it will indicate that she might be available.

'Voulez-vous faire une petite promenade avec moi?' Tom repeated grimly.

Anna frowned. 'What are you saying?'

'Didn't you understand me?' Tom demanded.

'No, I don't think I did.'

'Then she wouldn't understand me either,' Tom said

triumphantly. 'You've got the wrong man for this job. I wouldn't get to first base.'

'You'll do it,' Anna assured him serenely. 'It may take you a little time, but there are more girls along the Riviera than there are fish in the Mediterranean.'

Tom was silent for a few moments. He thought of the money he had won gambling in Monte Carlo, which was surely enough to carry him along until he heard something from New York about his novel – more than enough. But what if the news was bad when it came? In his own mind he had already earmarked his winnings as a nest egg to finance the writing of his next book. If he frittered it away now while he waited, what would he have to go on with? Besides, this blind search for a natural blonde might be rather amusing after all. If he were careful he couldn't get into too much trouble, and if he were lucky enough to find the right girl she certainly would be able to take care of herself and her own interests.

'All right,' he said resignedly, 'when do I start?'

Anna smiled. 'Since you don't want me to pay you a visit this evening, Tom, you can start immediately.'

'How do I get a list of the sort of places where I might find such a girl?'

Anna opened the desk drawer. 'As you know, Hugo Forchet knows this part of the world very well,' she said smoothly. She looked at the two sheets of paper in her hands. 'This is quite a complete list, by categories, of the most likely spots for your rendezvous. You'll need expense money.'

'I've still got plenty,' Tom grumbled. 'What's the time element, Anna? How soon do I have to find your specimen?'

'We hope you can find her very, very quickly,' Anna said. 'She is essential if Paul's plans are to progress and if his project is to succeed.'

Tom rose. 'I think Diogenes had an easier job,' he observed.

'That is quite possible, Tom,' Anna said gravely. '*Au revoir*.'

And so with the top of his Simca convertible down, Tom Welles began his prowl along the Côte d'Azur. For the first few hours he felt a strange feeling of guilt. Of course, no one knew what he was up to, and his actions were perfectly innocent and unobjectionable, but he kept thinking of that good old-fashioned word 'masher'. He felt as though ever gendarme were on the point of coming up to him and sternly forbidding him to proceed with this outrageous quest. He imagined respectable women looking at him askance.

Then he began to develop a conviction that this search would most certainly be completely futile. Ordinarily, one thought of the Riviera as teeming with attractive females. Now the whole place seemed to be deserted. There scarcely seemed to be a woman anywhere other than respectable French housewives.

He finally decided he needed a drink and stopped the car in front of a café halfway between Nice and Cannes. He ordered a Cinzano. He also decided that he would have to lay out a definite plan and abandon any idea of flopping into this place and out of that place like a chicken with its head off.

The big question seemed to be where one would be most likely to run across Venus. He got as far as naming the girl Venus. Why, he didn't quite know, unless it had something to do with the Botticelli painting of the blonde and the sea shell. Botticelli's Venus might have been a bit older than his would have to be but the resemblance was close enough for all practical purposes.

Maybe he should get a dog, he reflected. He always understood that a friendly dog on a leash, preferably of some strange, esoteric breed, was a great convenience in establishing contact with a member of the opposite sex. You could always manage a leash so that it got twisted around the victim's leg, and that necessitated apologies. With the ice broken, you could discuss the dog, and one thing would lead to another.

Also, any respectable or semi-respectable girl would not hesitate to go into ecstasies over a dog when nothing in the world could have persuaded her to address the dog's master directly.

Then, of course, if the girl had a dog, too, it was even easier. The dogs either approached each other in a friendly way and became intimate at once or they attacked each other. In either case, a strong bond was immediately established between the respective owners.

Then he decided he'd have to really consider the matter of a dog.

His biggest difficulty, naturally, was that on the Riviera unattached, unchaperoned French girls of distinction were not found everywhere. If it were America, the search would be much easier. At nineteen an American girl was on her own. If the field had been open to American and English girls, it would have been easier. But no, Venus had to be French.

Anna's idea of the casinos was ridiculous. A French girl of nineteen in the casinos might be with her family, but more probably under the wing of her *ami*. He wasn't even sure that they let unescorted girls of that age into casinos. No, he decided, in the casinos it would be bad hunting.

Anna had suggested the 'houses'. He consulted his list that had been furnished by Hugo. In spite of the law, there still seemed to be a number operating in Nice, one or two in Cannes, and some in Monte Carlo. Tom imagined that when you arrived at the door you rang the bell and said: 'Jake sent me,' following the speakeasy technique of prohibition days in America. Well, he supposed he'd have to case the houses sooner or later. He could do that late some night.

He was doubtful, too, about the hotels. What would such a girl be doing alone at a good hotel unless she were of the demi-monde, and a success at that. If she were successful, she probably would not be interested in any proposition that Paul had to make, whatever it might be.

The shops and stores that had models might be fertile territory – as a matter of fact even the good stores that did not use models. He had seen some damned good-looking store clerks in his time. That idea really appealed to him. A poor but honest girl working in a store in order to earn a living in a respectable way, supporting an old grandmother who was deaf, dumb, and blind. The grandmother would have to be deaf, dumb, and blind or obviously the girl could not leave without explanation. If she were deaf, dumb, and blind, Venus could hire anybody to take care of the old lady, put up a stake for the expenses, and

58

her absence would not even be noticed. Good jewellery counters would be likely spots to find such a girl with the grandmother. Perfumery counters, too. He certainly must investigate all the perfumery departments along the coast, and there must be a lot of them.

The night clubs and cafés and restaurants that had any sort of show were obvious spots. That was where he would probably find Venus! She was a singer in a small restaurant. She was a sweet girl. Her voice was true but too small for the concert stage or for opera. She was struggling hard, because she was unappreciated. In fact, she was in terror of losing her job. She would certainly welcome the attention of a rich young American, and once a carrot of gold was dangled in front of her nose, she would accept joyfully any proposal made to her.

Tom paid for his drink. He decided before starting out seriously after Venus, he would drop into the post office. Perhaps there would be a letter there to solve all his problems and he would be able to forget the quest for Venus.

He drove around to the post office and parked the car.

'*Rien aujourd'hui,*' he heard as usual. He turned away and settled down behind the wheel of the Simca.

Now, if that girl up in the inn at Vence were about nineteen. If she were only blonde. If she were only distinguished-looking instead of merely entrancingly pretty. If she were only un-attached instead of obviously being surrounded by townsfolk who had known her all her life.

Well, he supposed there was time to wander around some of the better stores this afternoon to see if there was anything there that looked worthwhile, and then he had a thought which caused a spasm in his chest. Suppose he did see a likely-looking candidate for Venus. What next? Wait for her outside the store? Follow her home? The chances were four out of five that she would have a family or a husband or, according to Anna, a lot of illegitimate babies.

He started the Simca and began threading his way among the bicycles.

'Here I come, you lucky Venus,' he said to himself, but his face was very grim.

59

There was one thing about the next three days: Tom Welles lost all his self-consciousness about women. He had decided that it would be necessary to develop a technique for establishing contact with Venus if and when he came upon her, and he might as well practise a little whenever he got the opportunity along the way, even if the girl was not blonde, nineteen, or aristocratic-looking. He hobnobbed with salesgirls, and they were remarkably friendly he discovered. He even asked two of them to have a drink with him after they finished work, and they accepted with pleasure. The problem then, of course, was to get rid of them. They took it for granted that the drink was just the overture to an opera, but Tom Welles could not spare the time for any opera.

Impersonally and as a connoisseur he examined all the inhabitants of the houses on his list. He found the houses quite unproductive and concluded that attractive, aristocratic nineteen-year-old blondes did not have to shut themselves up in such houses. Now if Paul would have been satisfied with a sleek raven-haired little mulatto, or robust redheaded Amazon of thirty-five to act as bodyguard, or a tiny brown Italian wench with cherry-coloured lips, it would have been very simple. Perhaps things had been better in the old days when the government had tolerated if not encouraged these palaces of pleasure, or houses of joy, but if so, things had certainly degenerated.

There were plenty of girls in the bars, *most* friendly girls. But there weren't many who could pass as nineteen. He had spotted one the night before he thought might qualify. He approached her warily, but she heard him coming, turned and opened her mouth in a warm, welcoming smile. Tom turned on his heels hastily and beat a retreat. Her mouth had been full of gold teeth. Somehow he did not think Paul and Anna would like those gold teeth.

He had spent hours in various *couturiers*, pretending to be searching for a gown for his nineteen-year-old sister in America. It was her birthday shortly, and he wished to send her a French gown. No, he was not sure of exactly what sort of gown, but he thought probably an evening dress. It was important, however, to have anything that they were showing him modelled by a girl as much like his sister as possible. Yes, his sister was nineteen, blonde, and she would like something not too extreme or flamboyant because she was a girl of distinction.

The *vendeuses* were most helpful and cooperative, and Tom was sure that he had seen every evening gown and every model on the Riviera.

Well, there was nothing to do now but telephone Paul and confess again that he had not struck gold. To comfort himself, he thought back to stories that he had heard as a boy, of prospectors who had spent decades looking for a vein of gold and had found it after many years. He also remembered wryly that a good many of the old prospectors had died of thirst in the desert. Well, he would telephone Paul, get something to eat, and go to bed. Tonight Venus, wherever she was, would have to buy her own dinner or go hungry. Tom Welles had had enough for the day.

7

IT WAS a beautiful day when Tom awoke the next morning. There was a gay breeze blowing in over the deep blue sea, the sun was shining, and in a tree near the window of his room he could hear the birds making love – or at least he supposed they were making love.

Considering the fact that he still had the quest for Venus hanging around his neck, Tom felt strangely gay. As he dressed, he wondered why. Perhaps it was a case of extrasensory perception telling him that there was a letter waiting for him at the post office with the news that someone had bought his novel and that a cheque would be forthcoming .

That most certainly must be it, or why would he feel the way he did? He actually hurried his dressing and, without bothering to get the Simca out of the garage, made his way hastily around to the post office.

His luck was in. There wasn't even any queue there this morning. He walked confidently up to the wicket and announced: 'Thomas Welles, *s'il vous plaît*.'

But a few moments later came the familiar '*Rien aujourd' hui, monsieur*.'

Tom swore to himself and made his way out.

At breakfast, however, he still felt his spirits high. Once the momentary disappointment at the post office had passed, he seemed to be feeling just as cheerful as he had when he woke up.

To hell with Venus, he decided. If I find her, I find her, and if I don't, I don't.

And he left the little restaurant deciding on his plans for the day. There were some stores he had not yet inspected. He supposed it might be worthwhile to drive up and down the Promenade des Anglais a few times, and he had more ground to cover in Cannes.

He had certainly learned more about the resort towns on the Côte d'Azur in the last few days than he had learned in the preceeding four months.

And then, still undecided as to where to start, he caught a glimpse of the green trees blowing in the park just down the street. He decided to take half an hour in the park over his cigarette as he used to during those months when he was writing. He wouldn't find Venus in the park, of course, but it wouldn't hurt Venus to wait for half an hour. Heaven knows he had spent enough time running around after her the last few days. 'Venus in the park,' he said to himself. 'Not a bad title for a light novel.' It reminded him of some of Maxwell Bodenheim's titles.

He wandered slowly down the street, relaxed, looking in the shop windows, and then found his favourite bench by the big sycamore tree on the corner. He had not been there for a long time.

It *was* a beautiful morning.

And the park was still quite empty.

It had been a good breakfast, and perhaps today he would find Venus, tie her up with a blue ribbon, and turn her over to Paul.

And tomorrow he'd hear from New York. That extrasensory perception of his must be even stronger than he suspected because obviously it had reached him from the letter a long way away and not just from the post office around the corner.

Across the park four children were playing a strange, involved game with sticks and chalk that he did not understand. The first part of it seemed to be a form of Still-Pond-No-More-Moving, with one child in the centre covering up his eyes. Then there would be a shrill cry and everyone would talk at once.

It reminded him of a game he had made up himself when he was very young. He had played it alone, and it helped sometimes when you were lonely. You could play it at a window overlooking the street or you could play it in the park or in any strange place. You covered up your eyes and counted up to a certain number. While you counted you guessed what you were going to see when you opened your eyes. It was not very exciting if you only counted to ten or twenty because not much could happen in the time it took you to count slowly to ten or twenty. The real way to play was to count to fifty or even to a hundred slowly. Of course you wanted to open your eyes long before you reached fifty or a hundred but that was against the rules. As you counted, you tried to guess what the first thing would be that you would see, and when you got near to the final number, tension would grow within you and you'd feel your heart beating, and it was terribly difficult not to open your eyes before you actually reached the final number.

Of course, sometimes you did not see anything worthwhile at all. As a matter of fact, that happened often. Of course, the first thing you saw when you opened your eyes hardly ever turned out to be what you had guessed it would be, but that just made the game harder, and there was always the hope that it would turn out to be exactly what you had guessed it would be.

Suddenly, without any conscious volition, Tom found himself sitting there on the bench, his legs spread apart, his elbows on his knees, leaning forward with his face in his hands, his eyes tightly closed. He was counting: 'One, two, three,' very slowly.

Should he make it fifty or should he make it a hundred? Well, he'd make it a good one this time. He'd make it a hundred. And what would he see when he opened his eyes? 'Thirteen, fourteen, fifteen ... perhaps a black poodle ... twenty-one, twenty-two, twenty-three ... an old man picking up papers with a stick ... thirty, thirty-one, thirty-two, thirty-three ... a boy rolling a hoop ... thirty-nine ... the black-haired girl up in Vence ... no, that was ridiculous, he'd settle on the black poodle ... forty-six, forty-seven ...'

'*Pardon, monsieur! Vous êtes malade?*'

It was a soft, low voice, and at the instant he was not sure whether it was very near him or very far away.

Without raising his head he peeked through his fingers and saw the bottom of a black pram and two small rubber-tyred wheels. And then out of the corner of his eye he saw two small white canvas shoes and slim ankles in white cotton stockings.

He raised his head slowly. A white starched skirt, a slim waist, something blue hanging down her back like a veil. The hands were holding the handle of the pram very tensely and the arms were rigid. The veil down her back fell from some sort of tight coif that came down low on her forehead and completely covered her hair and ears. It was a frame for an exquisite face, at the moment rather nervous and alarmed.

Tom's expression must have confirmed her suspicions.

'*Vous êtes malade, monsieur?*'

Tom rose quickly. He made a supreme effort. '*Non, mademoiselle, je ne suis pas malade.*'

And then desperately he demanded: '*Quel est le couleur de vos chevaux.*'

Her face was startled for an instant, and then her alarm and concern seemed to disappear, and although her mouth remained serious, he could see dimples flickering in her cheeks as she tried to restrain herself.

'*Je n'en ai pas,*' she replied demurely.

Tom forgot his French.

'No hair? You have no hair?' he blurted out. 'None at all?'

Then the miracle happened.

'You asked about the colour of my *horses*. No, I have no horses.'

It was halting English, a little stilted, with a strong French accent, but it was English.

'Your hair. It was the colour of your hair I asked about.'

'French is a very difficult language for all the English. So many words are so alike.' Her one concern now seemed to be that he feel no embarrassment about his mistake.

There was a cry from the pram, and for the first time Tom took his eyes off the girl and peered down. Good heavens, they must be twins, and they did not look very old. The girl was jiggling the handle of the pram, and the crying stopped. He remembered Anna's warning about illegitimate children.

'Those aren't yours, are they?' Tom demanded.

'They are mine – to take care of,' she replied a little stiffly. 'I must go now, monsieur. I am glad you are not ill. '

'But you can't go now,' cried Tom. 'I've got to talk to you.'

'One does not talk to strangers in the park,' she murmured, and her eyes dropped. Then she added: 'Unless they are ill.'

Tom grinned. 'Well, you are talking to me and I'm not ill,' he pointed out. She had already started to move away, pushing the pram. Tom took two long steps and reached her side. He noticed a slight blush on the girl's face. It was very becoming.

'Please leave me monsieur. Someone might see, and then I would be in trouble with my employers.'

'Not in nearly as much trouble as I am already,' Tom assured her.

'You must be an American. An Englishman would not be so – offensive.'

'I'm not being offensive at all,' Tom objected. 'I just want to talk to you. I've got to talk to you. Can't you do something with those children, get rid of them in some way?'

She looked at him, puzzled. 'Get rid of them?' she repeated.

'Yes. Drop them in the pond or hang them on a tree or something.'

'Monsieur is not very funny,' she said coldly. 'Will you please leave me now? Or shall I have to—'

'Look, mademoiselle, I made a mistake. I just realized that I am sick, very sick. I can feel a terrible, tearing pain right in here.' Tom thumped his chest vigorously. 'My heart is pounding. I think I'm falling. I think I'm falling. I need help desperately.'

She turned towards him, her face very serious. 'Monsieur, please believe me. The family I work for — Madame is very strict, very particular. If she were to see us or hear that I had been talking to a man in the park, I would be discharged.'

'That would be wonderful,' Tom said enthusiastically. 'You certainly don't want to go through life taking care of those two rather unattractive-looking babies, do you?'

She looked as though she didn't know whether to laugh or to cry.

Tom hurried on. 'You've admitted you haven't any horses, but, as a matter of fact, I don't think you've got any hair either. You are self-conscious about it, and you wear that head-dress to cover up your head so people won't know you are bald. You probably had scarlet fever as a child, and all your hair fell out and never came back. And *that's* why you won't talk to me in the park!' he went on triumphantly. 'It's not your job you're worried about at all. You're afraid that if we get to know each other better I'll discover that you haven't got a single hair on your head, and you'd feel ashamed!'

She certainly must have known he was joking, so it must have been the tone of his voice that infuriated her.

'I have hair! And very nice hair!'

'What colour is it?' Tom demanded quickly.

'I am a blonde!'

'I knew it!' he exclaimed triumphantly. 'Venus in the park!'

'What did you say, monsieur?'

'Nothing . . . See here, where are you going?'

She had turned the pram suddenly and was retracing her steps, walking swiftly now.

'Since you will not leave me alone, I am going home, monsieur,' and her voice was uncompromising.

'But, mademoiselle, mademoiselle, I must talk to you. Wait just a few moments.'

They had reached the edge of the park now.

'Monsieur, if you follow me out of the park, I shall report you for molesting me.'

The voice that Tom remembered as warm and sympathetic was very cold now, and he stopped abruptly as they reached the sidewalk. 'I am sorry,' he said quietly. 'I apologize.'

She bent her head gravely, accepting his apology, and started wheeling the pram down the street. Tom stood there watching her, but made no move to follow.

Then she halted for an instant and turned her head.

'*Au revoir, monsieur.*'

He watched her until she turned the corner and disappeared. Then he thrust his hands deep into his pockets and shuffled off down the street to the nearest café. He ordered a large *fine* and then another and then a third.

Tom was not thinking so much of the Ehrenhardts or the quest for Venus. He was thinking of the bluest eyes he'd ever seen, and high cheekbones, a wide, generous mouth, and the firm but sensitive chin, the colour that came or went on her face betraying every emotion, small, firm, capable hands, and a walk that put all the models he had been watching to shame.

And he thought about the tense excitement within himself that still had everything inside his chest twisted up in knots, and the feeling of despair that he felt when she had disappeared around that corner.

And Tom Welles wondered if he had fallen in love.

A few hours later Tom realized that he was getting drunk. There was a row of saucers lying on the table in front of him, tallying the number of brandies he had consumed. He counted them vaguely. There seemed to be quite a lot of them. Rather foggily he called for his reckoning.

He was not sure just how much the waiter demanded after counting the saucers, but he drew out a wad of bank notes and started putting bill after bill down on the table, one by one, until the waiter seemed satisfied. It did seem to him that the waiter was standing there rather a long time before he turned away.

He rose and headed for the door. Considering his condition, he thought he was walking rather well. The door seemed to be moving a little erratically ahead of him, from one side to the other, but he kept heading straight for it wherever it moved.

On the sidewalk he paused, and then automatically turned back toward the little park, made his way slowly down the street to the entrance near his own bench by the big sycamore

67

tree, turned in and sat down. He had done that *very* well, he decided, but it was good to sit down again. This air was what he needed. It was very good air, and the park was deserted. It must be the time for naps or siestas. In a few minutes he would go back to his room and go to sleep himself, sleep this off. It was a long time since he'd had too much to drink. It would be good to sleep.

And then he remembered the long, dark, steep stairs leading to his room. There were a lot of stairs and they were steep. How many stairs were there? he wondered. He would try to guess, and then when he got home he'd count them and see how close he had been able to come.

He dropped his head down into his hands and tried to visualize the stairway. Let's see, up to the first landing there would be one, two, three, four . . .

'*Pardon, monsieur, vous êtes malade?*'

The figure on the bench leaning forward, head in hands, did not stir.

The girl waited uncertainly for a moment or so and then she repeated in a louder voice:

'*Pardon, monsieur, vous êtes malade?*'

There was no response. She frowned and bit her lip. She could hear very heavy breathing, and occasionally the suggestion of a snore. She looked hastily around to see whether anyone was watching her and then leaned forward swiftly, put her head two inches away from Tom's face, and sniffed. Then she straightened up and stood there hesitating. She turned away and walked a few steps and then halted, looking back over her shoulder.

When she walked back to the bench it was very slowly and rather uncertainly. She stood squarely in front of the figure on the bench, reached out tentatively, and tapped Tom on the shoulder. Then she tapped a little harder.

Tom stirred, half groaned.

'*Pardon, monsieur, vous êtes malade?*'

Tom opened his eyes and peeked through his fingers. He saw a pair of bright red shoes with very high heels, slim, smooth, bare ankles, lovely, lovely legs, clinging yellow silk belted in at the waist with red leather, then more yellow silk cut down in a deep V, bare arms, a face he remembered under a curling mass of golden filament glistening in the sunlight.

Tom sat there motionless, staring up into her face. This was obviously a dream. He did not want it to end. At any moment she would disappear and he would wake up.

And the girl was silent, too, looking down at Tom with a rather strange expression in her eyes, waiting for him to speak.

Finally he did. 'That isn't hair. It must be a wig. Not even the good Lord could make hair like that.'

'Monsieur, you are very, very drunk,' the girl said severely.

'I suppose so,' Tom agreed.

'It is disgraceful to be in such a condition.'

He nodded in agreement. 'It's your fault, though.'

'*My fault?*'

'Yes. You wouldn't talk to me and went off and left me, so I got drunk. I see you've changed your clothes. Where are the babies?'

She ignored that. 'Do you always get drunk when you – when you – when your advances are repulsed?'

'No. As a matter of fact, this is the first time. You see, I think I've fallen in love,' he explained.

Her face was very sceptical.

'Mademoiselle, either you are going to have to sit down here on this bench or I shall have to get up. At the moment it would be much easier for you to sit down than it would be for me to stand up. You see, my head –'

'Disgraceful,' she murmured as she sat down tentatively on the far end of the bench.

'As a matter of fact, I'm completely sober now,' Tom assured her. 'My mind is working swiftly and clearly. The only trouble is my head. It seems to be whirling around, and thumping and thumping.'

'Much strong black coffee is indicated,' she said firmly.

'That might help,' Tom agreed. 'Mademoiselle, it is an outrageous suggestion, I realize, but do you think you could possibly help me get to the nearest café – and then perhaps stay with me for just a little while I drink your strong black coffee and until I feel a little better? My head really is terrific, and I'm not at all sure I can walk without help.'

Her face became very grave. 'You are very, very sick, aren't you?'

'I've never felt worse.'

'Then perhaps out of charity I should help you,' she decided.

8

WHETHER IT was due to the prescription of black coffee, or to a strong glandular reaction, or to the blood racing through his body cleaning up after the best part of a bottle of cognac, Tom Welles did not know, but he was feeling much, much better.

As a matter of fact, walking down to the same café where he had indulged in his recent bebauch, the girl had looked up at him reproachfully.

'You do not need me at all. You are walking as straight as I am. You are perfectly able to take care of yourself.'

'You're quite wrong, mademoiselle,' Tom protested, 'I need you desperately. You cannot possibly realize how much I need you. . . . How did you know I would be in the park if you came back?'

Colour flooded her face. 'I did not come back! I had no idea that you would be there on your bench. It was my free afternoon and – I was on my way to the house of a friend.'

'Oh.'

'And to walk through the park was the shortest route.'

'If that's really a true story, then there is a God,' Tom decided. 'My name is Tom Welles. Do you have a name?'

'Yes monsieur, I do have a name.'

'That's nice,' Tom said. 'I've always thought there's nothing like having a name.'

'I am called Angèle Corton,' she said kindly.

'Angèle Corton,' he repeated softly.

At the door of the café she had hesitated. 'I shall leave you now, monsieur,' she had announced. 'Here is your café, and remember, *much* black coffee.'

Tom had taken her by the arm. He was very serious. 'If you leave me now, I shall get drunk again, stinking drunk. I mean that.'

'You are impossible,' she murmured. But she entered the café as he held the door open for her.

There were four saucers on the table now, but this time they tallied *café noir*, not *fine champagne*.

Much of Angèle Corton's caution and reserve seemed to have been dissipated. She was calling him Mr Welles now, not monsieur, and she ignored the fact that he was calling her Angèle.

Yes, she liked babies and children or she wouldn't be acting as a nursemaid. No, she had not been a nursemaid long, but when she had finished her schooling she had wanted to learn English and had taken the position with an English family who lived in Nice. And what was Mr Welles doing in Nice ?

'Angèle, you won't believe me, but I really don't know what I'm doing at the moment. I *was* writing a book, but I finished that. And now I just don't know.'

'Enjoying yourself enormously, no doubt.'

Tom shook his head. 'No, not really, not until today. Angèle, will you have dinner with me tonight? I have a car, and we could drive up into the mountains and find a quiet little inn for dinner.'

'Most certainly not, monsieur.' Her chin was very firm and her voice was indignant.

Two hours later Tom Welles swung the Simca off the middle Corniche on to a narrow causeway.

'I have heard of the Château Madrid,' said Angèle, 'but naturally I have never been there. It is said to be very expensive.'

'The food is excellent, the view is even better. It hangs over the cliff. You have to keep telling yourself either that you are an eagle or a mountain goat. Otherwise you get dizzy and fall down over the cliff into Beaulieu.'

'I shall be a mountain goat,' Angèle decided, 'covered with

warm fur.' She drew Tom's coat more snugly around her. 'It is not warm here at all, Mr Welles.'

Tom swung the car into the cramped parking-lot.

'I do not like to be called Mr Welles,' he told her. 'Why can't you call me by my first name, Tom?'

She thought that over for a moment and then shook her head. 'That would be too informal,' she decided finally. 'It sounds as though I had known you for a long time. But if you like, I think I could call you Thomas.'

'My father used to call me Thomas when I had been bad and punishment was called for.'

'Then I shall most certainly call you Thomas,' Angèle decided.

As Tom had prophesied, dinner had been good and the view even better.

They sat there at a table inside the glass screen, and below them, far, far below them were the lights of Beaulieu and then a chain of other lights running along the coast on either side, with brighter glows over Monte Carlo and, in the distance, Cannes and Nice.

There had been a silence between them, Angèle looking out into the black night with the fairyland below, Tom intent on Angèle.

'Thomas, it is curious that you came to the park this morning on a day that happened to be my afternoon and evening free,' she said dreamily.

'Are you glad?'

'Yes – I think so. But tomorrow it will be strange to go back to the babies and the uniform and the "Yes, madame," "No, madame."'

'It sounds dreary, if you ask me,' observed Tom.

'No, Madame is very kind, and the twins are sweet, and I have learned English. My English isn't very good, is it, Thomas?'

'Excellent, but every time you call me Thomas I think of my father and a spanking.'

Angèle turned to her companion and her eyes were twinkling.

'Did your father spank you very often?' she demanded.

'Often enough. Do they spank children in France? Did your father use to spank you?'

'I don't remember my father.'

'He died when you were very young?'

'I don't know. I was brought up by the nuns in what you call an orphan asylum.'

'Your mother?'

Angèle shrugged. 'No one knows even who my mother and father were,' she said quietly. 'I was a young girl when I was taken to the convent, and all I remember is my life there. They hoped I would become a nun, but a year and a half ago I decided it was not the life for me. When they learned that I did not want to go on in the convent, they taught me how to take care of babies so that I could get a position as a nurse.'

'How old are you, Angèle?'

'I'm not sure even of that. They tell me that I was about six or seven or eight when they found me, and that was twelve years ago.'

'And you remember nothing of your life before the convent?'

'No, nothing.'

And then suddenly Tom came back to earth. For hours he had forgotten the search for Venus. He had forgotten Anna and Paul Ehrenhardt. He had forgotten everything except the enchantment of the moment. It had been as though he and Angèle had been in a world apart. But now he suddenly realized that the incredible and seemingly impossible had happened. Here was his Venus – he shuddered now at the name – and there could not possibly be a more perfect person for Paul's purpose, whatever it was.

'And your name?' he asked.

'The nuns gave me my name. Corton is an old name in these parts, and they called me Angèle.'

'I don't wonder,' Tom muttered. 'And your future?' he demanded.

'Oh, Thomas, how can I know? There seems to be much in life that I have missed, but I have been happy. Often I feel as though I must do things that I cannot possibly do. I would like

73

to play and be gay for a change. There is not much gaiety or playing for a nursemaid. I have one afternoon and evening off a week and a time to rest, but I do not think I could go on this way forever. Perhaps some day—'

Tom's mind was in a turmoil now. What the devil was it Paul Ehrenhardt wanted of his girl? Was it for a part in some play? Was it another case of a Max Reinhardt and *The Miracle*? He found himself strangely reluctant even to tell the Ehrenhardts about Angèle. But if he didn't? Perhaps they could offer her an opportunity that she could never otherwise have, a change of life in a world far removed from the one where she now lived. He remembered Paul's reassuring words about what would be ahead for the right girl if she could be found.

There were complications, though. He had always thought of love at first sight as a romantic concept rather than a reality, but here he himself was in the very midst of the experience. He, Thomas Welles. His one desire at the moment was to throw Angèle over his shoulder and flee to the highest hills where no one could reach them.

'Have you many friends?' he asked abruptly.

Angèle shook her head. 'I go back to see my friends the nuns often,' she said. 'I have met a few servants in the park. I have met a few other people casually, but, Thomas, you do not make many friends either when you're living with the nuns or working as a nursemaid.'

'Then you were *not* on your way to see a friend this afternoon,' he challenged.

Angèle's deep-blue eyes regarded him steadily. 'No,' she said simply. 'I am a silly, foolish girl, I suppose, but I was on my way to your bench to sit there and dream of what might have happened if I had not run away this morning. Thomas, you will take me home now. I'm expected to be back before the big front door is locked for the night. I am not usually late.'

'This is all very unexpected and very strange,' Tom said slowly.

'Yes, Thomas, it is very unexpected and very strange,' Angèle agreed.

After driving Angèle home, Tom Welles drove directly to

the Negresco. Strangely enough, he found that the Ehrenhardts were in, and he went up to their suite. Paul admitted him, and Tom stalked into the room without a word.

Anna looked at him curiously. 'Tom, what is the matter with you?' she demanded. 'You look five years older, your face is grim, and your eyes look as though you were in trouble. What is it?'

Tom shook his head. 'Paul, can I have a drink? A big drink? I need it.'

'Well, certainly, Tom,' Paul said suavely and rang for the waiter. 'What is it, *mon vieux*?'

'I want to give up this job,' Tom blurted out.

'But no, Tom! I know that what you're doing now must be wearisome and irritating, but as soon as you find our girl—'

'I have enough money to pay you back for my clothes and my expenses.'

'Then you have heard from New York, Tom! The news is good?'

'No, I have not heard from New York,' Tom said shortly. 'I have not had any good news, but I had a bit of luck gambling.'

That was about all he would explain about that, he decided.

Anna was looking up at him with narrowed eyes. 'What is happening to you, Tom?' she murmured softly.

'I just don't think I can go on working for you, Paul, and do the things you want me to.'

'Tom, I don't understand,' Paul protested.

'Can I ask you a few questions?'

'Certainly, but I don't promise that I shall answer them.' Paul smiled.

'What is this project of yours?' Tom demanded.

'That I cannot tell you,' Paul said.

'That being the case, if I found the sort of girl you are looking for, I don't think I would want to be responsible for her getting involved in this mysterious hocus-pocus of yours.'

'Perhaps the girl should decide for herself,' Paul suggested.

Anna swung back her head and burst into laughter. 'Oh, Tom, my dear Tom!' she cried. 'If it weren't for Paul, I think I could fall in love with you. You are *such* a baby.'

'And what do you mean by that?'

'I mean that you're sweet, even if you are very obvious. I mean that you have found a girl that you think might do for Paul's purpose and that you have become emotionally involved with her yourself and are now worried about what would happen to her if Paul took her on.'

'Nonsense,' Tom lied.

'Who is she?' Anna demanded. 'What is her name? What is she like? Is she fascinating, charming, and have you never seen anyone like her?' Her voice was teasing but affectionate. 'Was it love at first sight? Do you plan to marry her and take her back to the States?'

To Tom's relief, his drink arrived at that moment, and it gave him a moment of respite.

Paul approached Tom and put his arm on his shoulder, and a smile was on his face. 'Tom, I suspect Anna has hit your nail on the head. You don't have to answer her questions, however. They were very personal questions. Under the circumstances, if any prying female asked me such questions I should tell her to go to the devil. . . . Would you like another drink? I see you have finished that.'

'Please.'

Paul rang for the waiter again and faced Tom. His face was serious now. 'I want you to listen to me very carefully, Tom. I like you. I cannot tell you very much, but what I am telling you tonight is the truth.

'Anna and Hugo Forchet and I are involved in a – well, call it a project – which is very important to us. If it succeeds, it would mean a great deal. If it fails, we shall have lost a great deal of money which I can ill afford to lose.

'There are reasons why I cannot tell you what this project is or anything about it. I can promise you, however, that if it succeeds, those who are involved will be handsomely rewarded, and no one, no individual, will be hurt or injured in any way. It is not a search for buried treasure, but in many ways one might think of it as something like that – the recovery of a treasure which will never be recovered unless our plans succeed.'

'But why the girl?' Tom interrupted. 'Why do you need a girl?'

'That I cannot tell you, Tom. But I assure you that unless we find the right girl, we cannot proceed. If we do find the right girl, before she can be of any use to us, she will have to know everything about this project, her part in our plans, and what she is doing and why. I am confident that if she understood what was at stake, this girl you found would decide to join with us. The decision would be hers. If she did not voluntarily fall in with our plans, she would be useless to us.'

'You would tell her everything?' Tom demanded.

'We would *have* to tell her everything,' Paul replied.

Tom picked up his second drink. 'This is fantastic,' he objected.

'I quite agree,' Paul said. 'It is like something out of a cheap, melodramatic story of adventure and intrigue.'

'Is Ehrenhardt your real name?'

'No, but of course I would deny that I had ever admitted that fact to you. I am being very frank with you, Tom – telling you as much as I possibly can without jeopardizing my own plans.'

'Tom, my dear.' Anna's voice was soft and coaxing and affectionate. 'Tell me what she's like. Is she very lovely?' Then she turned to Paul with a *moue*. 'Paul, this must be a very special girl that Tom has found. I have been trying to seduce him ever since we met without any success whatsoever. He rebuffs me with protestations of his loyalty to you, but I suspect that our Tom is very particular and I do not appeal to him.'

Tom turned on Anna. 'For God's sake, shut up, Anna,' he growled.

There was another peal of laughter. 'I told you that you had become five years older since yesterday,' she observed.

Paul was ignoring the interruption. 'Well, Tom,' he asked, 'any more questions?'

'Paul, how do I know that you're telling me the truth?'

Paul shrugged. 'You don't know that I'm telling the truth. If you are intelligent, however, you would realize that if I were lying to you I could easily make up a much more convincing story. When I lie, I am a very skilful liar, and a skilful liar does not present an incredible story. Right?'

'I suppose so,' Tom muttered.

'If you should have happened to find the girl we're looking for,' Paul went on, 'she would be involved with us for a few months, just how many I do not know. No harm will come to her.' Paul smiled again. 'Her virtue would certainly be unimpaired. When our project is concluded successfully, which it will be, she would have a nest of golden eggs in which she could rest comfortably, if not extravagantly, for the rest of her life. I very honestly believe that this is an opportunity that any intelligent girl with a concern for her future would seize upon avidly.'

'I'll think it over,' Tom said abruptly. 'Thanks for the drinks. I'll come around in the morning at ten o'clock.'

Tom Welles slept very little that night. The next morning at nine o'clock he was on his bench in the park by the big sycamore tree, watching the near-by entrance.

A few minutes after nine Angèle appeared at the gateway in her uniform and her white cotton stockings and her coif, wheeling the big pram along, and as she turned in the gateway Tom saw her eyes searching the bench.

Once she had established the fact that he was there, her eyes concentrated on the babies in the pram, and she walked slowly down the path past the bench.

Tom had risen.

'Angèle,' he whispered, 'I have the most frightful pain.'

'Sit down and turn away,' she said quickly. 'The park is full of people. I'll stop just down here and you can talk to me over your shoulder.'

Tom sat down immediately and faced the gate. 'Angèle, when am I going to see you? I have to talk to you,' he said softly.

'I have made a dentist appointment for this afternoon at three o'clock.'

'I hate dentists, don't you?'

'I don't know,' she confessed. 'I have never been to one.'

'This afternoon—'

'Thomas, I have become very bold. I shocked myself,' she confessed, 'but I thought that, unless you have an engagement, if you were to be at the café at three o'clock this afternoon – I must go now. I have fussed over these babies so much that they will start roaring any moment. Will you be there at three, Thomas? Or shall I—'

'I'll be there at three, Angèle.'

Tom Welles was waiting just inside the café door that afternoon. He could see her walking swiftly down the street, and after a quick glance around she ducked through the doorway.

'This is very wrong of me,' she said. 'It was very wrong of me to say my tooth was hurting when I have never had a toothache in my whole life. And it was wrong to make plans to see you again – so soon.'

And then her face cleared. 'But I wanted to so much.'

It was as though that explained everything.

'Thomas, I said I could not eat because my tooth hurt so much, and now I am very hungry. Do you think I could have a sandwich and perhaps coffee?'

Tom nodded gravely and summoned the waiter.

'Thomas, one reason I had to see you was that after you left me last night I suddenly realized I knew nothing about you, except that you were an American – and that you were you. I do not know even where your home is, or what you do when you are not amusing yourself on the Riviera.'

'At the moment, Angèle, I am not amusing myself on the Riviera. I find that life has become very serious.'

'But tell me about yourself,' she urged.

Tom raised his head and began to check off the items of interest. 'I was born in Boston twenty-eight years ago.'

'Then you are about nine years older than I,' she interrupted.

'My father was a college professor.'

'Does he still call you Thomas when you are bad, and does he punish you?'

'My father and mother have both been dead for years. The only close relative I have is a married sister, and she's in California.'

'You are alone, then, almost as much of an orphan as I am. And what do you do, Thomas? Anything? Do you have any work?'

'When I got out of the Army after Korea I decided I would

try to learn to write. Before that, I was on a newspaper in New York. The only other really important thing about me that I can think of at the moment, Angèle, is that I think I have recently fallen in love.'

'That is very ridiculous,' Angèle said quietly.

'Haven't you fallen in love, Angèle?'

'Certainly not.'

There was a pause. Then she went on. 'It is just a case of you sitting in the park, bored and without anything to do, and you see a face that appeals to you.'

'You don't believe that!'

'That is what I have been telling myself all day,' she said to him.

'Then why did you meet me this afternoon?'

Angèle blushed. 'Because you are a rich young American,' she retorted. 'A most desirable connexion for any young French girl, particularly one in my circumstances of life.'

'Nuts!' said Tom firmly.

'Oh, Thomas,' she protested, 'I do wish you were not rich! It would be so much simpler. But I suppose all Americans are rich!'

'Don't let that bother you at all.' Tom grinned. 'I am not rich. Except for a few thousand francs, I literally haven't got a cent to my name.'

'But that car! That dinner last night! Your clothes!'

'Listen, darling, the car does not belong to me. I do not even pay its rental. That dinner last night was on an expense account, generously furnished by the man for whom I am temporarily working.'

'But you must be a successful writer and earn a great deal of money.'

'On the contrary, I only finished my first novel a few weeks ago, and I don't know whether it will even be published.'

'This is very difficult to believe,' Angèle observed.

'Listen, darling, up until a few days ago I was practically broke, without enough money to buy even a cheap passage home. I was so hungry that I tried to steal a roll off another man's table one morning. That is the way I met my present employer.'

'Are you telling me the truth, Thomas?'

'So help me God.'

Angèle sighed and relaxed. 'I feel so much happier,' she announced.

'Why?'

'I do not think you would understand, Thomas.'

'I could try.'

Angèle hesitated, and then as she began to speak, her face flooded with colour. 'It is – it is difficult to explain, Thomas.'

'Try.'

'I have told you I lived as an orphan with the nuns and then I worked as a nursemaid. I lived the life they wanted me to live in the convent, but I had always wanted so much more – music and excitement and pretty clothes, to travel and see strange places. I have wanted the things that only money can provide. I suppose it is natural for many people who are poor to want to be rich and to have the things that are beyond their reach. I am afraid that I am a very worldly person, Thomas. They always told me so in the convent, and they prayed over my soul.'

'It sounds perfectly normal and healthy to me,' Tom decided.

'I suppose so, but when I met you yesterday and came to know you a little last night and thought about you most of the night and all morning, I was confused and bewildered, not knowing – this is the difficult part, Thomas—'

'Go on.'

'Not knowing whether it was the rich young American that appealed to me or the very drunken Thomas, helpless on his park bench.'

Tom Welles was smoking furiously. 'And now you have discovered that instead of being rich,' he said rather grimly, 'instead of being rich, Thomas Welles, Esq., is an impoverished writer with a very uncertain future, who, if he ever proposed marriage and you accepted it, would look forward to being supported out of your wages as a nursemaid.' He laughed bitterly. 'Be sure not to lose your job, Angèle!'

'Your novel will undoubtedly be a big success, and you will go away and I shall never see you again.'

Tom Welles's hand shot out and covered Angèle's where it

lay on the table. When he spoke, his tone was light, but his eyes were troubled. 'Darling, perhaps it's as well that at the moment I couldn't possibly support a wife because if I could, I probably would already be urging you to marry me, come to America, and live happily ever after.'

Angèle made no effort to withdraw her hand. 'Thomas, this man you are now working for and this thing you are doing. What is it?'

'You won't believe me,' Tom grinned, 'but I haven't the slightest idea. I do what I'm told, and I don't ask questions. All I do know is that the job won't last long, and that today or to-morrow or next week I will be supporting myself again in the style to which I am accustomed.'

'I shall have to look for something else very soon, too,' Angèle said.

'What do you mean?'

'The English family for whom I work is returning to England very soon, and the people do not plan to take me with them,' she explained. Her eyes clouded. 'It is not easy to find such a position in Nice,' she said. 'Luckily, I have just a little money put by.'

It was as though fate were driving him to bring Angèle to the Ehrenhardts, Tom thought savagely. That morning, instead of going to the Negresco, he had telephoned Paul with a curt message that he would be in touch with him later on in the day, for his whole instinct was to keep the knowledge of Angèle's very existence to himself. And now, this afternoon, he found himself in the position of denying her the opportunity of reaching towards the luxuries and indulgences she admitted she had always craved. And now – the straw that could break the camel's back – she was very soon going to be out of a job and she was obviously worried about the future.

Of course he knew that Paul would never keep him on if he refused to divulge Angèle's identity, but his winnings at Monte Carlo were more than enough to carry him over for a few weeks in Nice, and by that time certainly he'd have news of his novel, and the news might be good. It had seemed worth the gamble, but now his hand was being forced.

'Angèle,' he demanded abruptly, 'what would you be willing to do? How far would you be willing to go to achieve your ambition of pretty clothes and luxuries and all the things that you say you have always craved?'

'At the moment I have forgotten about them,' she said simply. 'Today they do not seem very important.'

'Well, yesterday, then. As of yesterday, if you had seen the opportunity to acquire quite a lot of money, how far would you have been willing to go?'

'I would have been willing to do almost anything,' she said honestly. 'Certain things, no. I do not think I would steal money from someone. I would not have killed anyone for money or injured them.' She wrinkled up her nose as though she smelled something very unpleasant. 'Nor do I think I could have sold myself to some old man. Or some young man, either, for that matter.'

'If we only had a few weeks to decide,' Tom groaned.

'To decide what, Thomas?'

'I wish I knew. Angèle, if you chose to do so would it be possible for you to disappear completely for a few months without having anyone becoming too curious about what had happened to you, or where you were or what you were doing?'

Angèle laughed. 'That would be the simplest thing in the world, chéri. If you were to strangle me this afternoon, no one except my employer would even suspect that anything had happened to me as long as you kept my body locked up in a trunk. But these are most curious questions, Thomas.'

Tom ordered another drink.

'Angèle,' he said abruptly, 'listen to me carefully. I told you that I have a job that I couldn't explain. That is true. A man and his wife who are apparently wealthy commissioned me to find a certain type of girl. I would think that you would be very close to the girl they are searching for. What they want this girl for, I do not know. It might be for a part in a play or a picture. It might be for almost anything. I do not know. They assured me that the girl would come to no harm and that it would be very much to her advantage to cooperate with them. They indicated that there would be a very substantial amount of money as a reward for her cooperation. Whether they are telling the truth or lying, I have no idea.

'They emphasized that one essential condition would be that the girl could and would disappear completely for a few months without her disappearance causing curiosity or interest. You are an orphan, you have no close friends, you are of the right age and appearance. I have been trying to make up my mind whether to tell you about this or not, whether to give up my job or not.

'Then you told me that your work with the English family would be over shortly, and you seemed worried about the future. I have enough money for us both to live for a few months very modestly, but nothing more. I have nothing else to offer you except a completed novel which may or may not be published, which may or may not produce any income to amount to anything. Therefore, I felt I had to tell you and let you make up your own mind.'

'But, Thomas, this is the strangest thing I have ever heard. What in the world could they want me for – or a girl like me?'

'I haven't the slightest idea,' Tom confessed.

'What do you want me to do, Thomas?'

'What do *I* want you to do?'

'Yes, Thomas, *cheri*.'

'The only thing that I am sure I want at the moment is impossible,' Tom said shortly.

She looked up at him through veiled eyes. 'A few moments ago, Thomas, you said you had enough money for us to live for a few months only.'

'Yes?'

'If *I* were to make a great deal of money, perhaps—'

'Nonsense.'

'I think I should like to talk to these friends of yours, Thomas. What are they like?'

'Apparently rich, cosmopolitan, clever, charming, and in some ways, I imagine, thoroughly unscrupulous. They have working with them a Frenchman named Hugo Forchet. They did tell me, by the way, that if they found the girl they were looking for, she would be told everything about their plans in advance.'

'I think I shall have to see these people, Thomas, to hear what they have to say.'

Tom Welles already was almost sorry that he had made the decision he had. It was too late to alter it now.

'When could you talk to them?' he demanded.

'After this afternoon, not for several days. I do not have much free time.'

Tom rose and went to the telephone and called the Negresco, and Paul answered the telephone.

'Paul, I've decided to let you talk to this girl. But, so help me God, if any harm comes to her, I'll find you and cut your throat myself.'

'Tom, what I told you last night was the truth,' Paul assured him.

'Very well. I can bring her around to the Negresco right away.'

'Good God, no, Tom, she must not come here! She must not be seen here. And before I talk to her or have any contact with her, Hugo must look her over and see whether or not she could – play the part. Hugo is here now. When and where could he see her?'

'She is with me now at the Café des Deux Anges on the little park near the main post office.'

'Hugo will be there almost immediately. But, Tom, listen carefully. Hugo will pay no attention to you, and you are not to recognize Hugo. Do you understand that? If when Hugo leaves the restaurant he takes out his handkerchief and blows his nose, you will then immediately telephone me. If he leaves the restaurant without blowing his nose, it will mean that the girl is of no use to us. Be sure that the girl does not know who Hugo is or that he is examining her.'

The telephone clicked.

'Cloak-and-dagger baloney!' muttered Tom.

Angèle's eyes were questioning.

'We shall wait here for a little, Angèle. I think I shall have to telephone again in a little while.'

For the first time since they had met there was a strained silence between them. Finally, desperately seeking for a topic of conversation, Angèle asked Tom what his novel was about.

'About a beautiful young French girl who stuck her lovely blonde head into a lion's mouth and had it bitten off!'

'I do not think, Thomas, that that story will be very successful or make you much money.'

'I'm sure it won't,' Tom agreed.

'Thomas, on this what you call your expense account, could I have something to drink, something mild, perhaps a *crème de menthe*?'

'From now on, when I'm with you I'm using my own money,' Tom announced.

'But you must not spend that on drinks for me,' she said.

'Nonsense. Angèle, before I forget it, I must have your address and the name of the people for whom you are working.'

She gave them to him.

It was just as the waiter brought Tom's brandy and Angèle's *crème de menthe* that Tom, out of the corner of his eye, saw Hugo enter the restaurant. Without glancing up, Hugo seated himself at a near-by table and ordered a drink. Then he took a newspaper out of his pocket and began to study it. Tom saw the newspaper shifting slightly so that Hugo could peer around it at Angèle, and he seemed to study her for some time.

Then he abruptly put down his newspaper and finished his drink. He took a large white handkerchief out of his breast pocket and literally trumpeted into it. He rose and moved towards the door. Tom observed a very satisfied swagger.

'And now, Angèle, I must telephone once more,' Tom said quietly. 'By the way, what time do you have to be back?'

'What time is it, Thomas? I have no watch.'

Tom glanced at his wrist watch. 'It's a quarter past four.'

'I should be back by five thirty,' Angèle said.

Tom nodded, crossed to the telephone, and called Paul Ehrenhardt.

'Hugo blew his nose – very hard.'

'That is marvellous, my Tom, that is marvellous. Will you and your friend wait for me at the restaurant?'

'She has to be back at her job at five thirty,' Tom warned.

'That should give us time, Tom. I am already on my way.'

And the telephone clicked again.

Tom Welles dropped down beside Angèle. 'This man's name is Paul Ehrenhardt. He will be here in a few minutes.'

Angèle's eyes were excited. 'Thomas, this is the most exciting thing that has ever happened to me. No, I am wrong, it is the *second* most exciting thing that has ever happened to me.'

'That man who was in here a few moments ago was here looking you over,' Tom said heavily. 'That was Hugo Forchet.'

'I did not even notice him.'

'You weren't supposed to. When he left, he blew his nose. That was a signal that I was to call Paul Ehrenhardt again.'

'Oh, Thomas, my heart is hammering. This all seems so strange. Everything moved so quickly. Yesterday morning I had not even met you, and now—'

'Angèle,' said Tom quickly, 'it's still not too late. Let's get out of here and forget Ehrenhardt and the whole business. I don't want you mixed up in anything which is undercover or secret. I care for you too much to run the chance of your getting into anything that is messy or off-colour.'

'No, we will wait. My curiosity has been aroused, and I would never forgive myself if I drew back now. And perhaps, Thomas – just perhaps—'

The door of the little restaurant swung open, and Paul Ehrenhardt strode towards them purposefully. He swept his hat off his head with a gesture and bowed.

'Mademoiselle Corton, may I present Monsieur Ehrenhardt?' Tom said formally.

'Mademoiselle, I am delighted to have this opportunity of making your acquaintance. I assure you this means a great deal to me.' And then he turned to Tom Welles. 'Now, my dear Tom, I'm sure you realize that I wish to talk to Mademoiselle Corton privately.'

'Is that really necessary?' Tom demanded.

'I assure you that it is most necessary. I am sure Mademoiselle Corton will miss you, but I am also sure she will understand.'

Tom rose.

'And when shall I see you again, Paul?' The question was pointed.

'At ten o'clock tomorrow morning, of course, my dear Tom. As usual. Oh, by the way, Tom, Anna and I might need the Simca tonight. Would you have time to drive it around and leave it at the hotel and give the keys to the concierge? I would appreciate it more than I can say.'

Tom nodded. Then he turned to Angèle. '*Au revoir*, Angèle.'

'*Au revoir,* Thomas.'

9

T OM PICKED up the Simca and drove it down to the Negresco, turned over the keys, and left without calling the Ehrenhardts. He did not want to see Anna just now.

He thought of returning to the restaurant and catching Angèle on her way home, but there was not quite time enough to make it. He wandered around Nice aimlessly for a while, scarcely aware of where he was going. He was thinking only of one thing — seeing Angèle the next morning in the park and finding out what had happened.

He dined morosely and returned to his room and with grim determination decided that it was time to start actually working on his next novel.

He made a dozen false starts and at length gave up. When he finally went to bed, his sleep was tortured.

Tom's heart sank when he woke the next morning. Through his window he saw a steady, hard rain, rain driving down, rain that looked as though it had come to stay.

There was no possibility of Angèle being in the park with her charges on a morning like this. And when and how would he see her? He supposed that in the evening he might call at the house where she worked and ask to see her, but certainly not in the morning. There would be trouble over that, he was sure. To wait until evening for some word of what had happened was unthinkable. He would go to the park anyway on a chance that she would slip out alone and meet him. Surely the afternoon before, when they had parted, it had been understood without words that they would see each other in the morning. He was seeing Paul Ehrenhardt at ten, of course, but it was Angèle that he wanted to see, and Angèle's story that he wanted to hear.

Tom dressed hastily, flung on a raincoat, and without breakfast headed for the park. He realized that it was much too early, but his nervous anxiety propelled him through the downpour. Under the big sycamore tree there was at least some refuge from the rain.

The park, of course, was utterly deserted. Even the birds seemed to have disappeared. Tom knew that he was waiting in vain, but he waited. Now it was nine o'clock; then nine fifteen, and nine thirty. At a quarter of ten he gave up, and after a long search he found a bedraggled taxicab and drove to the Negresco.

Without ringing the Ehrenhardts he went up to their suite. As he approached it, he noticed to his surprise that the door was open.

In the doorway he paused. There were three maids apparently engaged in a thorough cleaning job, and he could hear a French voice from the bedroom. All the Ehrenhardts' personal belongings had disappeared. The room was completely impersonal, and it seemed very empty.

'Monsieur Ehrenhardt?' he demanded of one of the maids.

'Monsieur and Madame Ehrenhardt, *ils sont partis.*'

'Gone?' Tom repeated unbelievingly.

'*Oui, monsieur, ils sont partis.*'

He strode into the living-room, crossed to the bedroom door. It was as empty of any personal element as the living-room.

Swiftly he descended to the lobby and crossed to the reception desk.

'Mr and Mrs Ehrenhardt must have changed their room,' he told the clerk. 'Would you please tell me what rooms they have now?'

The clerk looked at Tom curiously. 'The Ehrenhardts have not changed their rooms, monsieur. They gave up their rooms last night and departed.'

'That's impossible!' Tom cried. 'I had an appointment with them at ten o'clock this morning. I have been working for Mr Ehrenhardt.'

'They left us very suddenly,' the clerk said. 'Mr Ehrenhardt said that he had received a telegram that necessitated their immediate departure.'

'But I saw him late yesterday afternoon and he said nothing about it,' Tom protested.

The clerk shrugged.

'Did they say where they were going? Did they leave a forwarding address?'

'Monsieur will have to ask the concierge about that.'

Tom crossed to the concierge's desk. 'I have been working for Mr Ehrenhardt,' he explained. 'I understand he left the hotel suddenly during the night. Will you please give me his forwarding address?'

'Monsieur, you will understand that we are not at liberty to give out a guest's forwarding address, but since Monsieur Ehrenhardt did not *leave* a forwarding address, there would be no breach in confidence in telling you that, would there?'

'Last night I left a rented Simca at the hotel and the keys at the desk here.'

'Ah, yes. Mr Ehrenhardt left enough to cover the rental, and the car has been returned to the garage.'

Tom's mind was whirling, and there must have been something on his face that aroused the sympathy of the concierge.

'What is Monsieur's name?' he asked.

'Thomas Welles.'

'Ah, Mr Welles. Mr Ehrenhardt said that you might call. He left a letter for you. Just a moment.'

A minute later Tom was crossing the lobby to a secluded corner, a thick envelope in his hands. He sat down and tore it open. He took out a thick sheaf of bank notes and a single sheet of Negresco stationery.

My dear Tom,
   It is to our great regret and embarrassment that we could not

*delay out departure long enough to bid you adieu and thank you
for all your kindness and help. Circumstances beyond our control
have necessitated a very sudden change in plans, and it would be
disastrous to delay even for a few hours.*

*We have had to abandon our project, and, I'm afraid, our
happy plans for retreating into the Castle Garac. By the time you
receive this letter we shall be far away.*

*With this sudden shift of plans, it is perhaps fortunate that
your little friend, Mademoiselle Corton, was unsuitable for the
part I had in mind for her. But I found her utterly charming,
and I wish you very good hunting.*

*Anna, who is now frantically packing, joins with me in wish-
ing you the best of luck possible with your novel, and you will
find enclosed a sum which I hope you will feel adequate compensation for your faithful and loyal services.*

With every assurance of our regard,

Yours very truly,
Paul Ehrenhardt.

This was impossible, Tom thought foggily. Had the police
run them out, or had they learned that the police were on their
trail? He supposed that was the sort of thing that happened to
adventurers. There was no other explanation of such a hurried departure leaving no forwarding address. Those stacked
notes in his lap were ten-thousand-franc notes, and there were
a lot of them, far more than his salary would have amounted
to for the time he had worked for Paul.

He read the letter over again, but the second reading brought
no clarity to his mind. He folded the letter up and shoved it
down into his pocket with the bank notes and closed his eyes
and tried to think.

The Ehrenhardts had disappeared. There was no question
about that. They were not going to use the Castle Garac. The
Ehrenhardts were definitely out of the picture from now on. He,
Tom Welles, was still in Nice, waiting for news of his novel. He
had no immediate financial problems, thanks to Paul Ehrenhardt.
He now had quite a decent wardrobe. And, last but not least, he
had found Angèle Corton, with whom he certainly seemed to be

in love, and, judging from her responsiveness, she wasn't herself indifferent towards him.

When you looked at it that way, Tom Welles had not done badly for himself in a few days, considering the fact that it all started with his attempted theft of a *petit pain*. Who was it anyway who had said that crime did not pay?

There was something else, too, in the back of his mind that he had forgotten. What the devil was it? . . . Oh yes, of course. He had a six-month option to buy the Castle Garac, with the right of occupancy in the meantime. The last thing in the world he wanted was to move into the Castle Garac, but it was rather nice to have it waiting there for him in case he ever changed his mind. If things continued as they had been going recently, he probably would be able to buy the Castle Garac, bring it back to life, and live as a feudal lord behind its walls! And he had wondered whether some of the events in his novel had seemed improbable!

Tom left the Negresco and hurried through the rain down the Promenade des Anglais to the café where he had met Paul Ehrenhardt. He had had no breakfast, and it was fit and proper that he commemorate the end of the Ehrenhardt episode on the spot where it had begun.

The same waiter was presiding over the almost empty restaurant, and he nodded at Tom without any enthusiasm.

'*Bonjour, monsieur. Il fait mauvais temps.*'

'On the contrary, it is a beautiful day,' Tom contradicted. 'One of the finest days I've ever known.'

It was obvious that the waiter understood him, because he looked at him most suspiciously. Was the young American drunk so early in the morning? That suit, though. The young man had had no such suit the last time he was in for *déjeuner*. And the shoes and the hat. *Monsieur l'Américain*'s luck at the tables must have changed. Well, perhaps he would tip more generously than in the past.

'*Vous êtes seul ce matin, monsieur.*' And his voice was more respectful.

He could have answered that in French, Tom congratulated

himself, but with this waiter who pretended to know no English there was a principle involved. 'Yes, this morning I am all alone,' he said clearly, 'and please bring me a copy of the *Paris Herald-Tribune*.'

Tom's mind went back to the morning when he had come upon Paul Ehrenhardt sitting there over his breakfast. That fatal *petit pain*! The luckiest *petit pain* in all the world. If it had not been for that little brown roll, in all probability he would have been by this time subsisting on the bounty of the American Consul, who would be trying to finance his return to the United States. He never would have met Angèle.

The waiter appeared with Tom's paper.

'*Monsieur, vous desirez quelque chose?*'

'Most certainly! A large orange juice – the juice of at least three oranges, you understand, and iced.' Tom emphasized the 'iced'. 'Then, *oeufs jambon, café crème*, no croissants, but a *basket* of *petits pains*.'

Croissants were really better, Tom reflected, but this morning out of sentiment he would stick to *petits pains*.

The waiter was regarding Tom with some amazement. The American *must* have done very well at the tables. He forgot that he only spoke French.

'Certainly, sir,' he replied in perfect English. 'Will you have the eggs fried on both sides, or sunny-side-up?'

Tom grinned at him. 'That's better,' he said. 'Sunny-side-up. You've learned a lot of English in a short time, haven't you?'

The waiter had the decency to flush, as he turned away.

'I'll have my coffee now,' Tom announced.

'*Oui, monsieur.*'

Tom took out Paul Ehrenhardt's letter and read it again carefully, but found nothing new. How many ten-thousand-franc notes were there in that stack? He supposed he had better count them. . . . Thirteen, fourteen, fifteen – good heavens! A hundred and fifty thousand francs! Paul *had* been generous. Tom still had left about a hundred and twenty-five thousand francs from his lucky banco that night with Anna Ehrenhardt in Monte Carlo. That made two hundred and seventy-five thousand francs – nearly eight hundred dollars. He was rich!

Tonight he would call on Angèle and insist that she come out with him for a little time at least. She would be in her uniform, of course, when he arrived. It would take her a few minutes to get permission to go out and she would want to change her uniform. If it was still raining, he would have to have a taxi, and he would keep it waiting because he did not want her to get wet. He would take her to some gay, fashionable bar, telling nothing until the champagne that he would order had been iced. And then—

Eight hundred dollars. How far would eight hundred dollars go in Nice, or perhaps in some smaller near-by town that might be less expensive. They could do with a very small apartment, and Angèle, being French, would be able to get one much more cheaply than he, an American, would. And Angèle would certainly know how to cook. He'd have to have a place to write. It would be nice if their apartment was on the sunny side of the building.

His orange juice was on the sour side but refreshing. He would not be ordering orange juice again, he reflected. It was expensive in France, and, after all, eight hundred dollars was only eight hundred dollars. They must plan to make it see them through the writing of another novel – four months certainly, possibly five months. If Angèle could find a suitable apartment cheap enough, and if they economized, perhaps they could stretch it to six months. But wasn't he taking a good deal for granted? What would Angèle's reaction be to all this planning of his? With all their ebullience, the French were apt to be cautious and realistic when it came to making important decisions. After just a few days, regardless of how she felt about him, would Angèle marry him? She was undoubtedly a Catholic. She must be a Catholic. And marriage was a much more serious matter to a Catholic than it was apt to be for a Protestant. What in heaven's name made him so confident that Angèle was ready to take a step that in the eyes of her Church would tie her up for the rest of her life? Even if she were really fond of him, perhaps she might prefer to come and live with him as his mistress, rather than enter into an irrevocable marriage.

Well, this being France, that would work out perfectly well, and they could always get married later. Certainly it couldn't take more than a few weeks for her to decide that she loved him enough to marry him. Would Angèle like America when they finally returned there, as they of course would? He thought so. And if he couldn't earn a living sufficient to support Angèle by doing creative writing, he could always go back to newspaper work.

Tom finished his eggs and summoned the waiter for more coffee. He had not even glanced at the newspaper.

It was queer about the Ehrenhardts. Where did they disappear to? Paris? Probably not. If it were a question of the law catching up with them, they probably slipped into Italy or took a plane for Madrid or London. Obviously he could get no information at the Negresco. He wondered if some ingenuous, innocent inquiries at the local police bureau would produce anything. Probably not, he decided, except the questioning of himself, which might be rather embarrassing. After all, if they were after the Ehrenhardts and had lost them, the police would be most interested in any friend of the Ehrenhardts. No, he'd forget them, he decided regretfully. He would always be nagged by curiosity as to what it had all been about, but the chances were he would never know.

Tom looked out of the window, and it was still raining. The whole day was ahead of him, and there was nothing to do but wait until he could see Angèle that evening. On a day like this, one could not go anywhere, and he certainly did not feel like working. Well, there was one thing he could do. He had not yet made his daily call at the post office. There would be no word from New York, of course, but if he failed to appear the old clerk with the long grey moustache would undoubtedly become alarmed, and call in the police to report that a certain young American had disappeared.

The rain had let up a little now. There was no taxi in sight, and Tom started walking quickly towards town. If it stopped raining, he would go to the park, he decided. After all, those babies needed fresh air, and if the weather cleared, Angèle would undoubtedly do her duty and take them out for an airing. The only trouble with that idea, he thought ruefully, was that the rain showed no sign of stopping.

By the time Tom reached the post office, the rain was working through his raincoat, and he thought he could feel dampness soaking through the shoulders of his jacket. After he had heard the usual *'Rien aujourd'hui, monsieur,'* he would have to go back to his room and change.

This morning there were eight people waiting in line at the Poste-Restante, all damp, morose refugees of the storm. The weak electric lightbulbs hanging from the ceiling were lighted, but the atmosphere was one of hopeless gloom and Tom felt his mood of excitement and anticipation slipping rapidly away. His shoulders were really wet now, and his shoes were soaked.

Why wait here in line for a letter that wouldn't be there? It would be more sensible to return to his room at once and change his clothes. His room would not be very warm, but at least he would be dry there.

The line was moving now, and Tom decided to wait. Finally he was at the window, and the old clerk was peering up at him.

'Thomas Welles,' he repeated mechanically.

The clerk's head bobbed in acknowledgement and he turned to the pigeonhole marked with a big black *W*. As always he sorted through the letters slowly and carefully. Now he paused as though he were having great difficulty in deciphering the address. There seemed to be a surprised look on his face, and he kept that envelope between his fingers as he ran through the envelopes remaining in his hands. Then he returned all but that one envelope to the proper pigeonhole and turned towards Tom with a flourish. There was a broad smile on his face, and he seemed to be very happy. It was as though he had been trying hard for a very long time and had at last succeeded. And Tom's heart began to pound.

Triumphantly the clerk pushed the long envelope across the counter.

'Enfin, monsieur!' he said in a stage whisper. Then he repeated: *'Enfin!'* and bowed his head.

'Merci, merci beaucoup,' muttered Tom and stepped away from the window.

He too examined the envelope carefully. In the upper left-hand corner was engraved the name and address of his agent.

The letter was addressed to 'Mr Thomas Welles, Poste-Restante, Nice, A.M., France.' There was an airmail stamp cancelled in New York two days before.

Tom's heart was thumping, but his mind was numb. He felt the envelope carefully, as though his fingers were probing for the news that would be inside. He turned the envelope over and started to tear it open. Then he stopped and stared at it again. After a moment he put it carefully in his pocket, buttoned his raincoat, and plunged out into the storm. He would have to have a drink on hand, he decided, when he opened that envelope. It was only a block and a half to the Café des Deux Anges. He headed for it automatically. The Café des Deux Anges seemed to be becoming an important spot in his life.

It was relatively warm and comfortable in the little restaurant. Tom shed his raincoat, sat down, and ordered black coffee and a cognac. He removed the letter from his pocket and put it on the table in front of him, staring at it uncertainly. Now that it was here, he did not dare open it. He had waited and waited and waited for news, and now he shrank away from it.

Perhaps there would not be any definite news, good or bad. Long ago he had had an acknowledgement from his agent that his novel had arrived, along with a guarded expression of enthusiasm, and this was probably to say no more than that his book was going the rounds and was still under consideration by some publisher or other.

Tom put three lumps of sugar in his coffee and poured in the cognac. He tasted it deliberately, then his eyes returned to the letter before him. Then he took another big drink of his coffee. Finally, very slowly, he slid his finger under the flap of the envelope. It was opening quite easily. The flap would come up without tearing. It couldn't be very good glue on the envelope, or it had been carelessly sealed. That was not a good omen. It told him that there wasn't anything of importance in the letter, that it really didn't matter if the envelope came open by itself en route, thus releasing the letter, which might very well be lost. The message wasn't important, and it did not matter whether he, Tom Welles, received it or not.

Thoroughly depressed now, Tom withdrew the single sheet of

notepaper and unfolded it. A green oblong paper fluttered to the table. Tom put the letter down and picked up the cheque. It was made out to Thomas Welles. It was a New York bank draft for five hundred dollars. Tom straightened up with interest and excitement. His first thought was that eight hundred dollars and five hundred dollars made thirteen hundred dollars. Then he picked up the letter again, and as he read it through slowly, the expression on his face changed from amazement to what was almost fear. He dropped the letter and drained his coffee cup in a few gulping swallows. He looked around the Café des Deux Anges in bewilderment and then turned back to the letter. He read it again even more slowly. He hit his hand sharply against the table. Yes, that hurt. He was conscious, and this was not a dream.

His agent, Lester Hotsom, apologized for not writing him before, but he had been away on a short vacation. On his return to New York a few days before, he found that there had been a good deal happening about Tom's novel during his absence. He would have written Tom immediately upon his return with the good news, but there had been the matter of contracts to negotiate and i's to dot and t's to cross. He had decided to delay writing Tom until everything was finally settled.

Everything had been arranged now to his, Hotsom's, satisfaction, and he hoped to Tom's. If Tom would cable his approval, the agreements and the contracts would be made out at once and forwarded to him to execute.

When Hotsom had read Tom's novel, he wrote, he had been excited by its possibilities and had had several copies typed. He had submitted the novel simultaneously to the most important weekly magazine and one of the best book-publishers in New York. And very luckily he had taken a copy of the manuscript with him on vacation, because in Las Vegas he had run into Randolph Brode, the famous picture star, whom he had known for a long time, and he had given the manuscript to Brode to read. Brode had been so enthusiastic about the possibilities of a picture – it was just the sort of part he had been looking for – that he had rushed the manuscript to his own studio with a demand that they buy it for him.

On his return to New York Hotsom had been greeted by the news that the magazine wanted Tom's novel for a serial and that the publisher was ready to make what seemed to be quite a decent offer for a first novel. The magazine would not pay their highest price for a new writer, of course, but Hotsom had been able to get them up to twenty thousand dollars. The publisher was willing to pay an advance against royalty of three thousand dollars. The price for the picture, subject to Tom's acceptance, was thirty-five thousand dollars.

It was impossible to prophesy, of course, how much the book would ultimately make for Tom, but if it were selected by a book club, which was quite possible, the novel would earn eventually a very substantial amount.

Hotsom felt quite sure that Tom would accept these offers, but would he cable Hotsom authority to close at the earliest possible moment? In the meantime, Hotsom was sending Tom his own cheque for five hundred dollars just in case Tom needed money or wished to celebrate the good news.

Thomas Welles was dazed and numb. He felt as though all the blood had been drained from his body.

'*Garçon,*' he croaked, '*encore du café!*'

Then, his hand trembling a little, he took a pencil out of his pocket and on the side of the letter wrote down the figure twenty thousand dollars. Very carefully he then added the figure three thousand dollars, the zeros meticulously lined up. Then he wrote down thirty-five thousand dollars and drew a line. Zero. Zero. Zero. Eight, and a five. Those three sweet figures added up to fifty-eight thousand dollars. At the moment he could not possibly have added them in his head. He looked at the cheque again. He must be careful not to add that cheque twice. That came out of the fifty-eight thousand dollars. Then he wrote down eight hundred under the fifty-eight thousand and drew another line. After all, he had eight hundred dollars right here in Nice. That made fifty-eight thousand eight hundred.

A lot of that would go for taxes, of course. What the devil was it Hotsom had written about taxes. Oh, yes, of course! Since Tom had been working on this book for some time and could prove it, his income could be spread over three years and his tax liability very much reduced.

But at the moment Tom Welles was not thinking very much about taxes. For some reason or other, he didn't quite know why, he divided the fifty-eight thousand eight hundred dollars by ten. The answer was five thousand eight hundred and eighty dollars. Tom frowned. He divided again by ten. The answer came out five hundred and eighty-eight dollars, and his face cleared.

'Now that's a figure I can understand,' he declared aloud triumphantly.

He straightened out his legs and shoved his hands deep down in his trouser pockets. He grinned down at Hotsom's letter and the cheque. He was now a rich young American, well able to support a wife. A novelist with a future. The first thing he knew, he would need a financial adviser to manage his affairs. That was probably what rich people always did. He could not possibly spare the time to look into investments or follow the stock market. He wondered where Angèle would want to live. Perhaps they would stay in France for a year or so, with a little villa up in the hills. Perhaps they would go back to America first, before they decided on any plans. It might be a good idea not to tell Angèle too much about his new position in the world before she married him. He remembered her doubts about falling in love with a rich young American, and there was no point in complicating matters at this stage. He would tell her that his novel had been sold, and it would be safe to show her the draft for five hundred dollars, and after they were married break the rest of the news.

Of course if she did not want to marry him now, they would have to stay in France because getting her into the United States except as his wife would present difficulties and delays. There were quotas, he remembered, and for all he knew, the French quota might be filled for years. That was another excellent reason for her to marry him at once. He'd tell her that he had to return to America on business about his book and that she must come with him, and to come with him she would have to marry him. . . . Bless Lester Hotsom. What a man! What an agent! In a few minutes he would have to go back to the post office and send a cable accepting everying, but at present he would just sit here for a little time, and think about it.

Thomas Welles sent off his cable and then treated himself to a magnificent luncheon of imported smoked salmon, *loup de la mer*, a bottle of white wine, green salad, cheese, and cognac, and then tipped the waiter extravagantly.

And *this* was the way successful novelists lived, he told himself happily.

Then he looked at his watch, which had so recently been pawned at the Mont-de-Piété. It was three o'clock and it was still raining. There was no point in going to the park to wait for Angèle.

What were the formalities about an American marrying a French girl? he wondered. Could it be done at once, or would there be a delay? That was something that needed looking into. Should he go round to the City Hall, which they called the Hôtel de Ville, or would it be better to go to the American Consulate? Certainly they would know all about it there. Was Angèle of age under French law? In the United States a girl became of age at eighteen, he thought, but here it might be twenty-one. If she had to have permission to marry, being an orphan, who would give her permission?

Tom rose abruptly. The sooner he found out about all this, the better. It would give him something to do this afternoon.

He looked up the address of the American Consulate in the telephone book in the restaurant. It was not far away. The rain had let up a little momentarily, and he decided to go on foot.

At the Consulate he demanded to see someone who could give him information about the procedure when an American wished to marry a French citizen.

'Probably you should talk to Madame Chiron,' the reception clerk decided. 'If you'll wait a few minutes, I'll see if she's free.'

The clerk picked up the telephone and, after a brief explanation to someone who apparently was Mme Chiron, gave Tom Welles instructions for finding her office.

Mme Chiron was an efficient-looking Frenchwoman of middle age, with her own tiny office.

'You wished information about marrying in France?' she asked in excellent English.

'Yes, please.' Tom grinned and sat down facing her across the desk.

Mme Chiron picked up a pencil and reached for a pad. 'It's a little complicated,' she admitted. 'I'll have to have some information first in order to answer your question. You are an American citizen and your passport is in order?'

Tom nodded.

'Your fiancée is—'

'I'm not actually engaged – I don't think,' Tom blurted out.

Mme Chiron controlled a smile. 'You are just thinking of becoming engaged, then?'

'Yes, I am thinking of becoming engaged,' Tom said hurriedly.

'Your – friend is French, a French citizen?'

'Yes.'

'Well, as in America, we have two forms of marriage. There must be a civil marriage, and then there is a church marriage. Is your friend a Catholic?'

'Yes, I believe so. As a matter of fact, she must be.'

'And are you a Catholic?'

'No, I guess I'm just a Protestant.' Tom's voice was almost apologetic.

'That complicates matters even more.'

'I could become a Cahtolic,' Tom suggested. 'I haven't a thing against the Catholic Church.'

Mme Chiron's smile was a trifle frosty. 'The fact that you have no prejudices against the Catholic Church in itself hardly qualifies you to become a Catholic,' she told him.

'It was just an idea,' Tom muttered.

'Protestants *may* marry Catholics,' Mme Chiron told him grudgingly, 'but of course you would have to sign an agreement that any children of the marriage would be brought up in the Church.'

'Yes, I've heard that. There would not be any difficulty there.'

'Next, your friend would have to have her parents' consent.'

'Even if she is of age?'

'Even if she is of age, she must ask her parents' consent to the

102

marriage once, twice, three times. If they refuse their consent three times, then by executing certain papers she may marry without their consent. How old is this girl?'

'She doesn't quite know,' Tom confessed.

'She doesn't *know*?'

'She thinks she's about nineteen.'

Mme Chiron settled back in her chair and sighed. 'Then she is not of age, and cannot marry under any circumstances without her parents' consent. She will not be of age until she is twenty-one.'

Tom Welles ran his hand through his hair. 'But she hasn't any parents,' he cried, 'or if she has, she doesn't know who they are.'

'Mr Welles, this gets stranger and stranger. This girl does not know how old she is, and she has no parents?'

'She is an orphan,' Tom explained. 'She was educated in a convent by the nuns.'

'Don't they know how old she is?'

'No, she turned up somehow at the convent as a little girl and seemed to be about seven years old. That was twelve years ago.'

'But don't the authorities who took her to the convent know more about her?'

'I don't think so,' Tom admitted vaguely.

'Does this girl live in Nice?'

'Yes.'

'I take it she has left the convent,' Mme Chiron observed dryly. 'She works?'

'Yes. She works,' Tom repeated.

'Mr Welles, you will find that she has a legal guardian – what is called here in France a *tuteur*. For an orphan without any family, the *tuteur* must take the responsibility and step into the place of the parents.'

'And to marry she would have to have the permission of this official?'

'Yes. I can't tell you who it is, but you could find out at the Mairie. He would undoubtedly consult with her priest.

'Now as to you yourself, Mr Welles. You would have to fur-nish information as to your profession, your father's and mother's full names. Your birth certificate you probably would not need, since you have your passport. Your friend's priest would undoubtedly wish to interview you before deciding whether to recommend consent to the marriage.'

'Well, that's all pretty complicated, but it doesn't sound impossible,' Tom decided. 'How long does it take to get married? Do you have to wait a period, or can you get married right away?'

'Oh, no. Once the formalities we've discussed have been complied with, the banns have to be posted for three weeks. Then, if there are no objections or complications, the civil marriage may be performed, and the religious ceremony on the same day if you wish.'

'Good heavens, you do take this business of marriage seriously in France, don't you?'

Mme Chiron's face froze again. 'Yes, Mr Welles, in France we take this matter of marriage very seriously. Then, of course, there's the matter of the marriage contract.'

Tom ran his hand through his hair again. 'What is a marriage contract?' he demanded. 'I thought by this time we'd be married!'

'Before you can be married, there's a question of settlement to be decided upon.'

'Settlement?' Tom frowned.

'Certainly. First is the matter of what your fiancée is contributing towards the marriage, her dowry; and her guardian will, in order to protect the bride's interests, want you to make a settlement on her.'

'What sort of settlement? How much would – well, would be considered suitable?'

'That I cannot answer,' Mme Chiron said. 'It is a matter that would have to be discussed with the authorities. It would depend upon your position in the world, your employment, your prospects.'

'I don't think she'd have any dowry.'

'You could always waive the matter of a dowry,' Mme Chiron said smoothly. 'Under the circumstances, however, there would certainly have to be a settlement on your part. Without a settlement, there can be no contract of marriage, and a contract of marriage can only be waived with the consent of all the individuals involved.'

Tom sighed. 'It would be a lot simpler not to get married, wouldn't it?'

'It would, Mr Welles. Marriage is a very serious step, and that step should not be taken lightly or precipitously.'

Tom Welles rose. 'Thank you ever so much for your help and advice, Madame Chiron. If I need some more help, may I—?'

Mme Chiron regarded him gravely. 'I would think that your next step would be to determine whether or not you're engaged,' she suggested.

'You're absolutely right,' Tom agreed, 'and I'll probably be back tomorrow.'

10

AT SIX O'CLOCK that evening the rain had stopped and the skies had cleared.

At seven thirty Tom Welles was studying the façade of a medium-size house on the Rue Peletier. He had a slip of paper in his hand.

'Twenty-seven *bis*,' he muttered. 'Yes, twenty-seven *bis*, and the name of the people is Morton.'

He approached the front door and rang the bell.

There was no response, so after a minute he rang again and waited.

Then he could hear footsteps inside on an uncarpeted floor. The door opened, and he was face to face with a woman somewhere in her late thirties. She was dressed in a severely tailored suit. She had short-cropped hair, just beginning to streak with grey, and a rather horselike face.

Tom Welles gave her his most winning smile. 'I'm sorry to bother you,' he said, 'but could I see Mademoiselle Corton for a few minutes? It is most important.'

The woman's face hardened. 'And may I ask who you are?' she demanded.

'My name is Thomas Welles.'

'An American?'

'Yes. Are you Mrs Morton?'

'I am Mrs Morton. And what do you want of Angèle?'

'I am a friend of hers.'

The woman regarded him suspiciously. 'Have you known her long?'

'No, not long,' Tom confessed.

'And what do you want with Angèle?'

'I want to talk to her,' Tom explained.

'Well, you can't,' Mrs Morton snapped.

'I realize that this is probably not her regular time off,' Tom apologized, 'but if I could see her for just a few moments – I assure you that it is urgent.'

'How long have you known Angèle?'

'Only a few days,' Tom admitted.

'How did you meet her?'

This was a very strange inquiry, Tom thought to himself. Either he could see Angèle or he couldn't see Angèle. What business was it of Mrs Morton's how long he'd known her or where he'd met her? She stood there in the doorway, however, implacable.

'I was in the park and feeling quite ill,' he explained. 'She saw that I was ill and asked me if I needed help.'

'Is that the truth?'

'That is the truth,' Tom told her coldly.

'And how many times have you seen Angèle in these past few days since you met her?' Mrs Morton persisted.

'Two or three times.'

Mrs Morton nodded to herself. 'On her day off, I suppose, and probably when she was supposed to be seeing the dentist.'

Tom was silent.

'Well, Mr Welles, you cannot see Angèle.'

'Not just for a moment?'

'Not just for a moment. You probably think it is because Angèle is working and that I am a hard taskmaster. The fact is, however – and that's why I was asking you all those questions – Angèle is not here.'

'Not here?' Tom repeated incredulously. 'Where is she?'

'I don't know, and what's more, I don't care. She left me last night without notice, bag and baggage, what there was of it.'

'I don't believe it,' Tom blurted out.

'You'd believe it if you'd had my two babies on your hands all day,' Mrs Morton said grimly. 'It is the most outrageous behaviour I've ever known. Angèle was well treated here, and had been with us for some time.'

'Why did she leave?' Tom cried.

'I haven't the slightest idea. She wouldn't tell me.'

'Where has she gone?'

'I don't know. She wouldn't answer any questions.'

'Mrs Morton, please believe this is very important to me,' Tom said quietly.

'If we're going on talking, you'd better come in,' Mrs Morton said grudgingly. 'It's cold here in the doorway.'

Tom entered the hall and stood there. Mrs Morton made no gesture towards the living-room. Obviously the interview was to be concluded there in the hall.

'Would you mind telling me exactly what happened?' Tom asked.

'Not at all,' Mrs Morton said crisply. 'Angèle returned from her supposed visit to the dentist about five thirty. I noticed that she seemed rather on edge and nervous, but I thought nothing of it because I thought she had probably had a bad time at the dentist's. She gave the twins their six-o'clock feeding and put them to bed. She then went up to her room and did not re-appear until it was time for her supper.'

'Did you see her then?' Tom interrupted.

'I saw her on her way down to the kitchen, where she eats,' Mrs Morton said. 'We dined at eight. About nine thirty Angèle knocked at the living-room door, where I was sitting with Mr Morton, and asked if she could speak to me privately. I came out into the hall, and, to my surprise, Angèle was dressed in her street clothes, and her suitcase was there beside her on the floor.' Mrs Morton pointed to the approximate spot where Tom was standing.

'I don't understand,' Tom murmured.

'Neither do I,' Mrs Morton said. 'Angèle then told me that there was a sudden emergency and that she had to leave immediately. She seemed very nervous and rather upset. She apologized profusely for leaving me without notice, but she said that she had no alternative.'

'And she didn't explain, or say what it was, or tell you where she was going?' Tom demanded incredulously.

'No. I was furious, of course, and told her she couldn't possibly leave without notice, and that I expected her to stay with us until we returned to England very shortly. Her only response was: "I cannot, madame, I cannot." I know she has no family. I know it couldn't have been a question of a close relative being dangerously ill. There was absolutely no excuse for her behaviour.'

'And then she left?' Tom asked.

Mrs Morton nodded. 'She said she would not expect me to pay her for the few days since she'd been paid last, because she was leaving so suddenly and was inconveniencing me. She looked very strange and her face was very white. She opened the door, and I watched to see where she was going.'

'And where did she go?' Tom asked quickly.

'She walked down the street, carrying her suitcase, and turned the corner. And that is the story, Mr Welles.'

Tom stood there silently, his mind in a turmoil. It was all incredible, but he would have sworn Mrs Morton was telling the truth.

'Mrs Morton,' he said at last quietly, 'this is even more of a shock to me than perhaps it was to you. You see – although I've only known Angèle a few days, I am very fond of her.'

'She seemed to be a nice child – or at least until last night,' Mrs Morton said grudgingly. 'After last night, however, she could be ten fathoms deep in the Mediterranean without my giving it a second thought. You'll undoubtedly be hearing from her, though, Mr Welles. She'll probably get in touch with you.'

'Angèle,' Tom admitted, 'doesn't even know my address.'

'Well, you'll probably run into her somewhere.' There was a ghost of a smile on her face. 'Try the park again, Mr Welles.'

'Mrs Morton, could I leave my address with you just in case—'

'If you want.' Mrs Morton shrugged. 'You're wasting your time, though. She'll never come back here. She wouldn't dare.'

'I'd like to leave my address, nevertheless.'

'Well, write it here, then, on this piece of paper. And if I do ever see her again, which I very much doubt, I'll give it to her.'

There was nothing more to be learned here, so Tom thanked Mrs Morton and left. Instinctively he walked down to the Café des Deux Anges, ordered a drink, and tried to think. It took him a few minutes to recover from the shock of Angèle's disappearance, but as the pieces of the puzzle began to fit together he saw the light.

It had to be. There was no other answer. The interview the afternoon before, between Angèle and Paul Ehrenhardt. The Ehrenhardts' sudden departure from the Negresco the previous night, destination unannounced. Angèle's state of mind as reported by Mrs Morton. Her sudden and inexcusable departure. Her refusal to answer questions. And again, destination unannounced, if indeed she knew herself what her destination was to be.

Paul Ehrenhardt had spun his web and Angèle was in it. And he, Tom Welles, had been played for a fool. He laughed loud and bitterly when he thought of his interview with Mme Chiron at the American Consulate that afternoon. Mme Chiron had been quite right. His questions about marriage were premature, very premature.

Months, Paul Ehrenhardt had said – perhaps longer. But what difference did time make? He had seen the last of Angèle. She had gone off with the Ehrenhardts without even leaving a word of goodbye. Why couldn't she have waited for at least a day so that they could have seen each other again? But that was probably Paul Ehrenhardt's doing. He was taking no chances on Angèle's seeing him again, or seeing anyone else to whom she might talk, for fear some link might be established between them which would interfere with his plans for Angèle. Or perhaps he was afraid that if she had time to think over her decision she might change her mind.

Ehrenhardt might have told Angèle that it must be that night or not at all. Paul was a winning, persuasive person when he wanted to be. And where could Angèle have left a message for him, under the circumstances of such a sudden departure? She did not know where he was living. The only way to find him would have been through the American Consulate or the French police, who, of course, had a record of his domicile. At short notice, it was impossibly complicated.

Then Tom Welles had a sudden thought. He rose quickly and crossed to where *la patronne* sat behind her antiquated cash register.

Tom was too disturbed to cope with French.

'Excuse me, madame, do you speak English?'

'Yes, a little, monsieur.'

'Perhaps yesterday or the day before, you noticed that I was here at your restaurant.'

'Yes, monsieur. The day before you were here twice, and on your first visit you had a great deal to drink.'

'Did you notice the girl who was with me here yesterday and the day before?' Tom asked eagerly.

'Yes, monsieur, I noticed Mademoiselle. She was very striking looking.'

'Did Mademoiselle by any chance leave a note for me or a letter last night?' Tom asked tensely. 'My name is Welles.'

The *patronne* shook her head. 'No, I am sorry, monsieur. I have not seen Mademoiselle since she left the restaurant yesterday. As you know, that was after your own departure.'

'Could she have left a note with anyone else here?'

'No, monsieur. If she had left a message, it would have been with me.'

'Did you by any chance notice the tall, dark man who joined us yesterday afternoon?'

'Certainly, monsieur. It is my business to notice everything here at the restaurant.'

'Did Mademoiselle and my friend leave together?' Tom asked.

'No, which surprised me a little.'

'I've lost Mademoiselle,' Tom said simply. 'She has disappeared.'

'I'm sorry, monsieur. Perhaps your friend could tell you where to find her.'

'My friend has disappeared, too,' Tom muttered.

'Ah.' The one syllable was expressive. The *patronne's* face was very sympathetic. This attractive young American evidently was very much disturbed. His eyes, in fact, were quite tragic. 'Mademoiselle and your friend talked together for a long time, almost an hour, I should think, their heads close together. Your friend did most of the talking. Mademoiselle listened. She seemed to be asking a question now and then, but she did not talk very much.'

'Madame, you are most observant. Is there anything more you can tell me?'

She thought a few moments. 'Very little,' she finally admitted. 'It seemed to me that your friend, if he is your friend, was making a proposal that at first did not appeal to Mademoiselle very much. Then later her eyes became excited and her manner changed.'

'You heard nothing, madame?'

'No, I heard nothing. They were talking very low. Then finally your friend took a piece of paper from his pocket, wrote something down on it, and handed it to Mademoiselle. She put it in her purse. Your friend arose, shook hands with Mademoiselle, and left alone. Mademoiselle departed perhaps five minutes later. She seemed to be hurrying.'

'Madame, you have been very kind. I thank you.'

Her eyes were very sympathetic. 'I'm only sorry that I could not be of more help, monsieur.'

Tom Welles paid for his drink and went out into the night.

That was another bad night for Tom. He paced up and down in his tiny room under the eaves. His emotions vibrated between anger, because Angèle had fallen in with Paul Ehrenhardt's plan and had vanished without a word to him, and a desolate feeling of loss. At one moment he would decide to catch the first plane to America and wash his hands of the whole business. Angèle had obviously dismissed him from her mind and had gone off with that golden carrot in front of her nose. A few minutes later he would convince himself that she was the victim of some diabolical plot, that he had betrayed her by introducing her to Paul, that she was helpless in his clutches, and that he must start searching the seven corners of the world in order to rescue her from the consequences of his own stupidity. In spite of the fact that he had told her he knew nothing about Ehrenhardt's plans, she might be thinking of him as hand and glove with Paul. She might be thinking that all that had passed between them was merely a build-up for whatever this Ehrenhardt project might be, and that she was doing what he would have her do. How could he know what Paul had told her?

His mind was not working clearly. It was confused and bumbling about, trying to juggle objects that he couldn't see or define. He had forgotten completely about his novel, the news from New York, and the fact that suddenly his whole position in the world had changed.

Strangely enough, it was not until deep into the night that he suddenly thought of the Castle Garac and its possible place in the picture. Then he took a long, deep breath. The passage in Paul Ehrenhardt's letter, saying that their plans had changed radically, Tom had ingenuously accepted at face value, and he had not associated the Castle Garac with the Ehrenhardts' sudden departure. Paul Ehrenhardt had, however, a letter from Tom giving him right of occupancy during the term of the option. Perhaps Paul's plans had not changed. Surely they had not changed. Paul's letter to him was only a blind. He was sure now that Angèle's disappearance was closely tied up with the Ehrenhardts, and what could be more probable than that they had departed for the Castle Garac with Angèle? It was a simple, logical conclusion, and it was amazing that it had not occurred to him before.

So what? What if he were right? Paul and Anna Ehrenhardt, and probably Hugo Forchet, and certainly Angèle, would be at the castle. It was a reasonable supposition, but it led to nothing.

Why were they at the castle? What part did the Castle Garac play in this project of Paul's? What part did an extraordinarily good-looking nineteen-year-old blonde play in the picture?

But, his acceptance of the Castle Garac as an important element in the problem gave Tom a sense of relief. At least here was something tangible, something one could think about. It at least opened the possibility of knowing where Angèle was and how she could be reached, if he wanted to probe further into this strange business.

He would consider this further in the morning when his mind was clearer. Now he realized he needed some sleep desperately, and he went to bed.

Thomas Welles' subconscious mind must have been working that night while he slept, because when he awoke that morning he knew exactly what he was going to do.

As soon as he had had breakfast he went to the American Express office and cashed his draft for five hundred dollars, added to it half his hoard of French bank notes, and opened an account on which he could draw.

He then found a sporting-goods shop, bought a small flashlight, and examined hunting-knives, finally selecting one which bore some resemblance to the Army knife he had been trained to use in Korea.

Next he acquired a pair of heavy rubber-soled walking-shoes, a pair of corduroy trousers, a blue fisherman's shirt, an ill-fitting French jacket, and a beret.

Then Tom found an artist's-supply store and bought the cheapest folding easel that he could find, a large pad of drawing-paper, and what he thought might be a proper selection of pencils and crayons. He hoped that there would never be anyone watching him when he put pencil to paper, because he had not dared even to try to draw since that horrible and painful experience in his first year of school when he had laboured vainly day after day in an attempt to create something that resembled that repulsive red apple on the desk in front of him. Tom had always rather liked apples up to that point. He had avoided them ever since.

With his purchases he returned to his room. He sought out

the concierge and paid the rent on his room for two weeks in advance, saying that he was going on a walking-trip up in the mountains and that she should not expect him back until he re-appeared.

Into a very small duffel bag that he could easily carry with one hand, he put two clean shirts, changes of underwear, socks, a razor, and other toilet equipment. After a moment's thought he added a heavy sweater. He had determined to travel light, but that sweater might be important.

Then he changed into the motley garments he had purchased that morning, threaded the sheath of his knife on to his belt and shoved it around to a position where it would not be conspicu-ous, and regarded himself in the mirror. He no longer looked like Thomas Welles, the rich young American, he decided with satisfaction. He picked up his duffel bag and headed for the bus depot. That morning at the American Express Company he had been told there would be a bus that went through Latire leaving at three o'clock, and Latire was the village nearest the Castle Garac. It was a slow bus that wandered here and there en route, and it would take him the best part of five hours to reach Latire, but it would be better arriving there after dark anyway, he had concluded. Besides, there was no other bus.

On the way to the bus station he decided to buy a small flask of cognac and some sweet chocolate. Vague as his plans were, these might come in handy.

And then, as he passed a bakery, with a grim smile he entered and bought one *petit pain* and shoved it down into his coat pocket.

To Tom Welles that bus seemed to be exploring every town in the Maritime Alps between Nice and the Italian border. It would roar along the highway, slow down, career into a narrow dirt road, and after bumping along for kilometres, happen upon a little village, drop a small sack of mail, perhaps leave a pas-senger or pick up a passenger, and after the complicated manoeuvre of turning around in the small village square, rumble back to the highway. At times it would stop in a village and just seem to wait while the driver disappeared. Perhaps they were running ahead of schedule, Tom thought, and time for departure was being scrupulously observed. Or perhaps the driver merely was thirsty and wanted a glass of wine. The other passengers seemed to be indifferent as to whether or not they ever arrived at their destinations. It was either that, or they'd had experience with this particular bus and were resigned to its uncertain progress. To Tom Welles, however, it was one of the most maddening, frustrating journeys he had ever made.

Dusk crept over the land. It grew darker and stars appeared. Tom had no idea how far they were from Latire. He had decided that he would be travelling on this bus for the rest of his life and that he would be lucky if he ever arrived at his destination. He began wondering whether there was an inn at Latire, and, if not, where he would spend the night. His recollections of the town were vague, his business having been transacted at the Mairie and without regard to the little village itself. He consulted his watch. If the American Express schedule had been correct, the bus was very late. It was almost nine o'clock.

When the bus finally stopped and the bus-driver announced Latire, although that was what Tom had been waiting for throughout these hours, it came as a shock and a surprise. He rose stiffly to his feet and sidled his way down to the door of the bus. Before descending, he peered out into the dark. There were but few lights, and the town seemed deserted.

'Est-ce qu'il-y-a une hôtel ici?' he demanded.

'Une petite auberge, monsieur. La première rue à droite et puis à gauche.'

'Merci bien.'

Tom wondered whether he would find a room. He was not in a hopeful mood.

Yes, there was a small room free. Perhaps not what Monsieur would choose, but it was all they had. No bath, of course, but Monsieur could have a pitcher of hot water. Dinner? Monsieur must understand that it was very late for dinner, but if he could be content with some cold meat and cheese and a bottle of wine, perhaps it would serve until the morning.

Monsieur was grateful and would be very content. Could it be served immediately?

Most surely. In five minutes it would all be waiting. While he ate Tom Welles learned from Madame that it was indeed a pleasure to welcome a stranger. They had very few visitors at Latire, especially foreign visitors. Was Monsieur here on business, perhaps?

No, Monsieur was not here on business. He was an artist and had heard much about the beauties hereabouts and had come here to sketch.

Yes, this was certainly one of the most beautiful corners of France. Monsieur would undoubtedly find much that would interest him. There was not only the natural scenery, but there were many interesting ruins in the vicinity, some going back even as far as the Roman invasion.

Yes, he had heard much about Roman ruins and medieval castles, Tom assured Madame gravely. It was because of the ruins and castles that he had been drawn to Latire. Did Madame have any specific recommendations about what he would find most interesting?

Madame did. In her swift, provincial French, she rattled off a long list of celebrated landmarks.

There was a certain castle that he had heard spoken of, Tom observed. Was there a Castle Garac near by?

There was indeed a Castle Garac just a few kilometres from Latire, Madame assured her guest. It was not as old as many of the more venerable ruins, of course. As a matter of fact, it actually had been lived in until recently. It had not been more than twelve or thirteen years since the de Garac family were inhabiting their ancestral castle. Not all the time, of course, but a great part of the year. And in the last few days, as a matter of fact, she had heard rumours about the possibility of the castle being bought by some rich young American who fancied the place and who was considering remodelling it for his own use. Monsieur was perhaps an American also?

No, Tom assured Madame, he was not an American. He was English, here in the mountains for a short holiday.

There had been some talk, Madame went on, of this American moving into the castle before he decided whether or not actually to buy, but that obviously was mere rumour and untrue, because certainly not even an unpredictable American in his right mind would even consider spending a night at the Castle Garac in its present condition. It was a desolate spot and going to rack and ruin. It was said that wandering gypsies occasionally used it as a rendezvous, but not even a self-respecting gypsy would be comfortable living at the castle as it was now. . . . Was Monsieur intending to stay long in Latire?

A few days perhaps, Tom said vaguely. He did not really know. It would depend partly on the weather and partly on how interested he became in sketching this particular spot.

And then Tom had an idea.

The use of a bicycle might be quite convenient, he observed. A bicycle would enable him to move about much more freely and cover much more ground. Did Madame perhaps know whether there would be a bicycle available for rent in Latire?

Madame did not know for sure, but she thought it would be very likely. If Monsieur wished, she would make inquiries in the morning. There were a number of bicycles in Latire, of course, but it was a question as to whether there would be one not in use.

Her inquiries would be most appreciated, Tom assured her, and now he thought he would retire for the night if Madame would excuse him. The *repas* had been delicious, and he regretted having had to inconvenience Madame at such a late hour.

As he climbed upstairs to his room, Tom Welles marvelled at himself. He realized that his French had been ungrammatical, halting, stiff, and uncolloquial, but even to have floundered through such a conversation, making himself clear, was a miracle, and most of what the old lady had said to him he had understood. There were only two explanations. Either necessity was forcing him through a more rapid acquisition of the language than seemed possible, or, more likely, he had been a Frenchman in some previous incarnation and now it was coming back to him.

Tired as he was after that gruelling trip on the bus, Tom Welles had but one desire that night: to go on to the Castle Garac and settle the burning question as to whether or not he had run his quarry to earth. But he realized that even if the Ehrenhardts had moved in, by this time of the night they would be in bed. There would be no lights and no outward indication of occupancy, and being very uncertain of his ground, Tom realized that he must postpone his reconnaissance until tomorrow and he forced himself to undress and to sleep.

Tom Welles descended the next morning for an early breakfast, but Madame had already been out scouting for a bicycle and reported with triumph that there was waiting a most excellent bicycle with almost new tyres. It belonged to the baker, M. Malgret, but M. Malgret had been persuaded to give it up for a few days. If Monsieur was pleased with the bicycle, he could rent it for two hundred francs a day.

Madame waited expectantly, for if Monsieur decided to rent this bicycle, M. Malgret would pay her fifty francs a day commission.

Tom went out and looked at the proffered bicycle. It was a bob-tailed affair like all French bicycles, but if he raised the seat a bit he would be able to manage, and he assured Madame that it would be most satisfactory and that he would be very content to pay two hundred francs a day for its use.

Tom Welles was feeling excited this morning. It was very much the same feeling he had experienced from time to time in the Army when he knew there was action ahead but had no idea as to what exactly would be happening. There was an element of fear, of course, but also one of anticipation, and that tinge of fear intensified the intense excitement of such a moment.

After a breakfast substantial enough to last him all day if need be, he thrust the *petit pain* and the chocolate down into his coat pocket and descended to cope with the bicycle. The seat arranged to his satisfaction, he tried the bell. It was a lovely bell, the sort of bell bicycle-riders had been ringing at him for months to scare him out of their paths. Now he would do the bell-ringing. He strapped his easel and drawing-equipment to the handlebars of the bicycle, told madam not to expect him until he reappeared, and pedalled off on the road to the Castle Garac.

It was a hilly road. It was true that you could ride down the hills without effort. It was also true that almost immediately you would have to descend your bicycle and push it up the next hill. Tom wondered whether the bicycle had been a sound idea or not. He couldn't leave it here beside the road, however, so the only thing to do was to proceed and make the best of it.

As he remembered, it was something over three miles to the Castle Garac from the village of Latire. Today it seemed much longer. At last, however, from the crest of a hill, he could see across a lower hill ahead of him a grey mound of stone that must be his destination.

Tom Welles had no plan. He had no idea what he was going to do when he reached the Castle Garac. He supposed the first thing to do was to reconnoitre and find out if possible whether the Ehrenhardts were really there. Intellectually he admitted the possibility that this might be a wild-goose chase, but emotionally he was convinced that within that bleak grey pile he would find the Ehrenhardts, Angèle, and probably Hugo Forchet.

After that there was but one thing to do – namely, draw four cards to a lone ace, and pray. In this game he could not call for a brand-new hand, and he had too much in the pot to throw in what he had, and withdraw. There was nothing to do but play whatever cards were dealt.

From the crest of the next hill he could see the Castle Garac more clearly. He stopped at the side of the road and lit a cigarette. Ahead of him lay a rough, wooded valley. There was no sign of cultivation and, from where he stood, at least, no sign of a farm or even any animal shelters. It was as though the entire valley had been deserted. As he remembered from papers he had seen at the time he was negotiating for the option on the castle, quite a lot of land went with the castle itself; but because he hadn't been interested, he could not remember just how much.

Almost in the centre of the valley, perched on a steep hill that looked almost as though it had been built up there purposely as a foundation, was the Castle Garac itself. The sides of the hill were, for the most part, rocky except where they were streaked with irregular but broad ribbons of trees so densely planted that, looking at them with one's eyes half closed, they seemed to be ragged strips and irregular patches of a mottled green carpet dropped down carelessly to break up the monotony of the sheer grey rock.

From where he was, Tom could estimate only very roughly

119

how high the hill rose above the valley floor, but it must have been two hundred and fifty or three hundred perpendicular feet from the valley to the crest where the castle walls rose straight up from their foundation, concealing the lower floor of the castle itself.

He could see where the narrow road to the castle swung off the highway he was travelling, and then the road lost itself as it twisted into the forest at the base of the hill.

Perhaps half a mile away from where he watched, Garac showed no signs of life or habitation. Tom cursed himself for not having bought or rented a pair of binoculars.

He decided to go on with his bicycle to the bottom of the hill and work on foot from there on. It was probably safe to stay on the road for the time being, but he did not want to be seen by anyone in the neighbourhood. If he had to leave the road and plunge into the fields, he wanted to be able to do so quickly.

At the bottom of the hill he found a clump of bushes close at hand, concealed the bicycle, and unstrapped his artist's equipment. He was sceptical about it proving effective camouflage, but it was better than nothing.

As he started down the road he told himself that he should not walk too fast. If anyone should notice him, it wouldn't do to have it seem as though he had any particular destination. It would be a good idea to stop now and then and study the landscape and surroundings as though he were searching for a subject that would appeal to his artist's soul, careful, however, not to seem too aware of the Castle Garac itself. In spite of a heightening of the tension he was under, he felt slightly ridiculous, and he recalled a period of his early boyhood when for weeks he had lived the life of an Army scout working for General Custer in the days just before the great massacre. His school marks had been very bad during those days, for even during the hours when he was not actually out playing and scouting for Indians, his own mind rejected anything but the enthralling life on the great plains and nothing else had any importance.

He had not laughed at himself in those days, but now he was very self-conscious at the figure that he must be cutting, wandering along the road there with his elaborate precautions, without knowing whether there was any excuse for his pretence or not.

He wondered whether the turn leading to the castle road would show tyre marks. Whether it had rained here two days before he did not know. There was certainly no sign now that it had rained for weeks, but that proved nothing. If it had rained the day before yesterday and there were tyre marks, it would be significant. If, however, there had been no rain, the tyre marks on the road might well have been from the Simca he had driven in himself a number of times when he was negotiating for the Garac option. He jumped across an old ditch into a field and felt the ground. It seemed to be normally damp, but certainly not wet.

'Kit Carson, you have a lot to learn about this business,' he said out loud. 'You're a hell of a scout.'

The road into the castle was just ahead now. What the devil should he do? Should he walk up the road? Should he try to sneak through the woods? Perhaps it would be better to come back after dark after a general survey of the surroundings.

When he came to the castle road, he studied it carefully. It was baked and hard and told him very little. There were marks there in the road that might have been tyre marks. They might have been anything. Tom shook his head and swore again. Why hadn't he made more inquiries at the village? Certainly someone there would know whether or not anyone had moved into the Castle Garac. But if his quarry were there, it could only have been since yesterday, and if they had not been out for supplies, their presence was probably still unheralded.

He decided to try the road for a little distance at least. Telling himself that he must be very alert, he started walking slowly along the road, broken, rough but open to the fields on each side of him. Then he remembered his training as one of Custer's scouts and realized that on open ground he should be running so as to reduce the time of danger when he might be observed, running and probably zigzagging in case someone was shooting at him. He controlled himself, however, and kept on with his slow, deliberate pace.

Of a sudden there was a rustle and a sharp crackle close by in the field to his right. To his mortification, Tom found himself flat on the road with his head down. Instantaneously and instinctively he had flattened out. He raised his head, and with a grin saw a great wild hare loping across the field.

This time he laughed at himself out loud without concern over who might hear him.

He rose, dusted himself off. When he reached the bottom of the hill where the woods began he lit a cigarette and thought things over. If he followed the road up the hill, he would certainly be able to hear any automobile descending before the car got too close. And he was even more effectively protected from his rear because any car climbing that hill would be making plenty of noise. A pedestrian, therefore, was the only real hazard for the time being, and from what he knew of Anna and Paul Ehrenhardt, he doubted very much whether they would choose to walk up and down a rutted gravel road unless it was a case of dire necessity. If he should meet Angèle, nothing would fit in more perfectly with his desire and his purpose. That left Hugo Forchet or some unknown. Hugo was something else again. With those big feet of his and that physique, he might be anywhere. Tom decided he'd have to take a chance on Hugo for the time being.

He started up the hill now, and the road immediately began to wind. It would circle slowly upward for a few feet and then switch back after a sharp hairpin curve. On this particular section of the hill there was practically no open ground. The woods were heavy, and the road above and below was densely shrouded.

Tom recalled the lie of the land on top of the hill. The woods ended abruptly about fifty feet from the castle wall, and except for the road hewn out of rock to the castle gate itself, the immediate surroundings were rough rocks with practically no vegetation. Tom supposed that in days gone by the open strip that circled the castle had been kept clear, so that the defenders could see more clearly to pour their boiling oil on any attackers unlucky enough to have reached the crest of the hill. He suddenly found himself wondering where all the boiling oil came from in days of yore. Everyone seemed to pour vast quantities of boiling oil on everyone else up until the time when they really got going with gunpowder. And if he remembered correctly, it wasn't until well on into the nineteenth century that oil as he knew it had been discovered in Pennsylvania. Before that, wasn't most oil whale oil? Certainly whale oil was too precious to go pouring around indiscriminately. But he had better get his mind back to the business at hand and look into this matter of oil some other time. ... They certainly didn't get all that oil from olives, though, he reflected. There was only one other answer. They must have melted up all their fat cows and sheep. No wonder these people in Europe lived mainly on vegetables and bread. It was in the blood.

A most curious person, he decided, this chap Tom Welles with whom he was out walking. Here he was engaged on a secret and dangerous mission, involved in a venture that was most important to him, and having arrived at a point where in a few minutes he might find himself in a more or less serious crisis, this chap Welles had become absorbed with a ridiculous, inconsequential, irrelevant inquiry into the source of oil hundreds of years ago. It occurred to Tom that it might be a good idea to send this chap Welles home and go on alone.

He was almost to the crest of the hill now and proceeding very cautiously. Then he decided it was time to leave the road, and plunged into the woods. The going was difficult here. Obviously no one had cleared in these woods for years. There were broken limbs barring his path and tangles of fast-rotting brush. The trees were too thick for there to be much undergrowth, but tangled vines were twisting aimlessly everywhere, ranging from tree to tree and effectively barring any straight progress. There was a deep and unnatural stillness, except for the occasional snap of a twig under Tom's foot as he worked his way up what was now a very steep grade.

The edge of the woods was just ahead. Tom could see the light belt of open space between the trees and the castle wall. He estimated that he would emerge about thirty or forty feet from the gate itself, well out of the line of vision of anyone who might be looking out through the open gateway. He thought of the gateway as open because on his various trips to the castle the mammoth wooden gates had never been closed. He did not even know whether they could be closed, after these many years of disuse. Cautiously Tom drew himself up behind a tree at the edge of the clearing where he could peer out towards the gateway. To his surprise and shock, he saw that the gates were firmly closed.

He could feel his heart thumping now. There was certainly someone behind those gates in the Castle Garac, and it could only be the Ehrenhardts. And if the Ehrenhardts were there, Angèle Corton would be there too.

What next? The great grey walls towered over his head; those gates were firmly closed and probably locked. The only chance of entrance would be to find a breach in the wall low enough for him to scramble over, and what the devil would he do once he was inside? He had to find Angèle, and talk to her, and get some explanation of this fantastic business, and try to persuade her to return with him to Nice, regardless of what this plan of the Ehrenhardts' was. But how would he find Angèle alone, with Anna and Paul and Hugo on the scene?

He had the wild idea of returning to the village of Latire and reporting that the Ehrenhardts had kidnapped Angèle and had her locked in the Castle Garac, but he realized that even if he escaped being locked up as a madman and could persuade the local authorities to investigate, the Ehrenhardts could prove that they were there with his permission and authority, and if Angèle had gone off with the Ehrenhardts voluntarily, she would not be likely to substantiate the kidnapping theory.

No, he must find Angèle secretly and talk to her without the Ehrenhardts' knowledge. The only chance of doing that would be at night under the protection of darkness. He would have to come back to the castle that night, but first he would have to discover some easy way to pass those walls. Damn Paul Ehrenhardt and his walls! It was almost as though Paul had known that he would need a wall to bar Tom's way.

Using the edge of the woods as a screen, Tom wormed his way slowly and with difficulty around the hill, looking for a breach in the wall that he could possibly scale. It would have been easy with a ladder, but how would he ever get a ladder up the hill and into the woods? A rope might help, but there was no certainty that it would. The chance of slinging a looped rope over a wall and having it anchor on anything secure was very remote. These walls really had had a utilitarian purpose, he decided, and the sweat and labour of raising them had undoubtedly paid off.

At last, almost halfway round the hill, Tom saw a wide, crescent-shaped depression in the wall, the lowest point of which was much lower than any dip he had yet noticed. He tried to measure the height of the low point with his eye. It would certainly be quite a bit above his head if he was standing by the wall, but perhaps within his reach. Even so, and even if there were anything up there which he could grasp and which would carry his weight, he doubted very much whether he would be able to pull himself up and over. A strong man in the circus undoubtedly could have managed it, or perhaps a trained gymnast. He was in fairly good condition by the standards of modern civilized life, but he reflected wryly that he was, at the moment, not living a civilized life.

Perhaps he would be able to pile up some rocks and stones by the wall under that low spot, and stand on the resulting mound. He glanced about. Yes, there were plenty near by that could be moved, but he did not dare to do anything about that now. If anyone spotted him it would be disastrous. He would have to do that tonight. If it was a clear night, there would probably be enough moonlight for him to see.

Tom wondered what there was just on the other side of that low spot. What was he going to drop down on to or into? Tom decided that question was unanswerable until he came to the actual drop – if he got that far.

Tom then retreated a little into the woods, sat down to rest, and decided it was safe to light a cigarette.

If that letter from Hotsom had only come one day sooner, things might have turned out quite differently. If he had known about the sale of his novel, he probably would have decided not to tell Paul Ehrenhardt anything about Angèle. By this time he even might have proposed to her and she might even have accepted him. Or if she hadn't accepted him, perhaps not turned him down cold. Tom sighed. His arms and his legs were aching from the unaccustomed exertion. His first excitement of finding the Castle Garac occupied had died down. His mind now was filled with an unemotional, dogged determination to find Angèle, and find her that night if possible.

He realized that even after he passed the castle's wall he would be floundering about inside without any idea of where or how to look for Angèle. He remembered vaguely the ground floor of the castle. There was a high hall with an arched ceiling which at its highest point must have been more than twenty feet above the floor. Facing the front door of the hall was a great stone hearth certainly large enough to roast a whole ox. Leading off from one side of the hall, not far from the hearth, there was a wide passageway. Stairs mounted from the passageway to the rooms above, sweeping up in a semicircle. Then there was a medium-sized room, opening off that passageway to the right, that had apparently been used as an informal dining-room; a small empty room was on the opposite side near the stairs. The door at the end of the passageway led into the kitchen and the scullery, with open but roofed sheds beyond.

Tom's mind went back to the great hall. The left wall was broken by a wide stone staircase leading to what was obviously the family's living-quarters above. There were an upstairs hall-way, two large rooms, and a number of smaller rooms. Tom couldn't remember how many. It was on that floor that the primitive bath had been installed.

Tom closed his eyes and returned to the reception hall. There were two large rooms off to the left, each with its door into the main hall, connecting with each other through a Gothic stone archway. The room at the back, with its altar at the end and several shaky *prie-dieux*, was obviously the family chapel. The walls of the castle were of stone, but he remembered handsome oak panelling in some of the rooms.

The second floor over the service end of the castle he remembered only vaguely. There was a narrow hallway, he remembered, with a jumble of small rooms irregularly arranged. The hall twisted here and there, but Tom did not remember the pattern.

Then he asked himself how, once being upstairs in the castle, you crossed to the other side of the great reception hall without descending to the first floor. He remembered no passage at the time he inspected the Castle Garac, and it had never occurred to him to ask. It might be important to know whether those two sections of the castle were isolated from each other. There certainly was not any third floor to the castle, or he would have remembered it. Then there was the great square watch tower which loomed up thirty or forty feet above the roof itself. It jutted out at the main corner of the castle by the large front room that opened off the great hall. He remembered now that one could reach its narrow circular staircase either from that big chamber on the ground floor, or from the big corner bedroom upstairs. Like all the other stairways in the house, those stairs leading up the tower were of stone.

Tom decided that when he got back to his room at Latire he would make some use of his artist's equipment and try to draw a floor plan of the Castle Garac. It might help him recall some of the details, and if his plan were at all accurate it would certainly help to fix the layout of the castle in his mind.

It would be easier, he decided, to cut down through the woods from where he was rather than return to the castle road. Going down through those woods would not be too bad. He started carefully picking his way down the hill.

Three quarters of an hour later he found his bicycle undisturbed, and realized for the first time that he had left his folding easel and his paper and pencils in the woods on his first stop. Well, he probably would not need them anyway, and it was out of the question to try and retrieve them. The chances were that no one would run across them.

The road back to Latire was long, but at last the village emerged ahead of him.

Madame greeted him at the door. Monsieur's easel and paper? Where were they?

Tom explained that in order to save carrying them back and forth, he had left them where he planned to sketch the next day.

Had Monsieur had his *déjeuner*? It was late, but if he was hungry there was still some excellent stewed rabbit, and with a bottle of wine—

Tom Welles greeted the suggestion with enthusiasm, and he told Madame that he was famished and that he would be at her table shortly.

After luncheon he dropped wearily down on his bed, realizing that the night ahead of him was bound to be a fiasco unless he got some rest in the meantime. Kit Carson may have been able to do this sort of thing day and night without rest, but he, Thomas Welles, was not cut out for it.

II

PANTING HEAVILY, Tom Welles rolled the last big heavy rock up the sizeable pile that he had built at the foot of the castle wall, settled it into position, and with his eyes measured the distance between the crest of his mound and the top of the wall.

That should do it, he decided. If there was anything up on top of the wall that he could really get hold of, he would be able to pull himself up until he could get his elbows over the wall, and then—

When Tom had come to life early in the afternoon, he had found himself filled again with that tense nervous excitement that he had felt that morning. Madame had provided him with an early supper, and he had explained that one of his vagaries was an irresistible passion for moonlight walks.

But Monsieur surely had had enough exercise that morning! The night was for sleeping or for— Madame broke off with an expressive gesture.

No, there was nothing like walking by moonlight, and if the moon was bright enough, he often sketched by moonlight.

And what time would Monsieur be returning?

Monsieur did not know. Madame was not to wait up for him. If he was not back by her usual bedtime, she was to retire and forget her guest.

And how would Monsieur enter after the *auberge* was locked?

The key would have to be hidden where he could find it, Tom told her firmly.

But Monsieur must realize that there was no key that could be hidden. There were only bolts on the front door which were manipulated from within.

Then Madame would have to leave the front door open, because he did not expect to return before she retired.

The matter was most irregular, Madame protested. To leave the front door unbolted would be most dangerous.

But certainly there were no thieves in such a village as Latire, and for one night surely Madame could make an exception.

Naturally there were no thieves in Latire, there was not a dishonest person in the whole village. But what of the gypsies?

Gypsies?

Certainly, the gypsies. Madame admitted that she had not seen any in the last few weeks, but there were often small bands of roving gypsies in the vicinity, and, as Monsieur must know, all gypsies were thieves and murderers, and their women were just as bad. She, Madame, would certainly not sleep a wink if she thought her front door had been left open.

There was one thing about Tom Welles: he knew when he was beaten.

Very well, Madame must certainly lock up the *auberge* when she retired and dismiss him from her mind. If he was late, he would spend the night in the hayloft over the shed in the rear. Or he might spend the night in the open. He had often done so, but Madame must not worry if he were not back in the morning. She should expect him only when she saw him.

Tom decided against the bicycle and started down the road towards the Castle Garac, taking his time because it was not yet fully dark and the moon would not be up until some time after nine. The moonlight he would certainly need.

Building up that cairn of rocks had not been easy. He had started with small stones that were easy to move, but, working so, progress was very slow. He worked as quietly as he could, but in the dead stillness of the night he seemed to himself to be making a great deal of noise. Then he switched to larger rocks that he could just manoeuvre by straining every muscle. With their irregular shapes, they would slip and slide. One small boulder actually escaped him and rolled crashing down into the woods below.

Tom froze and waited motionless for several minutes after that, praying that the noise had not reached any other ears. Finally he had resumed work.

Gingerly Tom mounted his cairn. Yes, he could just make it. His hands groped over the top of the broken wall. It was very thick and he could not reach the other side, but there was a jagged point about eight inches in from the outer surface that seemed to be solid and secure.

He grasped it with both hands and inched his way up the side of the wall. His elbow was over the edge now. He drew himself up a little farther and swung up his leg.

From the top of the wall Tom peered down into the darkness. The sky had clouded up and there was no moonlight now. As far as he could make out, below him was a mass of tangled, over-grown shrubbery. He had no idea how high it was, and he could not estimate how far the drop was to the inside of the castle wall. He would have to let himself down as far as he could, drop, and pray his landing-place would be soft.

Perched on the wall, Tom surveyed his surroundings. The castle itself was perhaps seventy-five yards away and rose bleak and forbidding, without any sign of light. This would be almost the back of the castle. Even so, it was strange that there were no lights whatsoever. Tom waited there a few minutes until he was breathing normally, alert for any sign of life or activity. Then he worked his way over the inside edge of the wall, his hands clutch-ing the same jagged, pointed rock that he had used in his ascent. When his body was flat against the wall, using one hand at a time he sought a finger hold on the very edge of the wall so as to cut his drop by a few more inches.

Then the edge of the wall crumbled suddenly, and Tom crashed down into the bushes. As he hit the ground, he felt his ankle twist under him, and a sharp pain. An instant later he heard a rustle in the bushes close by, and then he felt wiry steel fingers around his neck.

Instantaneously and instinctively Tom lurched up and over so as to free his hands. He clutched for his assailant's face. The man was heavy and strong. Those fingers were tightening, and in a few moments—

The American fighting force in Korea had been taught some very nasty tricks. Contact with the enemy was often personal and frequently unexpected, and the Marquess of Queensberry's rules were not observed. Tom's thumb was prying into his attacker's eye socket. If he could force it in a little farther through those desperately contracted muscles before he lost consciousness. There, almost—

There was a sharp cry of pain, the man's fingers relaxed, and he leaped away. Tom could see him as a huge grey hulk trembling there above him for a moment.

Reaching for his knife, Tom struggled to his feet. But he had forgotten his ankle, and as the pain flashed up his leg he realized that he would be very lucky if he lived through this one.

Suddenly the man turned and plunged away into the bushes. He must have seen Tom's knife. Tom could hear him crashing through the underbrush for a few moments, and then there was complete silence. He stood there, his weight on his left foot, waiting tensely. Had the man gone for help, or had he had enough?

All was utterly still now, and Tom could hear his heart beating. *Welcome to Garac,* he told himself grimly. Then, gingerly, he tried putting a little more weight on his right foot. Apparently nothing was broken, but, judging by the pain, it was a bad wrench. The sooner he found out whether he could walk on it, the better.

He could feel a trickle of blood running down his cheek, and he wiped it away. He noticed that his sleeve was torn, and there was a rip in his shirt. Crashing through those bushes had not improved his appearance.

Knife in hand and alert for any ambush, Tom tried a short step. Then another. His ankle hurt like the devil, but, for the time being at least, he could use it.

As quietly as possible, and very slowly, he began pushing his way through the undergrowth towards the clearing beyond. The bushes extended right up to where the great grey paving-stones had been laid in a huge circle around the castle. The paved courtyard extended out from the castle walls in a regular arc perhaps fifty feet wide. In the shadow of the last bushes, where he felt reasonably safe from any surprise attack, Tom halted to think things over.

The whole business was inexplicable. Obviously he had been overheard working outside the wall, because whoever his assailant was had been waiting for him just within the wall. Almost five minutes had passed since the attack. Why had there not been an alarm? Why had not the occupants of the castle been aroused? All he knew about his attacker was that he was tall and heavy and his breath had smelled of garlic. He knew it wasn't Paul Ehrenhardt. And Hugo Forchet was a much smaller man. But why had the man fled? It was almost as though he were the intruder, not Tom; as though he wished to conceal his own presence here at Garac.

Tom stood there at the edge of the pavement waiting, resting as much of his weight as possible on his left foot. The throbbing in his right ankle was getting worse, and he realized that he would have to keep using it or it would stiffen up and be almost useless.

Perhaps they were waiting for him inside the castle, thinking it would be easier to handle him within than in the open. There was no sign of anything outside, and apparently there would not be. There was no use in waiting longer.

Tom limped across the courtyard to the shadow of the castle itself, and then cautiously proceeded around towards the front of the structure. As he turned the corner, a dim light from an upstairs window caught his eye. He proceeded a few steps farther. That was the only light that showed. The great oaken door into the big hall was closed.

He realized that he would have to investigate that lighted window before proceeding further. It would be important to know just which room it was, and if he worked his way back towards the flagged courtyard he would perhaps be able to see part of the room.

It was risky playing around there in the open, but he had to take the chance. He moved slowly away from the castle, his head turned, watching over his shoulder. It wasn't a very bright light in the room. It must be either candlelight or an oil lamp.

Tom stopped and waited. He could see a small section of the room, but the light was not bright enough for any details to be perceptible. Then the light seemed to shift a little, as though someone had moved his candle or his lamp. The shadows were different.

That window would be in the big corner bedroom by the tower, the one over the front salon, with the entrance into the tower itself.

Unexpectedly a figure crossed the lighted window, and Tom Welles could feel himself trembling. He was almost sure, almost sure, that it had been Angèle. The excitement of the moment was almost unbearable. If that room were only a little brighter! The figure had been indistinct, but he was almost positive that it was Angèle. If she would only cross the window once more.

And then, as if in answer to his wish, the figure appeared in the window again and stood there looking out.

He could not distinguish her face, but he could see the outline of her hair and the set of her shoulders and her slim waist. She seemed to have on some sort of dressing-gown with long sleeves, tightly belted in at the waist.

He stood there breathlessly. The silhouette at the window was very still as it peered out into the night.

Tom stood rigid as a statue, afraid to move lest the slightest movement should catch her attention and frighten her into a cry of alarm. At last Angèle turned away and disappeared. Tom Welles relaxed and breathed again.

He moved slowly back to the shadow of the castle wall near the big front door and tried to lay out an intelligent plan of campaign. He had two choices. He could hide himself somewhere around the castle grounds until the next day and wait for Angèle to emerge from the castle, which she certainly would do sooner or later. Or wouldn't she? He did not suppose they had her locked up, but he actually knew nothing, and would he be able to hide in a place from which he could accost Angèle secretly? The other alternative was to go into the castle and seek her out. If the front door was bolted against Madame's gypsies, forcing an entrance might be impossible.

But, if he were able to penetrate into the castle and escape notice, from that corner chamber on the first floor he would be able to climb up to Angèle's room by the winding tower staircase. That would be much safer than using the main stairway from the big hall to the upstairs gallery from which opened all those bedrooms.

All right, he had entered the castle, he had not been observed, he had gone up the tower stairs and was at the door of Angèle's room. Would it be locked? If it was, he would have to work upstairs the other way.

Now, in imagination, he was opening the door from the tower into Angèle's room. Would Angèle be terrified by the unexpected appearance of a man in her room? Would she scream and arouse the Ehrenhardts? That would be fatal. Perhaps it would be safer to wait until she was asleep, steal into her room, and try to awaken her gently and softly by speaking to her. She still might cry out in alarm, but he decided that it would be a safer procedure.

He would wait until her light went out and then give her a half-hour to get to sleep. He glanced at his watch and frowned. He should put that watch in his pocket. The luminous dial was too dangerous for anyone who wished to enter a house surreptitiously. God, that ankle hurt!

It was only a few minutes later that the lighted window blacked out. Tom waited a full thirty minutes and then, from where he had been lying on the cold pavement close by the castle wall, struggled to his feet.

He limped slowly towards the big oak door. He halted, his hands grasping the big wrought-iron knob, hesitating and reluctant to try the door lest it be locked.

His grasp tightened, and he turned the knob. There was a soft, grating noise of rusty metal. Tom pushed gently. At first the door did not yield, but as he pushed harder it swung open slowly in front of him. He slipped in and heard the heavy iron hinges grating as he closed the door behind him.

The great hall was dark. High on the wall at the farther end he could make out the grey vaulted rectangles of the leaded windows. It was so still that it was impossible to believe that there had even been the sound of a step or the sound of a human voice in that great black hall.

Tom took the small flashlight out of his pocket and prayed that it had survived his fall. It had. The narrow beam of light hit the floor at Tom's feet, and he sighed with relief.

Swiftly he turned the light on the doors leading into the hall. They were all closed except the door into the tower room on his left. So far so good, but that ankle was getting stiffer and paining him much more.

His rubber-soled shoes made no sound as he crossed the stone floor to the door of the tower room. He had shut his light off. There should be no one in there, but there just might be.

He could not remember about the furniture and where it was in this room. He was afraid to cross to the entrance into the tower without reconnaissance, so he snapped on the flashlight and swept it around the room. As he expected, there was no one there. Tom shivered, and he wasn't sure whether it was the tension of fear or excitement or the chill damp of the old stone castle itself. The door to the tower staircase groaned protestingly as he opened it, but he did not think that the noise was loud enough to be heard upstairs. Slowly he mounted the stone steps, putting as much of his weight as he could on the iron rail that curved up on the outside. He reached the landing on the second floor and paused at the door that led into Angèle's room. He had passed the disruptive stage of excitement now. Every sense was alert, and his mind seemed to be calm and waiting. This door was the last potential obstacle between him and Angèle, and in just a minute now—

Very cautiously, so as not to arouse her, Tom tried the door. It moved. Putting all his strength into a lift under the knob so as to reduce the noise that the hinges might make as the door swung open, Tom pushed. The door opened, and he entered the room. He had closed the door through which he had entered the tower. He decided to leave this door open. There were no curtains on the windows, and from out of the night came just enough light for Tom to be able to distinguish a shape in the middle of the room which must be a table, two shadows near by that were probably chairs, a great bureau against the wall, and a lighter mass across the room which would be the bed. He listened intently, but he could not hear Angèle breathing. The last thing in the world he wanted at the moment was his flash-light, so he slipped it back into his pocket. He must creep across the room now without waking her.

The outlines of the bed became clearer as he slowly took one step after another across the room. It was a big canopied bed, but the canopy and the draperies were missing. At the foot of the bed he paused. He could just make out the outline of a body stretched out and very still near one side of the bed. Softly he worked his way round to that side. Now he could hear her breathing, and he knew she was still asleep.

Beside the bed and close to her, Tom dropped to one knee. He could see the outline of her face now. Tom's mouth was very dry, and it seemed difficult to swallow.

'Angèle,' he whispered softly. The figure did not stir. 'Angèle.' His voice was a little louder and urgent. She stirred, but her eyelids did not open.

Tom put out his hand and gently stroked her cheek. 'Angèle, it is me, Thomas.' And he heard himself pronouncing his own name as she pronounced it.

Angèle's eyelids seemed to hesitate for a moment. They half opened, and she regarded him as in a dream. Then a white hand and arm crept out from under the covers and circled his neck.

'Thomas, *chéri*,' she murmured. And then her eyelids dropped again, and she sank back into sleep.

Thomas Welles was trembling. 'Angèle,' he whispered, 'Angèle. This is not a dream. This is Tom, Tom Welles. Wake up, Angèle.'

His eyes were on her mouth and his hand was ready to stifle any sudden outcry that she might make.

The eyes opened again, this time wider. 'Thomas!' she cried in a low voice. 'It is really you! It is not a dream!'

'Angèle, be very, very quiet,' he whispered. 'No one must know that I'm here.'

'Thomas, *chéri*,' she repeated. 'You are here.'

Her arm tightened around his neck and drew his face down to hers, and her mouth was waiting for his.

And again for a few moments there was utter silence in the Castle Garac.

Then Angèle drew away from him. 'You are *here*,' she repeated as though she were still half asleep.

'Yes, Angèle, I am here, but do you understand that we must be very quiet and not arouse anyone?'

'Yes, but I do not understand why.'

'Because no one but you must know that I'm here.'

'Paul Ehrenhardt said that you would come – but not for several weeks.'

'Paul told you that I would come?' Tom asked incredulously.

'Yes. He said he had work for you elsewhere that would keep you busy for several weeks, but that then you would be joining us here. But, Thomas, can we not have a light? I want to see you.'

Tom reflected. He thought of the lighted window and realized that the dim light in the room would not be noticeable except from outside the castle.

'Where is the light?' he asked.

'You will find candles on the table.'

Tom lit his flashlight and started awkwardly for the table in the centre of the room.

'Thomas, you are limping! Have you hurt yourself?'

'Just my ankle. I twisted it when I fell climbing over the wall.'

'You climbed over the wall?' Angèle's voice was bewildered. 'Why did you climb over the wall?' Tom had lit a candle, and the light shone up his face. 'Your face! Thomas, you are covered with blood, and your clothes are torn! What has happened to you? *Chéri*, you are hurt!'

Angèle leaped out of bed, completely unconscious of her attire, and crossed swiftly to Tom.

He looked down at her frowningly. 'Where did you get that nightgown?'

Her eyes instinctively glanced down at the wisp of a garment she was wearing.

'Anna. Anna lent it to me. What matter? Give me that robe there on the chair.'

Swiftly she wrapped herself in a long woollen robe. 'Thomas, what is the matter? What has happened to you? I do not understand. Are you badly hurt?'

Tom grinned. 'These are just scratches I got when I fell into the bushes. My ankle's bad, but not too bad.'

'Why should you have to climb the wall and fall into bushes?' Her eyes were bewildered. 'Why not summon someone and come in through the gate?'

'Because I did not want the Ehrenhardts to know that I was here.'

'Oh, I see. You should be somewhere else, and Paul would have been angry at your coming here now.'

'You say Paul told you I was coming here in a few weeks?'

'Yes, Thomas. You do not think I would have told Paul that I would work with him, and disappear with him and Anna, unless you had been joining us very soon, do you?'

'I think I begin to understand,' Tom said slowly.

'I wanted to say goodbye, but Paul told me there was no time and that he would give you my message. Oh, Thomas, I am so glad to see you, even if you are bloody and dirty and hurt. I am glad that you came.' Then she stopped speaking suddenly. 'You did come to see me, didn't you, Thomas?' she asked slowly.

'Yes, Angèle, I did come to see you.' Tom smiled.

'And you must leave again without Paul knowing that you are here?'

'That will have to be decided later,' Tom said thoughtfully. 'Angèle, I must sit down and get off this ankle.'

'Oh yes, *chéri*. I am so excited that I forgot. Here, sit here and let me examine your ankle.'

She put the candle down on the floor and knelt there by Tom's feet. She pulled up his trouser leg and then very gently tried to roll down the sock.

'This is not good, Thomas. This is not good at all.'

'You're telling me,' Tom muttered.

'It is very red and very swollen.'

'I'm not surprised.'

'It should have a wet compress and be bound up.'

'There's no time for that now, Angèle. It will have to do as it is.'

'But—'

'No *buts*.' There was something serious in his voice that stopped her.

Angèle put the candle back on the table and drew up a small chair close to where Tom was sitting. 'What is it, Thomas?' she asked quietly.

'That's what I came here to find out,' he told her. 'Angèle, you will have to tell me what it is all about.'

'I don't understand, Thomas. What is it you want to know?'

'I want to know what you are doing here with the Ehrenhardts. I want to know everything they have told you.'

Angèle was looking at him as though she did not understand his words. 'But surely you must know even more than I do, Thomas. You have been working with Paul and Hugo. Paul told me that you had even helped him in working out many details of the plan.'

'Angèle, don't you remember I told you that I knew *nothing*, absolutely nothing, of Paul's project?'

She nodded. 'But Paul said he had told you that you *must* say that, until it was decided whether I was the right girl or not, and that I was to hear everything first from him.'

Tom shook his head. 'Did Paul Ehrenhardt tell you that I was working with him and Anna, that I knew all about their project, whatever it is, that I would be away only temporarily and then would join you here at the Castle Garac?'

'But certainly. I told you, Thomas—'

Tom interrupted her. 'And you entered into this plan because you thought that I was involved in it, too?'

Angèle nodded.

Suddenly Angèle's gaze shifted away from Tom. The expression on her face had changed to one of tense alarm. She seemed to be looking at something above Tom and behind him.

Tom swung around swiftly in his chair. Paul Ehrenhardt was standing there in the doorway. He was dressed in a red brocaded dressing-gown. There was a lighted cigarette in his mouth. In his right hand, extended slightly, was a revolver. Paul Ehren-hardt's face was an expressionless mask. For a few moments it was a still tableau. Then he bowed courteously to Angèle. 'May I join you?' he asked.

He walked casually across the room, picking up a small wooden chair as he approached the table. Paul was very careful not to turn his back on Tom during the manoeuvre.

He looked Tom over with some curiosity. 'My dear Tom, what in the world has happened to you? You look as though you had been fighting and had not come out of it very well.'

Tom made no reply. He was staring at Paul Ehrenhardt.

Paul turned to Angèle. 'We did not expect Tom here so soon, did we, my dear?' His face broke into its most charming smile. 'I could not help but overhear a little of your conversation,' he admitted. 'There seems to have been a slight misunderstanding about certain matters. I'm afraid things have become a trifle more complicated than I anticipated. The present situation seems to call for a little thought.'

Paul was looking at Tom now, his eyebrows raised expectantly, waiting for Tom to speak. Angèle was watching the two men tensely, but, like Tom, she did not speak. Paul Ehrenhardt shrugged and turned back to Angèle. 'My dear, perhaps a drink would loosen our tongues. I certainly think a drink is in order. I dislike having to ask you, but do you think you could find that bottle of cognac we had after dinner tonight and three glasses? I believe you will find it on the shelf in the passageway just off the main hall. I would get it myself, but I think perhaps that Tom and I should stay here together.'

Paul took a flashlight out of his pocket and handed it to her.

'This will be better than a candle,' he told her.

Without a word, Angèle took the flashlight, rose, and dis-appeared out into the hall.

Ehrenhardt was surveying Tom broodingly. 'This is really most unfortunate,' he murmured. 'By now you should be on your way back to America.' He glanced down at the revolver in his lap. 'I hate these things, you know,' he said. 'They always make me feel so primitive and uncivilized. I hate any form of violence, and I lose respect for myself when I have to resort to the use of it.'

Then he frowned. 'What *did* happen to you, Tom? All that blood. Your clothes.'

'Didn't your welcoming committee tell you?' Tom asked wryly.

Ehrenhardt looked puzzled. 'My welcoming committee?' he repeated. 'I don't understand.'

'Why did it take you so long to find me?' Tom demanded.

Ehrenhardt looked even more puzzled. 'I did not know you were here until just a few moments ago, when I happened to be passing in the hall. There was a glimmer of light from within the bedroom, and I paused and heard your voices.'

'What about the man who attacked me when I dropped down from the wall?' Tom demanded.

'A man attacked you? What man?'

'One of your people, I suppose.'

Paul Ehrenhardt shook his head in bewilderment. 'There is no one here at the Castle Garac except Anna and I and Hugo Forchet and his sister. Oh, and of course the girl!'

'Well, it wasn't you and it wasn't Hugo. So Hugo's sister must be very tall and very strong and she must dress in men's clothes – and smell of garlic.'

Paul Ehrenhardt shook his head. 'This gets stranger and stranger,' he observed. 'You say you dropped over the wall and a large man attacked you?'

Tom nodded.

Ehrenhardt's eyes were very thoughtful. 'Another matter that will have to be looked into,' he murmured. 'Please believe me, I have no idea who it was. Whoever it was, he was not, to use your expression, one of my people.'

Angèle reappeared with the bottle and three glasses and silently put them down on the table.

'My dear, will you act as hostess and pour us three rather large drinks? I think we need them. But, Tom, something has just occurred to me! I realize, of course, that you two know each other. In fact, you seem to know each other rather intimately, considering the few days since you met. I do not think, however, that you have been formally or properly introduced.'

Paul turned towards Angèle. He still held the revolver in his right hand, but his left hand raised the glass of brandy as if in a toast. 'Comtesse, may I present my friend, Mr Thomas Welles?' His manner was very formal. 'Tom, the Comtesse Renée de Garac.'

Tom stared at him blankly. 'What the devil are you talking about?' he demanded finally.

Paul was frowning as though he did not understand the question, but Tom thought that he could see his mouth twitching a little. 'You have just had the honour of being presented to the Comtesse de Garac.'

'What sort of a game is this?' Tom muttered.

'I can assure you that it is no game.'

'Thomas,' Angèle broke out. 'Thomas, I—'

Ehrenhardt turned on her almost savagely. 'Stop!' he ordered. 'Comtesse, before you say another word, I would like to remind you of a promise you made and an oath you took.'

Angèle's face was very white.

'It was a very solemn oath, and it is imperative for your own sake as well as mine, and perhaps even for the sake of your friend Tom Welles, that you abide by that oath.'

'Yes.' Angèle's voice was a very low whisper.

'Apparently Tom Welles has some doubts about your identity. Will you resolve them, and yourself tell Tom what your true name is and who you are?'

Angèle's eyes turned to Tom. Her mouth opened, closed, opened again. It was as though she were trying to speak and could not. 'I am Renée de Garac,' she said in a low voice, 'the Comtesse de Garac.'

Tom stared at her for a moment, and then slowly and deliberately took a cigarette out of his pocket and lit it. He blew out a narrow funnel of grey smoke. 'So this is just a variation of the shell game,' he observed. 'Now you see it, now you don't. Are you a member of the de Garac family, too, Paul?' he asked sarcastically.

'I do not have that honour,' Paul Ehrenhardt answered stiffly.

'That's tough,' Tom sympathized. 'So this is the Comtesse de

Garac and she has returned to her ancestral castle! What next?'

Paul Ehrenhardt now looked sincerely worried. 'That is the question, Tom. It is a very serious problem. Now that you have unexpectedly and inadvisedly appeared on the scene, there seem to be only two possibilities. Either you will join with us and become – to use your own phrase again – one of my people, or you will have to – well, say disappear – for a very long time.' Paul Ehrenhardt looked regretfully down at the revolver in his hand. 'You are too intelligent not to realize that it would not do to have you out in the world, sceptical of our good faith and intentions and possibly casting doubt on Renée's identity.'

'So you propose to cut me in on the racket, is that it?'

Paul Ehrenhardt smiled. 'There is no racket, my dear Tom. But of course you probably already realize that I am not an ungenerous man, and if you were to ally your interests with mine and continue working for me, there would undoubtedly be proper compensation.'

Tom nodded thoughtfully. Then he turned to Angèle.

'Angèle,' he said quietly, 'I know nothing more about all this than what I told you that afternoon at the Café des Deux Anges, except that whatever Paul is engaged in must be crooked as hell, and the sooner you and I get out of it the better. Supposing you get dressed, and you and I will move out of this high grass – and fast.'

'That is not one of the alternatives that I mentioned,' Paul Ehrenhardt pointed out gently. 'There is no reason for the Comtesse de Garac to leave her ancestral home.'

'What is the purpose of this masquerade?' Tom broke out angrily. 'The whole thing is fantastic. Why, in front of me, who knows that it can't possibly be true, do you pretend that Angèle is the Comtesse de Garac or the Comtesse of anything else?'

Ehrenhardt turned to Angèle. 'Will you try to convince Tom that you are the Comtesse de Garac?' he asked quietly.

'I am the Comtesse de Garac,' she repeated automatically.

'Have you hypnotized her?' Tom demanded.

'Comtesse, will you answer that question, too, please?' Paul Ehrenhardt requested.

'No, Thomas, Paul has not hypnotized me,' she replied quietly.

'I have always observed that Americans are unimaginative and that it is difficult for them to accept – well, let us say, the improbable.' Paul's voice was almost purring. 'You see, Tom, yesterday when the Comtesse saw Hugo Forchet – not the meeting in the restaurant, of course, but when she saw him later, close to – the cloud that had been shrouding her memory since infancy suddenly lifted. Here has been a classic case of amnesia. Contact with Hugo has restored the Comtesse's memory. She remembered her childhood and her identity. For twelve years she has been living in a fog, under the name of Angèle Corton, the name the nuns gave her because at the time they took her into the convent they had no idea who she was. And now she has returned to live on her family estate, and she has asked Anna and me to stay with her for a time as her guests.

'Comtesse, is not this – substantially – correct? Certainly Thomas will believe you, even if he doubts my words.'

'Yes – I think that is – what happened,' she murmured.

Tom looked at Paul Ehrenhardt with real admiration in his eyes. 'You're wonderful,' he admitted. 'I wouldn't have believed it. But if I may ask, just how do you propose ever to make this story stick? I know all about the long arm of coincidence, but this one is really too long.'

Paul regarded Tom blandly. 'That is all very simple, my friend. Do not let it worry you. Every detail has been most carefully considered. There is but one real difficulty – yourself, Tom Welles.'

Tom rose to his feet and leaned on the table to take some of the weight off his bad ankle. 'Angèle,' he demanded, 'are you really lending yourself to such a scheme? Are you—?'

Paul Ehrenhardt interrupted him sharply. 'Tom, when you are addressing the Comtesse, will you please address her by her correct name and forget that she was ever called Angèle?'

Tom had not taken his eyes off her face. 'Suppose you tell me what I am to call you,' he said almost brutally. 'Are you Angèle Corton, or are you the Comtesse de Garac?'

Her eyes fell. She could not meet his gaze. 'I am the Comtesse de Garac,' she said.

'I see,' Tom said grimly. 'And you're going to continue to – to be the Comtesse de Garac?'

She nodded mutely.

'And what about us,' he demanded.

Now her eyes were back on his. 'Thomas, I care for you. I care for you a great deal.'

'But not enough to become Angèle Corton again. Is that it?'

Her eyes were clouded. 'Thomas, perhaps there is something you do not quite understand. I think I *am* perhaps Renée de Garac.'

Tom's mind was stunned with disbelief and pain. He needed a few moments to recover from his shock. He shifted his weight as much as he could, then finally dropped back into his chair. 'I think I have everything straight now,' he said quietly. 'It has been a great pleasure to have had the opportunity of meeting you, Comtesse. I trust that you will fulfill all the ambitions that you once told me about, and find the gaiety and excitement in life that you craved. It is very late, and I realize that I have disturbed your sleep, Paul. So I'll say goodbye, and—'

'I'm afraid it isn't as simple as that, Tom.' Paul's eyes had narrowed. 'You see, from my point of view it would not be very – well, practical just to let you walk out of the Castle Garac. Since you will not join with us, you might be tempted to talk indiscreetly and perhaps say something that might affect the Comtesse's good name. We couldn't have that, could we?'

'You mean you're going to try to stop me from leaving?' demanded Tom.

Paul looked down unhappily at his revolver. 'I'm afraid so,' he admitted. 'I have no alternative.'

The girl was on her feet now, standing over Paul Ehrenhardt. 'Do you mean,' she demanded, 'that you are going to do any harm to Tom?'

'Renée, my child, I am very fond of Tom. I find him a delightful and charming person. But surely you understand that if he left the castle alive, the sword of Damocles would be hanging over our heads – yours as well as mine.'

Angèle was very pale. 'If anything should happen to Thomas,' she said quietly, 'our pact is at an end.'

'But, Renée, surely—'

'You will never see the Comtesse de Garac again,' she said calmly, 'if anything should happen to Thomas.' She paused a moment. 'Furthermore, Paul, I would see that you were convicted of murder.'

Paul studied her thoughtfully, and then he shrugged. 'These personal emotions are most inconvenient,' he admitted. 'This is nothing but one attractive young American. I like him. So do you. But there are thousands that have been turned out of the same mould. Renée, my child, you are letting a silly, childish romanticism jeopardize your whole future. It does not make sense.'

'Leave Thomas alone,' she warned him, 'or you and I are through — except that I shall watch your execution,' she added.

Paul Ehrenhardt sighed, thought for a moment, and then he turned to Tom with his winning smile. 'May I congratulate you, Tom? You seem to have evoked a strong and violent affection on the part of the Comtesse. I only wish my dear Anna felt so vehemently about me. It seems that you are to leave the Castle Garac after all. That being the case, the sooner the better. I only hope that you will remember that Renée has saved your life tonight and that you will not ever do anything or say anything that might injure her. For myself I ask nothing. But this is none of your affair. What I told you once is the truth. What we are doing will injure no living soul. If you should ever talk about this business, you would be responsible for a grave injury to — to the Comtesse de Garac, to whom you now owe much.'

'I understand,' Tom said.

'Once more,' Paul persisted. 'Will you not join with us? It would be well worth your while.'

'No, thanks. I don't think I'd be very good at this sort of game,' Tom said lightly. 'I'll just be on my way.'

The girl rose quickly and crossed to stand very close to Tom Welles. 'Thomas,' she said softly, 'you cannot walk on that ankle.'

'I'll make it all right,' Tom said shortly.

'Why must you go?'

'I told you – Comtesse. I don't think I like the game, and I do not choose to take a hand.'

'Yes – I understand. I would not want you to do anything which you did not think was right, Thomas.'

Then she drew herself up. She looked at Paul Ehrenhardt speculatively, then back at Tom. 'Thomas, will you stay, please, for just a few days, until your ankle is better?'

'Renée, you are mad!' Paul burst out. 'He must leave here immediately. And lucky he is to be leaving.'

She drew herself up almost regally and turned to Tom with a warm smile. 'Thomas, as the Comtesse de Garac, I bid you welcome to – my home. I am glad you are here. I want you to stay. I want you to stay very much.'

'But, Renée,' Ehrenhardt broke in impatiently, 'this will not—'

She silenced him with an imperious gesture. 'And my other two guests, Anna and Paul, I'm sure will be as delighted to have you here as I am.'

Paul rose in protest.

The girl stamped her foot angrily. 'There will be no discussion about this, Paul! Is the Castle Garac my home or yours? Are you a de Garac or am I? Answer me once and for all. I would like to get this settled here and now.

Ehrenhardt studied her, unwilling admiration in his eyes. He realized that he had lost this round. He smiled ironically. 'My apologies, Renée,' he said. 'You are indeed the Comtesse de Garac, and I assure you that Anna will be even more delighted than I that Tom is to be your guest for a few days.'

She turned swiftly to Tom Welles. 'Thomas, you will please stay as I ask. There are perhaps things that you do not understand. Thomas, I need you. Will you stay?'

Tom thought that over for a long time. There was complete silence in the room as they waited for his answer. Finally he looked up into her face. 'As your guest, Comtesse? Merely as your guest?'

'Yes, as my guest, Thomas.'

Tom Welles was torn between the instinctive desire to put as

147

many miles as possible between him and the Castle Garac and all it held, and the emotional pull he felt towards Angèle. He looked down at his ankle.

Then he shrugged. 'I don't suppose I'd get very far with that foot anyway,' he observed. 'So if Paul will put that gun away, I'll stay – if you really want me.'

'Thank you, Thomas. And, Thomas, please do not call me Comtesse.'

'I understood very definitely that I was not to call you Angèle,' Tom said stiffly.

'No, not Angèle,' she agreed. 'But, Thomas, you will call me Renée, please.'

'Because Renée is your name?' Tom asked mockingly.

'Yes, because Renée is my name. And now, Paul, because Tom's welcome to Garac has been most inhospitable and not at all what it should have been, would you be so good as to arouse Hugo and ask him to prepare a room for our new guest? Perhaps the next room to this, which I believe is empty.'

Paul bowed with exaggerated grace and disappeared.

Renée crossed swiftly to Tom Welles and put her hand on his arm. Her voice was low, tense, urgent. 'Thomas, *chéri*, please do as I say. Something has started that I cannot explain now. It is all very strange, but for the time, play this little game. I am frightened.'

'Come away with me now, at once, Angèle.'

'I cannot leave now. I cannot leave. I have started something that I must finish. Will you stay near me for a time at least? I need you.'

From the darkness of the hall came Ehrenhardt's voice again. 'Tom's room is being prepared,' he called out. 'I hope he has a comfortable night. For my part, I am now going back to bed, and to my rest that was so unhappily interrupted.'

'Before you go, Paul, tell Hugo that Tom will need hot water, and we will need cotton or something with which to bandage his ankle.'

Again there was that puzzled expression on Paul Ehrenhardt's face. 'I will give Hugo your orders, Comtesse.'

'Thank you, Paul,' she said gravely.

12

THOMAS WELLES slept very late the next morning. He had been completely exhausted physically and emotionally.

His ankle was still badly swollen, but when he tried it out carefully from the edge of the bed, it seemed to be a little easier to stand on than it had the night before. Over a chair near the door he saw a pair of grey slacks, fresh underclothes, and a sports shirt. They looked as though they might belong to Paul Ehrenhardt. Someone, obviously, had decided that he needed an outfit other than the torn garments in which he had arrived.

On the old-fashioned washstand in the corner he saw a razor and a can of water which he discovered was still warm, although it must have been standing there for some time.

With his bad ankle, dressing took a little time, but half an hour later Tom was standing at the head of the broad stairway descending into the great hall. From where he stood he could hear voices below, but he could not distinguish who was talking or what was being said.

Quietly he started down the stairs. The voices grew louder. He recognized Hugo Forchet's guttural French. Apparently he was talking to Angèle – Renée, rather. He could only think of her as Angèle, but he must remember to call her Renée. Occasionally she would ask a question or make some comment. He stood there out of sight, listening. The voices seemed to shift now and then from spot to spot. He could not understand everything that Hugo was saying, but slowly he began to get the drift of the conversation.

Hugo's voice was ceremonious, almost obsequious. He was apparently guiding her around the great hall from spot to spot on a detailed tour of inspection, almost as though he were a guide exhibiting the castle to an honoured visitor.

'And this portrait, Comtesse, is of your great-great-uncle, Alexander. He married a Razat – somewhat of a *mésalliance*, if I may say so. Your mother always—'

In bewilderment, Tom listened as Hugo's tour proceeded. He had become garrulous. Something would remind him of the old life at Garac, and he would describe that incident in detail. And here was the chair the Comtesse's mother always sat in when interviewing her servants. That started him off on a detailed account of the routine day-by-day life of the household.

At last Tom realized what was going on. The Comtesse, he reflected wryly, was getting a thorough coaching on her childhood background. Well, now that her amnesia had so happily disappeared, there would be much that the Comtesse de Garac would have to remember out of her childhood.

Tom started down the stairs again, and paused on the last step.

'Good morning, Renée,' he said gravely. 'Good morning, Hugo.'

Renée's face lit up, and she started swiftly across the great hall towards him. Tom noticed that Hugo had bowed and was already on his way towards the kitchen. 'I will see to Monsieur's breakfast.' The self-confident and assured Hugo Forchet of Nice, dealing with Paul Ehrenhardt and Tom Welles as equals, had disappeared. This was Hugo the old family retainer – major-domo of the castle, perhaps, but with quite a different personality from the person Tom had met at the Negresco.

'Thomas, you slept and you slept and you slept, and it was good for you. How is your ankle?'

'Definitely better, Renée.'

She flinched a little at the tone of his voice as he pronounced her name.

'Hugo, here, has been giving me a lecture on my family history.' She smiled a little. 'Things that I must have either forgotten or never knew,' she added.

'Most interesting and instructive, I'm sure.'

'He was even trying to teach me a nursery song that he says little Renée used to sing when she was very young.'

Hugo had re-entered the hall and was standing just behind her.

'That *you* used to sing, Comtesse,' he corrected her stiffly.

Renée ignored him. 'Come along and get some breakfast,' she

suggested to Tom. 'I will sit with you while you eat. Come along. It will be ready in a moment.'

The conversation over Tom's breakfast was desultory and, what there was of it, unnatural and forced.

Renée waited until he had finished and then rose abruptly. 'Tom, is your ankle well enough to permit you to come outside with me? I wish to talk to you, and one cannot talk very well here. I wonder if I could find you a cane to lean on.'

'It'll be all right,' Tom reassured her. They passed through the great grey hall into the open sunlight, and it was a different world. She led him around the castle along a narrow, overgrown path that cut through the shrubbery to an old stone wellhouse, where there was a bench.

They sat down.

'Thomas, put your arm around me again just for a moment. I would like to feel your arm. It is strong, and I am still frightened after last night. I have known fear before, but never terror. That pistol of Paul's! I could not believe that he meant to hurt you. Yet—'

'Paul must be playing for high stakes,' Tom decided. 'I think he would have shot me if he had to.'

Renée shuddered. 'But I do not understand. Paul told me that you – and yet today—'

Tom's face was grim. 'Listen, An – Renée. First Paul had me scouting for a walled castle in the mountains which he said he wished to use temporarily as a retreat, so as to create the right mood for some sort of production that he was involved in. I thought it was a movie or something. He sent me out with very definite specifications, based, I realize now, on the Castle Garac. It must have been important to him to create the impression that he had found Garac completely by chance. Next he told me he needed a certain type of girl for this project of his, and described her in detail. Then he sent me out in the highways and byways to find such a girl. You yourself know how we met. At first I hesitated to introduce you to Paul, because I was falling in love with you and I did not know exactly what he had in mind. Then you told me that you were losing your job. I had very little money. I was on the point of asking you to marry me, but I knew I couldn't support you.' He could feel her body tense in his arms. 'You told me the things you had dreamed of in life, and I felt I had no right to deprive you of your opportunity.

'You know the rest. Hugo looked you over and decided that you would pass as a de Garac. You are now here at the castle, being carefully coached on your family history and on your past, obviously so that when the time comes for the Comtesse de Garac to be unveiled to the world, you will not be spotted as an impostor.

'Having no further use for me – in fact, because of my feeling for you, I had become a liability and a complication – Paul left a letter at the hotel dismissing me, telling me that his plans had completely changed, and that you were of no use to him anyway. He doubtless expected me to take the first boat or plane to America with the very generous payoff that accompanied his letter. Paul never expected to see me again. He never expected you to see me again. That's all I know.'

'And I thought I would see you again very soon,' she murmured. 'I am in this very, very deep, Thomas. I wish I could go away with you now, but I cannot.'

'I understand,' he said shortly.

'Perhaps you do not understand,' she said. 'Thomas, I think you must despise me for what I am doing. You do, do you not?'

Tom lowered his arm. 'An – Renée, do you know the purpose of this intrigue?'

'I know what Paul told me.'

'Do you think he told you the truth?'

'About what I am thinking, yes. Oh, Thomas, I wish I could tell you, tell you everything, but I have sworn not to tell anyone ever. It was a very sacred promise.'

'Well, it's obviously to cheat somebody out of a substantial amount of money.'

'No, Thomas, not to cheat anyone.'

'What else could it possibly be?' Tom demanded. 'Paul has spent a small fortune on this scheme of his already. He is playing for big stakes.'

'Yes, the stakes are big,' Renée agreed. 'But, Thomas, something else has happened too, something that I do not quite understand myself and cannot talk about.'

'What do you mean?'

'I cannot tell you – yet.' She was looking at him strangely. 'Thomas, please do not despise me if you can help it. That would make me very unhappy.' Then her head straightened up. 'Here comes Anna.'

'I was wondering where she had been keeping herself,' Tom muttered.

Anna Ehrenhardt came down the path towards them. She smiled at Tom and held out both hands towards him.

'Tom, how perfectly lovely! There's no one that I would rather see. Paul told me that you had arrived last night unexpectedly.'

'That much is true anyway.' Tom grinned.

Anna turned to Renée. 'My dear, Hugo has been looking for you everywhere! There's an hour free before luncheon, and we haven't much time, you know. Do go in now!'

Renée hesitated. It was obvious that she did not want to go. Then she turned and retraced her steps towards the castle.

Anna looked after her. 'She is lovely, isn't she?' Anna admitted. 'But she's such a child.'

'It's what you were looking for, wasn't it?' Tom said shortly.

'Exactly what we were looking for,' Anna agreed. 'Tom, you are a fool not to join with us.'

'I don't join things unless I know what they are.'

'I hear you almost got into trouble last night,' she observed.

'Would Paul have killed me?' Tom demanded.

'Certainly, if he had had to,' Anna said calmly.

'And now?'

'After the scene the Comtesse de Garac put on last night, he'd be afraid to touch a hair of your head. This girl of yours is very important to us, Tom. Without her—' Anna shrugged.

Anna sank down on to the bench and Tom sat down beside her.

'Tom, have you noticed anything strange about Renée?'

'No.'

'It's probably that she is a little bewildered by what has

happened, but once in a while she seems to be very far away, almost in a daze.'

'I don't blame her. I'm in a daze myself. As soon as I leave here I'm going to delve back into the history of the de Garacs and see whether I can clarify things a little.'

'Yes, Tom, I suppose you will. Therefore, I might as well tell you what you are bound to discover very easily yourself. Would you like to hear a little of the de Garac history, Tom, the part that might interest you?'

'I certainly would.'

'The de Garacs, as you can imagine for yourself, are one of the oldest and one of the most aristocratic families in this part of France. Most of them seem to have been a rather decent lot, and they were enormously wealthy. In 1942, twelve years ago – as you will remember, that was during the worst part of the war – the Comtesse de Garac and her seven-year-old daughter, both reputedly very beautiful, were living here at the castle. The Comte de Garac had left France at the time of the surrender and was fighting with the Free French. He was a flier, and he was killed.

'At that time the Germans and the Italians were all through this part of the country, and the Italians in particular were not under very strict discipline. One night a small band of drunken soldiers invaded the Castle Garac. The Comtesse was there, her seven-year-old daughter, Hugo – who had been with the family all his life, and his father before him – and two other servants, both old men. The soldiers started to loot the castle. One thing led to another, and it ended in a massacre. The Comtesse de Garac was shot, and with his own eyes Hugo saw both the servants killed; and Renée, the seven-year-old daughter, Hugo thought at the time was killed too by a blow on the head. He saw her fall. Hugo had been knocked out early in the fight and came to just as matters came to a climax. It was a horrible business.

'Hugo lay there, pretending to be dead, and finally the soldiers staggered out of the castle with whatever booty they could carry. Hugo, with great difficulty, made his way into Latire and reported what had happened to the German military authorities who were quartered there. The authorities, of course, were enraged by such an outrageous breach of discipline. They rushed back to the castle and found things pretty much in ruins as Hugo had described them, but no bodies.'

'No bodies?' demanded Tom.

'No. Apparently some of the soldiers had sobered up enough to realize how serious their offence had been, and had returned and disposed of the bodies in the hope that if they were caught they would at least not have to pay the penalty for murder. The bodies were never found.'

'Good God, what a story!'

'Yes. Well, that was the end of the de Garacs. Curiously enough, there were no cousins and no relatives. The First World War, influenza epidemics, automobile accidents, and the Second World War had wiped out the family of de Garac completely – or at least it seemed to have wiped the family out completely until very recently.'

'I'm beginning to understand,' Tom muttered. 'It must have been a great surprise to Hugo when he walked into the Café des Deux Anges to see right there before his eyes Renée de Garac, who he thought had been killed twelve years ago, but who had merely been knocked over the head and lost her memory, an orphan brought up by the nuns without any idea who she was or who her parents were. It all fits perfectly.'

Anna nodded gravely. 'It is scarcely believable,' she agreed, 'but that is exactly what happened. The moment Hugo saw your friend, he recognized Renée, who now, of course, is the Comtesse de Garac.'

Tom burst out laughing. 'Wasn't it lucky that Paul selected me to find her? Considering everything, I think he grossly underpaid me. Probably nobody else in the world would have produced the Comtesse de Garac. And when her identity has been firmly established, she will, of course, inherit the enormous de Garac fortune.'

'Naturally.' Anna nodded.

'Anna, do you and Paul really think you are going to get away with this?' Tom demanded.

Anna regarded him blandly. 'I do not understand, Tom.

Get away with what? She *is* the Comtesse de Garac. She was not killed twelve years ago.'

'And you have told Angèle all this?'

'Angèle? Do you mean Renée? Yes, we have explained everything to her. Naturally she does not remember yet all the details of her childhood. She was very young when she went through that ghastly experience, but she already shows signs of recollection, and after a few weeks with Hugo here at the castle, it will probably all come back.'

'Well, I'll be damned!' Tom shook his head. 'And what happened to Hugo after the massacre?'

'Hugo made his way out of France, volunteered with the Free French, and after the war went to America. He got a position as headwaiter in a very good restaurant.'

'And whatever gave Hugo the idea that Renée had not been killed and was still alive?'

Anna looked amused. 'Well, Tom, you see, one night Hugo overheard two men talking in the restaurant where he worked. One was a private banker, and he was telling his friend about one of his problems. It seems that a French family named de Garac had been farsighted enough to transfer a very large part of their investments and property to America before the war, and convert everything into dollars, and the fortune was deposited with this private banker. Naturally Hugo pricked up his ears at the name of de Garac, and he took pains to hear the rest of the conversation. The banker's problem was that he had deposited with him a very large estate, and he had been unable to trace any de Garac to turn the property over to. It was one of those rare cases where a family no longer existed. He had spent thousands of dollars trying to find distant relatives, but he was convinced that there were no more de Garacs.'

'It was then that Hugo remembered little Renée, of course.'

'Yes, Tom, it was at that very minute that Hugo began to have doubts about whether little Renée had really been killed.'

'And then Hugo decided he needed help, probably financial help, and at that point Anna and Paul Ehrenhardt became interested in the de Garac problem. Is that right, Anna?'

'Yes. When Paul heard Hugo's story, he became most intrigued.'

'I'll bet he did. . . . Anna, I'm supposed to be a writer, but in my wildest dreams I could not conjure up anything like this.'

'I've seen many things in real life that were too strange to write about,' Anna observed.

'I see now what Paul meant when he said that what he was doing would hurt no individual.'

'No, eventually the de Garac fortune, I suppose, would have been turned over to the state, if we had not found Renée.'

'It's still crooked as hell,' Tom decided.

'And you, Tom, are an impractical idealist.'

'Anna, for God's sake, get Angèle out of this. You can find someone else. If you're caught – and you may very well all be caught – you'll all go to jail, and you know it.'

'But, Tom, you do not understand,' Anna protested. 'We are doing nothing wrong. We are doing Renée a great favour. We are helping her to re-establish her identity, her real identity as the Comtesse de Garac. She *is* the Comtesse de Garac.'

Tom dropped his head into his hands and groaned. 'And I am responsible for this mess,' he muttered. 'Anna, one more thing. Who the devil was waiting for me under the wall last night – the man who tried to choke me?'

'As I live and breathe, I have no idea, and neither has Paul. He was over there in that part of the close early this morning, to see whether he could discover anything.'

'That is difficult to believe,' Tom said slowly.

Anna shook her head. 'There is no one here at the castle, as Paul told you, except Hugo and his sister. It could only have been another intruder. After all, the castle has been empty for years, the gates have been open. Someone may have hidden something here some time, and just come back to recover it.

'And now that you know more, Tom, don't you think you should join us? There is a very large amount of money involved, and I know Paul would be generous.'

Tom shook his head. 'No, thanks, Anna, it's not my cup of tea.'

'And if you don't join us, Tom? When you leave here?'

'I'll start writing again,' Tom said.

'Will you be able to forget the Castle de Garac and the Comtesse de Garac?' Anna demanded.

There was silence for a moment. 'I don't think I shall ever forget the – Comtesse de Garac,' Tom said. 'And although I'm not joining you, Anna, I think you and Paul can be very sure that I would never do anything to injure or betray – Renée.'

'Mr Welles,' Anna said impulsively, 'I do like you. I really like you. And except for the fact that you led us to Renée, I wish you had never met her. And I wish you were not such a Puritan. And I wish a lot of things.' She rose. 'Come on, my stupid one, it is almost time for an *apéritif* and lunch.'

'You go in, Anna,' Tom said quietly. 'I'll be in in just a few minutes. I think I would like to be alone for a moment.'

A quarter of an hour later Tom Welles joined Renée and the Ehrenhardts in the great hall.

'What would you like, Tom?' Paul's voice was jovial. 'Sherry? Cinzano? Dubonnet?'

'Have you got any whisky?' Tom demanded.

'Certainly, but that's a strange drink for before luncheon,' Paul protested.

'No stranger than everything else around here,' Tom said grimly.

'Anna tells me that you and she have had a little talk,' Paul said. 'Anna seems to feel that it was a very satisfactory little talk,' he went on. 'Can I trust her judgement?'

'Anna's a very perceptive woman, as you know better than I do,' Tom replied.

'Tom, your ankle – how is it?' Renée spoke for the first time.

'It hurts a little, but it's improved enough for us to forget it.'

'That ankle is entirely your responsibility, Tom.' Paul's voice was decisive. 'If you'd come up to the front gate like any honest man and pulled on the bell rope, you would have no problem of an ankle. If, however, you choose to steal through the woods and make a dramatic entrance over a wall, you are responsible for the consequences. I warn you that if you attempt to sue the Comtesse de Garac in connexion with your injuries, I will testify against you.'

Tom turned to Renée. 'Have you learned your song yet?' he asked politely. 'The song that little Renée sang as a child?'

Renée flushed and turned away, and with a murmur left the room.

Paul turned to Tom with a little frown. 'Tom, my dear chap –' his voice was very conciliatory '– I know you well enough to believe that you will not resent a suggestion from a friend.'

'Go right ahead.'

'You are here as the guest of Comtesse de Garac,' Paul observed. 'As your hostess, Renée is doing everything possible for your comfort and pleasure. As her guest, perhaps you should not make remarks which distress her. Renée is in a very difficult position. She is confused. Her sensitive mind is torn between the present and the past. She seems to be fond of you, and—'

'Paul, you're perfectly right,' Tom said sincerely. 'I'm sorry.'

He put down his drink and limped across to the door of the salon through which Renée had disappeared.

He looked around the salon swiftly. She was not there. From the door leading to the chapel he surveyed the solemn interior. It was empty. She must have gone upstairs by way of the tower.

As swiftly as he could with his bad ankle, Tom climbed around the arc of the stairs until he reached the door to Renée's room.

He knocked, but did not wait for an answer, flinging the door open.

She was standing there in the centre of the room, facing him, with a rather startled expression on her face.

'My dear, I'm sorry,' he said very softly. 'I'm terribly sorry. I either hurt or embarrassed you. Which, I don't know, but I should not have done either.'

She stood there in the middle of the room, poised for sudden movement, but as though uncertain as to just what direction she should take.

A moment later she was in Tom Welles's arms.

'Oh, Thomas, *chéri*, I love you so. I am so miserable. You think badly of me, and that twists my heart. I have never loved anyone before. I would not lose you for the whole world. And yet every minute I feel you withdrawing from me further and further, and there seems to be nothing that I can do about it.'

'Angèle,' he murmured, stroking her hair, 'Angèle.'

'Give me time, Thomas. Do not mock me. Do not make fun of me. Wait, Thomas, wait just a little and we shall see.'

'I'm waiting, Angèle,' he said quietly, 'waiting to take you away at any moment you want to go.'

Late that afternoon Tom Welles was standing in his room in front of his window, moodily looking out over the irregular stone wall into the valley below. He felt rather washed out and beaten. Perhaps it was a reaction after the last two days.

Luncheon had been a rather stiff, unnatural meal, with Angèle very silent and Paul and Anna exchanging polite amenities and Tom brooding over the situation and eating very little.

Most of the afternoon Angèle had spent – Good Lord, he had to stop calling her Angèle even to himself or he would forget to call her Renée in public – closeted with Hugo in the tower room downstairs. Continuing her education as the Comtesse de Garac, Tom thought bitterly.

He had lain down on his bed and tried to sleep, but without success. His ankle was still bothering him, and now as evening approached, it seemed to be getting worse again.

Would Paul and Anna – and Renée – get away with this mad scheme? It seemed utterly impossible, but when you analysed it carefully, there being no relatives, it might succeed. Tom kept telling himself that it did not concern him, that in a day or so he would be leaving and that he would never see this girl again. She seemed to be fond of him, yes, but she also seemed to be dominated by something else, something of which he could not approve, which had crowded him into the background.

He swung around as he heard a hesitant knock on his door, crossed the room as swiftly as he could, and swung the door open. Renée stood there, very uncertain of herself. Her face now was not the face of a Comtesse. It was the face of an uncertain child. 'Thomas, would you like to come with me and explore the castle?' she asked. 'I know the rooms downstairs and these rooms here, but wouldn't it be fun to explore the whole castle and poke into the corners and discover what it is really like? I do not want to do that alone. Perhaps I'm a little afraid. Would you like to come with me, Thomas? We *might* find most exciting things.'

'Yes, there's no telling what we might find. Where do we start, Renée?'

'Perhaps in the rooms in the back of this wing?' she suggested.

So together they started their tour. In most of the rooms, except those occupied by the Ehrenhardts, they found very little except neglect and dust and an occasional piece of furniture that no one had bothered to move or steal.

'How can you cross from one wing to the other across the great hall?' Tom demanded.

'I don't know, Thomas. There is no passage on this floor. The hall thrusts up here, separating the two wings. There must be an attic or garret above this floor. Perhaps there is a passage there.'

'How do you get up to the attic?' Tom demanded.

'I don't know. There must be a stairway somewhere.'

At the rear of the left wing they walked into a very large bedroom, a corner bedroom with four windows. It was completely empty. Tom looked uncertainly around and then turned to Renée. 'That's queer,' he said. 'I was shown around this place, you know, when I was looking it over for Paul, and I remember this room. I would swear there had been a big oil painting on that wall over there. I remember it distinctly.'

He limped across to the wall. 'Of course there was. You can see the marks where it hung.'

'What sort of painting?'

'The portrait of a man and a woman and a little girl.'

The moment he spoke he realized who the subjects of that portrait might have been.

'An old portrait?' Renée asked.

'No,' Tom admitted, 'a fairly modern portrait.'

'Where has it gone?'

'I don't know, but I'd swear it was hanging there two weeks

ago, or whenever it was I was up here. I've lost track of time.'

'Perhaps it was moved somewhere else.'

'Perhaps, but not to any of the rooms I have been in today,' Tom said. 'I should have remembered it.'

'I imagine that through these years many things here have been stolen,' Renée observed.

'No doubt. The old woman who runs the *auberge* in Latire spoke about gypsies using the castle now and then as a rendez-vous. There's nothing here, Renée. Let's move on.'

Finally, in a little alcove off the hall, almost as though the builder had tried to conceal it, was a steep little stairway that led up to the attic.

'Do you want to go up there?' demanded Tom.

'Of course, if it is not too difficult for your ankle.'

'I'll make it all right.'

They climbed the steep stairs into the attic that reached up to the roof itself. It was in a state of utter confusion. Chests had been opened and their contents strewn about. Bags of feathers hanging from the rafters had been ripped open. Here were the castaways and the discards of many years, things that people no longer wanted but hesitated to throw away. Tom looked around in despair. 'Cleaning this place up will be a job for whoever comes to live in the Castle de Garac,' he observed.

'Isn't it awful!' Renée gasped. She crossed to a pile of what seemed to be discarded toys. 'Children's things,' she said absently. 'Here's a broken doll's bed and doll's clothing. There's a toy stove here, Thomas, a stove that looks as though it would really burn wood if the twigs were small enough.'

And then she suddenly fell silent. She was holding a large blonde doll. The arms had been torn off, and the doll's clothes were filthy, but the head was still there, and the blonde hair, and the legs. Renée was staring at the doll, transfixed. She held it there in her hands for several minutes while Tom watched her curiously. Then she rose slowly, still carrying the doll, and looked at Tom with a strange expression on her face. 'Let us go on, Thomas,' she said.

'Are you taking that doll with you?'

'Yes.'

They worked their way around the attic, the centre of which was blocked by the ceiling arches of the great hall below. Tom was leading the way. Suddenly he stopped. 'Renée!' he exclaimed. 'This is the portrait that I saw in that room downstairs that I spoke about!'

She came up to him, and together they stood looking at the portrait of a distinguished-looking man of perhaps thirty-eight or forty. He was dressed in formal riding-clothes, and the crop seemed to be tapping nervously against his boot. The second figure was a woman in her early thirties, very blonde and very beautiful. She was dressed in a simple morning dress that seemed now old-fashioned but which Tom placed vaguely as being what the fashionably dressed woman had worn not too many years before. And with them was a little girl of perhaps five with long blonde hair and deep-blue eyes and a chubby face.

Tom felt Renée's hand fasten on his arm, and he could feel her fingers digging into his flesh.

'That picture, Thomas! That picture!'

'What about it?' Tom asked quietly. 'It *is* the picture that was in the room downstairs, by the way.'

'That picture must be the last de Garacs,' Renée whispered. 'The clothes, that little girl, her father and mother. Hugo was telling me today that he was a great rider, that he rode whenever he could. Thomas, you will think I am going mad, but I swear to you that I have seen that picture before. I know that picture, Thomas, I know it!'

'If those are the last generation of de Garacs,' Tom said evenly, 'that is a portrait of you when you were a child.'

'Don't, Thomas, don't. I cannot stand it. Come here, please, and sit down on this chest. Put your arm around me. I need your arm, Thomas.'

There was a silence. Then she looked up into his face desperately.

'I don't know how to say this. Thomas, do you think that I am going mad? Or do you think Paul Ehrenhardt has me under some spell or hypnosis?'

'Why, Renée?'

'Because I have had such strange feelings and strange

emotions the last two days. When we first arrived here at Garac it was an utterly strange place. I walked into this old castle which I had never seen before. The day was just breaking, because, as you know, we drove up during the night. The Ehrenhardts sent me to bed so that I could rest and sleep. I was very tired.

'When I awoke about noon, I dressed and wandered out from my room, and it was as though I had been here before. In a sense it was strange and unknown, and yet familiar. That was what I was trying to tell you about this morning, and couldn't. Am I going crazy, Thomas?'

'You are overwrought and nervous and worried, Renée. That is all.'

She looked up at him and her eyes were defiant. 'Would that explain why I honestly keep asking myself whether Angèle Corton is not Renée de Garac?' she demanded.

'Probably. You are going through an experience like nothing you have ever known,' Tom said. 'You have been told to play a part and to feel as though you were the Comtesse de Garac. You have been told that you *must become* the Comtesse de Garac. Hugo, damn his eyes, is filling you full of family stories and family history and traditions, and you, your mind in utter confusion, feeling perhaps a little guilt, now are asking yourself subconsciously whether life would not be simpler if you really were Renée [Renée de Garac] Garac. I'm no psychologist, but I think a psychologist would explain it in some such way.'

'Thomas, that doll that I found back there! As soon as I saw her I felt that she belonged to me. She seemed to be part of me. That's why I had to bring her with me.'

'You probably had a doll like that when you were a little girl,' Tom explained. 'This doll reminded you of your doll.'

'Perhaps. You are probably right. But this picture that you say has been moved up from the floor below! When I saw that picture, that man in riding-clothes and that very beautiful woman, strange things happened to me inside, Thomas. I would swear that I had seen that picture before, that I had seen that man in riding-clothes and his wife.'

Tom was silent.

'You don't believe me, do you, Thomas?'

'I believe you,' Tom said slowly, 'but I don't think it all means what you think it means. I think your reaction to Garac and that doll and this picture must be explained in some other way.'

'*Am* I going mad, then?'

'No, certainly not.'

'Paul has *not* hypnotized me. One must be alone with a person and there must be concentration for hypnosis, mustn't there?'

'I believe so.'

'Then Paul has not hypnotized me. Thomas, I am frightened.'

'Renée, my dear, have you ever heard of self-hypnosis?' he asked.

'Yes, but I—'

'It is possible, I believe, for the subconscious mind to project itself so strongly that it can affect if not dominate the conscious mind.'

'And you think this is what has happened to me?'

'I think it is what may have happened to you.'

'But I must find out, Thomas. You do understand I must find out, don't you? Except for this ever-present question in the back of my mind, "*Are you Renée de Garac?*" I would have told Paul already that I would have to break my pledge, and I would have gone away with you as you asked me.'

'Do you mean that truly?' Tom demanded.

'Of course I mean it truly, *chéri*. I am speaking to you from my soul. But nagging at me, haunting me, is the question of whether I am Angèle Corton only or whether I am that child that you see in the picture there.'

'And do you think you can ever settle that question?' Tom demanded.

'I do not know, but I must try to find out the truth. Oh, I realize how ridiculous and absurd it sounds, that you by chance should have found me at Nice and brought me to Paul Ehrenhardt, who was looking for someone to play the part of Renée de Garac, and then that it would possibly turn out that I really *was* Renée de Garac, but yet, Thomas, improbable as it sounds, it is possible.'

Tom took her two hands that were clasped together under her

chin and covered them with his hands. 'Renée,' he said very soberly, 'are you telling me that you really believe that you are the Comtesse?'

'No, Thomas. I am only telling you that I am possessed by the question as to whether I am Renée de Garac or not, and until I settle that in my own mind, I must search for the truth. Will you be patient with me, Thomas? Will you try to understand? I need you so very much.'

'I love you, Angèle,' he said very quietly, 'and one day perhaps you and I will look back on this as a very bad dream that we have lived through.'

'Perhaps,' she agreed. 'Or perhaps in a few days you will leave me, and we shall never see each other again.'

She rose abruptly. 'Thomas, we should go down now. It is very dark up here. There is nothing more that we can see.'

And clutching the doll, she followed him towards the steep stairs that led to the floor below.

13

PAUL EHRENHARDT was standing alone by the fire burning in the big hearth when Tom Welles came down to dinner that night.

'Get yourself a drink, Tom, and then come over to the fire. You were quite right about these old castles being damp and unhealthy. We must keep this fire burning most of the time. It is a godsend. What are you frowning about, Tom? What is on your mind?'

'I was thinking of my room in the *auberge* down at Latire.'

'Your room?' Paul said swiftly. 'You didn't tell me that you had a room in Latire.'

'You didn't ask me,' grinned Tom. 'I do have a room at Latire, and I'm wondering what Madame is thinking about the fact that I walked out yesterday evening for a moonlight stroll and have not reappeared.'

'Good heavens, Tom, she has probably gone to the local *gendarmerie*, and they may be poking about all over the place looking for you!'

'That's what I was thinking,' agreed Tom. 'I've got some clothes there, too.'

'This is a problem,' Paul admitted. 'How is your ankle?'

'Not too bad, but I wouldn't want to walk all the way into Latire on it unless I had to.'

'Anna will have to drive you in close to the town, and you will have to walk from there,' Paul decided. 'It would be better to have Anna drive you than Hugo, or to do so myself. If you are seen in the car, your being with a woman will arouse less curiosity than it would if you were with Hugo or me.'

Paul was facing Tom now. 'And when you reach Latire, what then?' he demanded. 'Do you plan to return here, or will you go away?'

'I think I shall return here,' Tom said quietly, 'in spite of the dampness and discomfort of your castle.'

'As you will. Hugo put in a big stock of provisions, so although the menu is somewhat limited, there is plenty of food for another mouth. Anna had better drive you down after dinner. This business would be better conducted at night, I think, than in the daytime. And just what are you going to tell Madame about your absence?'

'That I sprained my ankle, and that it was so painful that I was not able to return to Latire until this evening. I spent the night in the forest.' Tom looked down at the clothes he was wearing. 'I do appreciate these clothes of yours, Paul, they're much better than mine, but I shall have to reappear in Latire dressed as I was.'

'Naturally.'

Anna sauntered down the stairs into the great hall.

Paul explained to her about the trip to Latire that night, concluding: 'And since Tom is returning to the castle, you'll have to wait for him outside of town until he can give up his room at the *auberge* and get his clothes.'

Anna nodded and looked up at Tom mischievously. 'All right, I'll wait for him,' she agreed. 'It's a lovely night, the moon is beautiful. I must say, though, that I'd look forward to this evening more if I thought Tom would be a little more responsive than usual.'

'Anna, you are shameless!' Paul cried.

'You have known that for a long time, *chéri.*'

'Paul,' Tom broke in, 'who moved the big portrait of the man and the woman and the little girl from the big bedroom upstairs to the attic?'

'I had Hugo dispose of it.'

'But why?'

'You have seen it, I take it?'

'Yes, I noticed it when I looked over the castle two weeks ago, and today Renée and I were exploring and I missed it in the bedroom, and we found it up in the attic. Why did you move it?'

'You have guessed, haven't you, who the subjects of that portrait are?'

'The late Comte and Comtesse de Garac and their daughter, I suppose.'

Paul nodded. 'Hugo and I decided that – well, let's say that that portrait was a little close to home, under the circumstances. We thought that, excellent as the likenesses are of the late Comte and Comtesse, it was a very bad portrayal of little Renée.'

'How do you know it was a bad likeness of Renée?'

Paul Ehrenhardt shrugged. 'After studying Renée as she is now, it did not seem to us that she ever could have looked quite like that moppet in the portrait. It will have to be destroyed eventually, but it seemed easier to put it in the attic for the time being. We discussed the matter at length, Hugo, Anna, and I, and finally decided the portrait would do no good and it might possibly do some harm.'

'If I were you, I'd talk to the Comtesse before destroying that portrait,' Tom said grimly.

Paul looked at him quizzically. 'Ah, Renée saw it too, then. And did it bring back memories of her childhood?'

'She reacted very strangely,' Tom admitted.

Paul Ehrenhardt sighed in satisfaction. 'Tom, the more I see of Renée, the more I realize just how grateful I should be to you for finding her. It really is amazing how quickly her past seems to be coming back to her. I never dreamed that in just a few days she would make such progress towards the resumption of her true place in the world. Most remarkable! It is almost as though she were an actress with a very great talent, an actress who enters so fully into the part she is playing that she loses all consciousness of her own identity. Yes, we are very grateful to you, Tom. Another drink?'

'Speaking of Renée,' Anna said, 'she is not coming down to dinner. She said she had a bad headache and was going right to bed.'

'We should sit down, then,' Paul decided. 'I think Hugo is ready, and if you are going to Latire—'

After dinner Anna drove a long, low, black limousine from the stone barn behind the castle, where the car had been garaged, and Paul and Hugo between them swung open the great gates of the castle wall.

'Anna, you will have to drive without lights – at least until you get on the main road,' Paul commanded. 'We want no head-lights seen on the castle road.'

Anna nodded. 'There's enough moonlight to see by.'

The great car started crawling cautiously down the narrow, twisting road to the valley below.

'But why the utter secrecy?' Tom demanded. 'Surely someone around here knows that you're occupying the castle, and the news will spread.'

Anna shook her head. 'We think not. We have seen no one, no one has seen us. Hugo brought everything up from Nice, and he had to make several trips back and forth.'

'But under the circumstances, why is it so essential that no one knows that you are in the castle? After all, it is known that I took an option to buy and have the right of occupancy.'

'True, Tom, but you are just another mad American, and there is no connexion between you and us or between you and Renée.'

'I still don't understand.'

'You are being a little dense, my friend. Once Renée's educa-tion has been completed, we leave the Castle Garac, and Renée goes her way and we go ours. No one will know that Renée has ever been at the Castle Garac, and no one will know that the Ehrenhardts and Renée have ever even met. That is why neither Hugo nor Paul could tend to the business of the castle or search for the Comtesse de Garac.'

'I see,' said Tom thoughtfully. 'When – Renée – leaves the Castle Garac, she will become once more Angèle Corton. Right?'

Anna nodded.

'And Hugo will again become, say, a maître d'hôtel some-where? And the Ehrenhardts will resume their normal life?'

'Light a cigarette for me, Tom.'

'And then,' pursued Tom, 'by chance Angèle Corton will go to the restaurant or the hotel where Hugo is serving as maître d'hôtel, and he will recognize her as Renée de Garac, who was thought to have been killed twelve years ago but who is obviously alive and healthy.'

'You've almost got it,' Anna admitted, 'but Hugo will not have a chance to recognize the Comtesse de Garac until the Ehrenhardts have by chance met Angèle Corton. At that moment I will be looking for a companion, of refinement and education, and Angèle Corton obviously would be a most excellent com-panion.'

'Unless something unexpected happens or there's some slip, it might work,' Tom admitted.

'Of course it will work, provided we can conceal the fact that there has ever been any contact between ourselves and Hugo and Renée up to the time we openly meet Angèle.

'The bankers will be very happy that an heir to the de Garac fortune has been found, and they will sigh with relief to be rid of this burdensome estate that has been hanging about their poor necks. Hugo and his sister will make most excellent witnesses, and there will be no one to question seriously Renée's identity. The matter will be settled to everyone's satisfaction when she is brought to the Castle Garac, not having been there since her seventh year, and proves that she is thoroughly familiar with her ancestral home.'

'But the castle has been taken over by the state for taxes.'

'Who cares anything about the castle itself?' Anna said indifferently. 'Let them hold it until the stone crumbles. The de Garac fortune is in New York, in American securities, beautiful stocks and bonds, and the French government cannot touch it. And there ahead of you are the lights of Latire. I think I shall stop here and pull off the road. Come back as quickly as you can, Tom. I do not enjoy waiting – even for you.'

At the *auberge* Madame was finally placated. Tom paid handsomely for the bicycle he had used but once, paid even more liberally for his room, and told Madame that he would catch the bus which was due now at any minute.

When he limped back to the car outside of Latire, he had to wake Anna up. She was sleeping as peacefully as a child. Tom put his hand on her shoulder and shook her gently. She opened her eyes with a yawn. 'You are a nuisance, Tom. Get in quickly, and let us get back to Garac. I am very, very tired. I do not think anything could keep me awake tonight except perhaps a new lover.'

At the bottom of the castle hill Anna put the car into first gear and, with the light off again, guided the big car up on its serpentine ascent.

The main gates were still open, and Anna drove directly around the castle over the paved court and into the old stone barn.

As they circled back and came to the castle door, Anna frowned.

'You'd think they'd be cold enough in there without leaving the door ajar, wouldn't you?' She pushed the door open, and Tom followed her into the hall. It was in complete darkness except for a few dying embers on the hearth at the farther end.

'Even if Paul couldn't wait up for us, he might at least have left a light,' Anna grumbled.

'Here, I've got my flashlight. We'll have to find that lamp.'

The beam of the flashlight searched for the lamp in its usual place on the long centre table. There was nothing there that Tom could see but what looked like bits of a broken china shade.

'What the devil?' he muttered, and crossed swiftly to the table.

'Anna!' he cried sharply. 'This lamp is lying on the floor with the oil running out. It's been broken. Someone knocked it over.'

She was beside him. 'Why in the world didn't they clean it up? We'll have to find candles. There should be some here in the drawer.'

She pulled open the drawer in the big table and took out two candles, and Tom lit them carefully.

'My God, Tom, over there by the fireplace! Look!' She ran across the hall. 'It's Paul, Tom! It's Paul! He's tied up and gagged!'

Paul Ehrenhardt lay there rigid, his eyes rolling, and they had a desperate and urgent message. The lower part of his face was tightly bound with a white cloth apparently holding a gag. The rope was wound around his body, tightly pinioning his arms to his sides. He was tightly bound at the knees and ankles.

'My God, what's happened, Anna? Here, hold the candle while I cut him loose.' Tom whipped out his knife and began sawing at the tough hempen rope.

'Get that gag off first,' Anna urged.

'Right.'

The knife cut through that cotton cloth easily. Tom ripped it off. Paul's mouth was wide open, and it had been stuffed with cotton rags. Swiftly Anna started pulling the rags out of his mouth while Tom went back to the ropes.

Paul's face was dirty and bloody, and Tom noticed a great rent in his right sleeve. It must have been a knife cut, because the sleeve was wet with blood that was beginning to cake.

'Good God, Paul, what happened? Tell us!'

Paul did not seem able to speak. It was as though he were trying to swallow something.

'Water or brandy quickly!' Anna exclaimed. 'Something so that he can moisten his mouth and his throat.'

In a few seconds Tom was back with a bottle of cognac from a passageway shelf off the hall. Anna raised Paul's head and poured the brandy into his mouth. Paul choked a little and then groaned.

'What happened?' Tom cried. 'Where's Renée?'

172

Paul shook his head. 'I don't know,' he croaked. His left hand raised in a vague gesture. 'She was running.'

Tom had Paul free of his bonds now. With difficulty he raised himself to a sitting position on the hearth. His right arm seemed quite helpless. 'More brandy,' he whispered.

'What happened, Paul?' Anna cried.

'Men – quite a lot of men – gypsies, I think – soon after you left.'

'But Renée!' Tom persisted. 'You say she ran?'

Paul nodded. 'They were after her – into the tower room there.' He made another gesture towards the front salon off the great hall.

Seizing a candle, Tom raced across the hall to the door to the tower room.

Renée lay there on the floor, her arms outstretched, very still. Her dressing-gown had come undone, and it splayed out over her on the floor as though it had been spread out for display. She lay face down, her head slightly turned.

Tom dropped to his knees beside her. Her eyes were closed. He felt her pulse and found it beating. Her hair was clotted with blood just above and behind her ear. Tom felt her pulse again. It seemed fairly even and quite strong.

Apparently she had been hit on the head from the rear and knocked out. Tom was afraid to move her. If there was real concussion, she should be moved only gently, carefully. He ripped off his coat and threw it over her. Then he found a slim pillow on the old-fashioned sofa and slipped it gently under her head. He straightened up. That was all he could do for her now.

Anna's eyes were questioning as he returned to where she was half supporting Paul by the hearth.

'Knocked out and unconscious, but I think she will be all right.'

Paul looked a little stronger.

'What about you, Paul?'

Paul looked down at his arm with a grimace. 'Not too bad, except for my arm. They slashed that pretty well open.'

'Where's Hugo?'

Paul Ehrenhardt's face was bleak. 'His sister, Margot, rushed in and said they had killed him. That was the first I knew that anything was wrong.'

'And Margot?'

Paul shook his head. 'I do not know.'

'Paul, where's your gun? I must look around, and I'd be more comfortable with that revolver of yours.'

'In the drawer of the little table by my bed.'

In a matter of moments Tom was back in the great hall with Paul's revolver in his hand. He picked up a candle and hurried out through the passageway towards the kitchen. He found Hugo there, slumped on the floor, half under the table, his right arm twisted around in an unnatural position. Tom examined him quickly. He was still alive, but he, too, was unconscious. Suddenly he heard something stirring behind him. He turned swiftly, the gun ready. Margot lay trussed up there on the floor like a fowl. She too had been effectively gagged, but she was very much alive. Her black, baleful eyes were snapping.

Tom waved to her. 'I'll be right back,' he said, and then hurried back to the great hall to report.

'Hugo is not dead,' he said crisply. 'He's unconscious, and I think he has a broken arm. Margot is very much alive, and very angry. Anna, you'd better take this knife and go out and cut her loose so that she can help us. I'll see if I can get Paul up on the sofa.'

With Tom's help, Paul staggered to his feet. He seemed very weak, for he had lost a good deal of blood. His face, however, was beginning to regain its debonair expression.

Tom got him into the chair and handed him a glass of brandy. 'Now, what happened?'

'I was in the hall alone, not long after you and Anna left. Suddenly I heard a commotion in the kitchen, and Margot rushed in through the passage screaming that Hugo had been killed. Men burst out of the passage just behind her. They looked like gypsies – probably relatives of your friend of the other night. They started for me, and Margot turned and rushed back towards the kitchen. It was ridiculous, of course, to try to defend myself, but what was I to do? They grabbed me, and I started to struggle, and then one of them lurched at me with his knife. Then my eye caught Renée on the stairs. She must have heard the uproar and was almost all the way down the stairs. One of the men swung around and started towards her, and Renée started running to the door of the tower room. By that time they had me down and were tying me up.'

'And then?' Tom demanded.

'I could see practically nothing from where I was lying. I heard them rummaging around, and I heard noises below in the cellar and the vaults. I could hear them dragging chests or boxes or something across the stones. After a time they disappeared.'

'Gypsies, you say?'

'I think so, Tom.'

'The old woman in the village told me that they had used this deserted spot as a rendezvous from time to time.'

Paul nodded. 'They may have hidden away stolen goods here,' he said. 'It would have been a good hiding-place. The man who attacked you the other night was probably reconnoitring.'

'I'm afraid to move Renée without help,' Tom said. 'She's on that cold floor, but she's better off there than she would be with any clumsy handling. My God, Paul, do you suppose there's any chance of their coming back?'

Paul shook his head. 'I doubt it. They came for what they wanted, and they must have found it before they left. They will not be looking for any more trouble than necessary.'

'As soon as Anna gets back with Margot I'll have to go for a doctor and some help.'

Paul shook his head. 'No, Tom. There probably is no doctor near by, and if there were, you could not bring him here under the circumstances. I have been thinking. Your little Renée is probably all right, or will be with rest and quiet. This arm of mine and Hugo's arm, if it is broken, need help. I do not think I can drive a car tonight. Anna will have to drive Hugo and me to Nice. You will have to stay here with Renée and Margot.'

'But Renée needs a doctor,' Tom protested.

'There's little a doctor can do in cases of concussion except keep his patient quiet. If Renée's condition is really serious, there will have to be a doctor, of course. But, from what you say, there is not yet any emergency as far as she is concerned. To bring any stranger here now would be to ruin everything for us – and for Renée.'

Anna reappeared in the doorway.

'Hugo is coming around,' she announced. 'Where's the brandy? Tom, take this out to Margot. I must look at Renée.'

Tom left the brandy in the kitchen with Hugo's sister and hurried back to the tower room. Anna was examining Renée's scalp carefully and gently.

'This is not too bad, Tom,' she observed. 'It was a hard blow, but the cut is not long. It has stopped bleeding. It will not be necessary, I think, even to have it sewn up.'

'Do you know anything about this sort of thing?' Tom demanded brusquely.

'A great deal. I was a nurse in the last war.'

Very gently Anna lifted one of Renée's eyelids. 'Her eyes are good, too,' she said. 'I think when she wakes up she will have a very bad headache and will want to be very quiet for a time. But there is nothing serious.'

'Paul wants you to drive him and Hugo to Nice to the hospital.'

'Yes, I thought that would be the plan. As soon as we can persuade Margot that Hugo is alive and not dead, the three of us will have to get Renée off this floor and into her bed. Get two heavy blankets, Tom, and lay them out flat here on the floor. We should be able to carry her up the stairs with blankets. She is not very heavy.'

'And I suppose Paul won't even report this raid to the police?'

Anna looked at him with surprise. 'Most certainly not, Tom. Can you imagine what that sort of investigation would be for us? Get those blankets, Tom. Renée has been here long enough.'

And so it was that three quarters of an hour later Anna Ehrenhardt started the big black car crawling down the hill again, with Paul beside her in the front seat, his face drawn with pain now that the numbness in his arm had worked off, and Hugo stretched out in the back seat, his broken arm tied to his body with a long, heavy scarf, conscious but very drowsy from the huge dosage of cognac that Margot had insisted upon.

Tom watched the car winding down the hill until he could see it no longer, then turned back into the courtyard. With difficulty he swung the great gates closed and shot the heavy iron bolts.

The castle door he bolted too, and then made his way up to Renée's room, where Margot was keeping watch.

Margot looked up at him. 'She does well, I think,' she said reassuringly. 'One must not worry.'

Tom nodded. 'You go to bed now. I'll take over. I'll stay here so that if she wakes up there will be someone near her.'

Margot nodded. 'If Monsieur does not mind, I think I shall sleep in one of the rooms up here tonight. I think I would feel safer.'

'By all means,' Tom agreed. 'And you'll be near by if the Comtesse needs anything.'

'Do you think Hugo's arm will be all right?' Margot demanded.

'I'm sure it will be, Margot. He won't enjoy that trip to Nice very much, but once a doctor gets hold of him he'll be all right.'

'I shall strangle the next gypsy I see,' she muttered, and disappeared into the hall.

Tom pulled the most comfortable chair he could find up near the bed and another chair for his feet. He must get that ankle up. He had been completely unconscious of it for the last hour, but now it was throbbing badly again. He made sure that there was a supply of candles in the room and left one candle burning so that he could watch Renée's face.

He settled down in his chair, lit a cigarette, and suddenly he was struck by a most curious coincidence.

Twelve years before, drunken soldiers had invaded the Castle Garac, there had been a massacre, and the seven-year-old Renée had been killed. Tonight there had been a strange gypsy raid. No one had been killed, true, but Angèle Corton, pretender to the de Garac name and fortune, had been attacked and knocked unconscious. He wondered whether Paul Ehrenhardt was thinking of this as he rode painfully into Nice.

Dawn was just breaking when Renée first stirred.

Tom had been cat-napping throughout the night. At the

moment Renée's head turned a little he happened to be awake. He bent over her anxiously. She sighed and sank back into her stupor. Tom settled down and continued his vigil.

The Ehrenhardts must be in Nice now. He wondered when they would return. He would get no news of them until they did. Certainly two or three days, anyway, and possibly not then. Anna might return alone, leaving Paul and Hugo in Nice.

Outside it was brighter now, almost full daylight, and there was a brighter light over a distant hill where the sun would soon appear.

There was a sound behind him. It was Margot in a long, old-fashioned woollen wrapper. She was carrying a small tray with a steaming cup of coffee.

'It has been a long night, monsieur.'

'Did you sleep, Margot?'

'A little, monsieur. And the Comtesse?'

'She moved a little not long ago, but is still asleep.'

'It is good,' Margot decided. 'The longer she sleeps, the better. There is no doctor like Nature, monsieur.'

'I shall be happier when she opens her eyes and can speak,' Tom admitted. 'Thank you for the coffee, Margot.'

'I will get Monsieur some breakfast in about an hour,' she announced, and disappeared. And in an hour she told him that his breakfast was on the table and that she would watch the Comtesse while he ate.

Tom hurried through breakfast and returned to Renée's room.

'Still asleep?' he asked.

'Still asleep, monsieur. I have bathed her face gently and straightened the bed. If Monsieur has need of me, he will call?'

'Yes. Thank you, Margot.'

The black, shrewd French eyes peered up at him. 'Monsieur, I am an old Frenchwoman. I have seen much. I think perhaps Monsieur is very, very fond of this little Comtesse?'

'I think you may be right, Margot.'

'There are complications, *hein*?'

'There are complications,' Tom admitted.

'Monsieur, you must remember that there is nothing in the world as important as the heart, and what it says to you sometimes is against all reason. If Monsieur is wise, he will ignore the other complications and listen only to his heart.'

And Margot disappeared.

Tom Welles stood there beside Renée's bed, looking down at her tenderly. She lay there on her back, her face an oval, and then suddenly, without there being a flicker of her eyelids, her mouth opened.

'I heard what Margot said to you, Thomas, but I pretended to be still asleep.'

Still the eyelids did not move.

'I must have been sleeping long, Thomas, and I remember a very strange dream. Perhaps I am still dreaming. I am afraid to open my eyes lest it is a dream and you are not here beside me.'

'Open your eyes, Renée. I am here.' Tom took one of her hands in his.

The eyelids fluttered, opened, and she stared up at him with her great deep-blue eyes. Her mouth smiled, and then she closed her eyes again. 'My head hurts. I had a headache when I went to bed, but it was nothing like this.'

Then her eyes opened again. 'Have I been ill?' she demanded.

'You had an accident,' Tom said.

Her eyes clouded. 'In my dream I remember the hall below and strange, swarthy men seemed to be attacking Paul Ehrenhardt, and then one of them started after me.' Then the eyes became very puzzled. 'What happened to my mother? She was being attacked, too. Where is my mother?'

Tom's heart was pounding. *What happened to my mother? She was being attacked, too. Where is my mother?*

'Everything is all right, darling,' he said softly. 'You had an accident, and you had a dream. You should go back to sleep now until your head is better.'

'Will you stay near me, Thomas?'

'Yes, I will stay near you, darling.'

'And take care of me?'

'And take care of you.'

'Then I think I shall go back to sleep for just a little while. My head aches so, and I am very tired.'

179

Her eyes closed, and she sank back into oblivion.

It was late that afternoon before Renée seemed lucid enough for Tom to feel that he could tell her what actually had happened.

Three times Renée had roused herself from her coma, each time being a little more alert than previously. She had asked for Anna and could not quite understand why Anna was not there. She asked about Paul and the attack, which was beginning to seem to her now more like an actual happening than a dream. She remembered her flight through the great hall and the swarthy giant who was pursuing her. And each time she awoke, Tom observed, it was all becoming less of a dream and more of a reality.

Margot had brought her a big, steaming bowl of chicken broth, and she had eaten it hungrily. There was a little colour back in her cheeks and her mind seemed alert.

'Thomas, *chéri*!' Her eyes were gleaming.

'Yes, Renée. Can I get you anything?'

'No, but sit down here, on my bed. You must tell me now what really happened, and where is Anna and where is Paul? I think that what I thought of as a dream was not a dream. Something very strange happened last night. I have been asking you questions, and you have been evading them. You must tell me now.'

In a matter-of-fact voice Tom sketched the events of the preceding night. Renée listened carefully, and when he finished she looked puzzled.

'And that is all that happened last night?' she demanded.

'Everything except some details that I haven't bothered with.'

'What about the soldiers?' she demanded.

'What soldiers?'

'Weren't there any soldiers? What about the two soldiers who were holding me, one holding each arm, and the third soldier who kept turning my face back and forth with his hand, looking at me?'

'You must have imagined that, Renée. There were no soldiers last night, only a few gypsies who apparently came back to

180

recover something that they had left here at the castle, probably stolen goods.'

'When will Paul and Anna be back?' she demanded. 'After all, you were not here when the gypsies came. Paul might know something more than you do.'

'I don't know when they'll be back. It certainly won't be long. Perhaps Anna will drive up from Nice tomorrow.'

There was a silence.

Relieved as he was to have Renée conscious again, Tom Welles was deeply disturbed. The shock of her experience the night before had obviously produced certain hallucinations. Angèle's mind, teeming with the story and the background of the de Garac family and her own impersonation, affected by the horror of the wartime massacre of the Comtesse and her young daughter, had associated the story she had heard with the events of the preceding night. Even he, Tom Welles, from an objective point of view, had been struck by last night's strange coincidental repetition of the events of twelve years before at the Castle Garac.

'Don't you think you should go back to sleep again, Renée?' Tom said gently.

She looked at him accusingly. 'You don't believe me, do you, Thomas?' she demanded. 'You think I am either imagining things or making them up. My mother had on a long, clinging blue velvet gown that swept to the floor. There was lace around her neck. She was standing near the fireplace, almost where Paul was last night, when she fell.'

'And what happened to you?' Tom demanded.

'I don't remember anything after those soldiers – one on each side of me, holding my arms, and the third man looking down at me, his hand grasping my chin, turning my face from side to side, and laughing.'

Involuntarily, Tom shuddered. 'And you remember nothing after that?' he persisted.

'No, nothing after that. Except of course I remember Angèle Corton at the convent and the last few years.'

Tom Welles shook his head helplessly. He wished he knew more about the way the human mind worked and more about psychiatry. That Renée was completely sincere in what she said, he had no doubt; but she had undoubtedly taken over stories that she had heard and woven them into her own actual experience of the night before.

'Thomas, I wish to talk to Margot. I must talk to Margot! Now! Will you call her for me and then leave us for a little while?'

'Of course, Renée. I'll send Margot right up.'

Margot was behind a closed door with Renée for a full half-hour. When she emerged, she looked very disturbed. Tom was sitting in the great hall, and he watched her descending the stairway.

'Is the Comtesse all right?' he demanded anxiously.

'Yes, monsieur, the Comtesse is much better.' Margot halted by Tom's chair. 'She asked me,' Margot went on evenly, 'whether Monsieur would be kind enough to bring down from the attic that portrait that you and she were looking at yesterday, the portrait of the Comte and Comtesse de Garac and their daughter.'

'Bring it down to her room?' Tom asked.

'Yes, she wants it where she can look at it,' Margot explained.

Tom was frowning. He did not know whether that particular portrait would be good medicine for Renée or not.

'Margot, does the Comtesse's mind seem to you – clear and rational?'

'Monsieur Welles, I think I know what is in your mind. I will admit that some things the Comtesse said to me came as a surprise and a shock. I know the story of Angèle Corton and how you met her and why you met her. I know about the plans of Monsieur Ehrenhardt and my brother. I also knew the Comte and Comtesse de Garac and their daughter Renée.

'If I were you, I would get the portrait down from the attic as the Comtesse requests. And, monsieur, I would ask myself very seriously whether the most strange and amazing turn of fate has not brought about in reality an event almost unbelievable. I am not sure, monsieur, I am not sure, because I know the mind plays the most curious tricks. Nevertheless, I find myself asking myself questions that are not easy to answer logically.'

Then Margot disappeared through the passage into the kitchen.

Ten minutes later the de Garac portrait, carefully dusted, was standing on the tall oak bureau facing Renée's bed.

'Thank you, *chéri*,' she said quietly. 'I feel very tired again. I think I shall go to sleep. But I did so want that picture there to look at when I woke up again.'

14

THAT NIGHT passed, and the next day, without any sign of Anna or Paul Ehrenhardt.

The time had passed very quietly. The following morning Renée had pleaded to get up, but Margot and Tom both insisted that she stay in bed. She seemed quite normal, if unusually quiet. She ate at least part of everything that Margot brought her. Her smile welcomed Tom whenever he appeared in her doorway, but, for the most part, her mind seemed to be far away, absorbed in some problem that only she herself could solve. She never referred again to the gypsy raid or the scene that she associated with that night. She seemed to avoid any topic that might lead to a discussion of the de Garac family or her own identity. She mentioned Paul and Anna casually, but only casually.

Tom felt her warm affection and her response, but at the same time he sensed a barrier that she had raised between them which almost seemed to carry a big black-lettered sign: PRIVATE PROPERTY. KEEP OUT.

Tom could guess at the struggle going on in her mind, but there was nothing that he felt he could do to help her in her trouble, and as she seemed to want to be alone much of the time now, Tom dropped in on her only occasionally, although he kept well within call.

Late in the afternoon of the second day he heard Renée calling him. He picked up a bottle of sherry and two glasses and ascended to her room.

She lay there in bed, her arms outside the covers lying in

straight lines parallel to her body. Tom thought he had never seen eyes so blue or eyes so big.

'Feeling like a glass of sherry?' he asked.

'That would be good, Thomas. Are you occupied just now, Thomas?'

'No, of course not, except that I'm now here with you.'

'Sit down, then, *chéri*. There is something that I must say.'

Tom dropped into a chair beside her bed. She was silent for a moment, and then she said: 'Thomas, before I begin, would you put your arms around me and kiss me? I should like to feel your arms around me once again.'

Tom leaned over the bed and circled her slight body with his arms. He half drew her up towards him and held her very tight. Their lips met, and they clung there together, each wanting the other, each needing the other, and yet both in the shadow of uncertainty.

'Sit down now,' she finally whispered.

'Thomas,' she began slowly, 'a few days ago I asked you whether you thought I was going mad or whether I had been hypnotized. You said no, but that you thought perhaps I had hypnotized myself with this thought of being Renée de Garac.'

Tom nodded.

'I explained to you what seemed to be happening to me here at the castle, the strange familiarities, the feeling of belonging here, and my sense of dim, vague shadows out of the past. I tell you now I believe I am Renée de Garac.'

She looked at the picture facing her from across the room. 'I believe I am that child. That man is my father and that woman my mother.' Her eyes turned back to Tom. 'I realize that such things do not happen in life and that you undoubtedly still think I am mad, or the victim of my own desires and wishes. I have tried to persuade myself that you are right, but what happened to me the other night, when the gypsies came to the castle, seems to have opened up much of the past that until now has been thickly veiled. Perhaps it was seeing men struggling in the great hall, perhaps it was the blow on the head. But I told you the next day, when I awoke, of things that did not happen that night, but things which must have happened twelve years ago.'

'You had been told that story,' Tom said very gently.

'Yes, I had been told that story, but not in such detail as I experienced it in my mind. I saw things that only Renée could have seen, and I felt things that only Renée could have felt.

'Thomas, I have talked to Margot. I have spoken to her of things that I remember, little things that no one has told me about, and she remembers them, too. Oh, *chéri*, I know you do not believe me and that you cannot believe me because of the strange circumstances of this whole series of events, but in my own mind I am certain that I really am Renée de Garac.'

There was a long, long silence. Finally Renée looked at him appealingly. 'Say something, Thomas, say something to me, even if it has to be that you think I am mad or still pretending.'

Tom put his hand out and stroked Renée's hand, which was lying on the counterpane. 'My dear,' he said, 'I myself do not know what to think about all this. I have become convinced of one thing, however. I am sure that you yourself believe that you are Renée de Garac. That is the important thing.'

'Please go away now, Thomas. I want to be alone.'

Without another word he left the room.

A little later, just as Tom was sitting down to the dinner that Margot had prepared, he heard the noise of a clanging bell from outside the castle.

'It is the bell of the castle gate!' Margot cried. 'Perhaps it is Monsieur and Madame Ehrenhardt and my brother!'

Tom had not heard that bell before. He hurried out.

Margot followed him, and together they swung the big gates open, and Anna, alone, drove the big black car through the gateway and drew up to the front door. She looked wan, and her face was strained.

'How is Paul? How is Hugo?' Tom demanded.

'They are all right,' Anna said absently. 'Paul had his arm sewn up and is in bed at the Negresco. Hugo is still in the hospital with his arm in a cast. They'll let him out tomorrow.'

She descended swiftly from the car and swept into the great hall. 'And Renée?' she asked.

'We've still got her in bed, but I think she's all right.'

Anna nodded as though it did not concern her very much.

'You're just in time for dinner, Anna.'

'Good. I'm hungry. I'll go up and speak to Renée first and be down in a few minutes.'

When Anna dropped down wearily into the chair that Tom offered her at the dining-room table, she sighed.

'Give me a drink, Tom. Whisky, and bring the bottle.'

Silently Tom did as she had asked, and put the bottle of Scotch down in front of her.

'Anna, you look awful,' he blurted out. 'What has happened?'

Anna's laugh was bitter. 'A lot,' she admitted. 'I'll tell you in a few minutes – as soon as I relax just a little.'

Tom nodded, and they began eating silently.

'Are you staying on here, Anna,' he finally asked, 'or will you be going back to Nice tomorrow?'

'I'm going back to Nice *tonight*,' she said deliberately, 'as quickly as I can pack up our things.'

'Won't Paul and Hugo be able to come back very soon?'

'Paul and Hugo are not coming back.'

'Not coming back?'

Anna looked around the room and made a sweeping gesture with both hands. 'The Castle Garac – finish!'

'But what do you mean? What has gone wrong?'

'Tom, do you remember warning me that we would never get away with this, and how sure I was?'

'Yes, but what could have happened now?'

Anna took a long drink. 'The morning paper,' she said calmly, 'announced a sensational failure of a well-known private banker in New York.'

'Not—!'

'Yes, the most respected and trusted banker, whom the late Comte de Garac selected as custodian for all his property, shot himself yesterday after writing a confession that he had for years been using his clients' resources for his own purposes, and that rather than face disgrace and imprisonment he was taking his own life.'

'My God!'

'Yes,' Anna said dryly. 'This was one possibility that Paul and I overlooked.'

'But perhaps there's something left. Surely he couldn't have absconded with *everything*!'

Anna's laugh was hollow. 'As soon as Paul read the news he telephoned a friend of his in New York. His friend confirmed the newspaper story. It appears to have been the failure to end all failures. It seems that there are no assets whatsoever left in the bank, either belonging to our banker or to his clients. He had taken one last desperate gamble to recover himself, after embezzling funds for years, but he ran true to form on his last gamble, and he lost that, too.'

'And so there is no de Garac heritage,' Tom murmured. 'Anna,' he went on abruptly, 'perhaps you won't believe me. You know what my feelings have been about what you and Paul were doing. But at this moment I feel myself really sorry for your sake.'

'Paul and I will make out,' Anna responded dully. 'We always have. I'll admit, though, this is something of a shock.'

'And Renée?'

Anna shrugged. 'Renée will have to take care of herself. Paul and I will need everything we have to make a fresh start.' And then her eyes flickered for the first time. 'If your novel sells, Tom, you might buy her the Castle Garac and give it to her as a wedding present.'

'Curiously enough,' Tom went on, 'I don't find myself feeling particularly sorry for Renée. I keep thinking of you and Paul, because it is a dream that you have had for some time, and you have worked for it and planned for it, and now the treasure has disappeared.'

'You are sweet, Tom. I have always liked you. Marry this girl of yours and take her back to America, and both of you forget that there was ever a Castle Garac or a fortune. To her I don't think it ever has been a reality, and, after all, she has lost nothing except a chance that she would not even have known about, had it not been for us.'

Tom nodded. 'And Hugo? And Margot?'

'Hugo will have to get himself a job as soon as he is able. We will, of course, leave him money enough to see him through his illness. And Margot will go back to her husband, whom she left temporarily to help Hugo and take care of us here at the castle.'

'And you and Paul?'

'We shall leave Nice in a day or so, as soon as Paul is well enough to travel.'

'What next?'

'Who knows what next? For some time Paul has been intrigued with an idea that would take us to Paris. On the other hand, there is a great deal going on in Rome, and now that things have really picked up in Germany— Who knows?'

Anna rose abruptly. 'I must get hold of Margot and get her to help me pack. I want to get back to Nice as quickly as possible. It is not good for Paul to be alone for long at a time like this. He needs me . . . In spite of my lovers, Tom, Paul is my man.'

'What about Margot? You are not taking her with you, are you?'

Anna frowned. 'If Renée is still in bed, she will probably need her for a few days. If I leave Margot here, will you see that she gets back to Nice? That is where she lives.'

'Of course.'

'Then she will stay.' Anna nodded briskly. 'And as for you, Tom, the Castle Garac is yours for the time being, and may I never see it again.'

Three hours later Anna started down the hill, and the great gates closed once more.

Very thoughtfully Tom Welles mounted the stairs. Renée's door was open and there was a light in her room.

He paused on the threshold. 'You should be asleep, Renée. It is late, very late.'

'I was waiting for you, Thomas. I did not want to go to sleep without seeing you.'

Tom entered the room and sat down. 'Anna said she had told you what has happened.'

Renée nodded. 'Poor Anna and poor Paul. It is a great blow to them.'

'And isn't it a blow to the Comtesse de Garac?' Tom asked.

'Thomas, since Anna told me, I've been trying to understand myself. I tell myself that I should be bitterly unhappy and disappointed. I suppose it is a cause for great regret. And yet, I wonder if I ever really believed in that fabulous wealth that Paul told me about. The idea was exciting, but it did not seem very real. And with the dream gone, things seem to be simpler, and my mind seems to be at peace.'

'You are a strange person, Renée.'

'Perhaps, but, Thomas, you know the thought that has been uppermost in my mind ever since Anna told me of what has happened, the thought that has been singing in my mind joyously? I have been telling myself that now, regardless of what you yourself think about this question, it will be impossible for you not to believe that when I say that I think I am the Comtesse de Garac, I am telling the truth. You have talked to me much about my subconscious mind and about self-hypnosis. Perhaps you are right, but at least there is no longer a motive for me to pretend to be someone I am not.'

'My darling, it doesn't matter to me whether you are Angèle Corton or the Comtesse de Garac or Medusa.'

'Thomas, will you take me away from here very soon? Could we go tomorrow?'

'Are you sure you want me to take you away, Renèe?'

'Yes. You must take me wherever you are going.'

'Will you marry me?'

'Yes, of course, Thomas, if you want me to. We can manage some way. You have a little money left, and I can get work. I think I should like to live with you, Thomas, whether you marry me or not.' There was a pause. 'It would be nice to be married, however.'

'It's very complicated,' Tom grinned, 'but I think it can be done. But why are you in such a hurry to leave Garac?' he asked curiously.

'I don't quite know, Thomas. I told you that I felt as though I belonged here, but that is something out of the past. It is the part of me that I do not know very well, and do not understand. . . . Can we leave here tomorrow, Thomas?'

'Perhaps. I'll go down to Latire the first thing in the morning and see what arrangements can be made about a car to Nice.'

'Will we stay at Nice?'

Tom nodded. 'We shall have to stay at Nice for a time,' he said, 'until we can make all the arrangements about our marriage.'

'Thomas, there is one thing. When we leave here, I want that portrait there across the room. The frame we need not take. I would like to have you cut that picture out, and I would like to keep it.'

'No sooner said than done, Comtesse.' Tom rose, crossed to the portrait, and, with the hunting-knife that he had bought in Nice, carefully cut along the four sides of the painting close to the frame. Then he rolled it up and walked back to the side of Renée's bed.

Her blue eyes were swimming in tears. 'Thomas, this has been a very strange, prosaic proposal of marriage.'

'I suppose it has.'

'You haven't kissed me, you have not said you love me, you have not held me in your arms.'

'I suppose it's been because we've just been settling details about something that we have both known for days would surely happen,' Tom said thoughtfully.

'But, Thomas, you *do* love me?'

He gathered her into his arms. 'Angèle,' he breathed, 'I've loved you since I first saw you in the park. I have thought of nothing else, I have dreamed of nothing else. Angèle—'

'Thomas,' she interrupted softly, 'beginning tomorrow morning, I shall of course be Angèle Corton until the day you marry me. From then on, if you like the name Angèle, for the rest of my life I will be Angèle Welles. But, Thomas, just for tonight – just for tonight, Thomas—' She drew him down on to the bed beside her.

'Just to humour me, use the name Renée.' Her arms became even tighter. 'Perhaps you will not understand, but I do not want you to go away from me tonight. I want our first night together to be here at the Castle Garac, and if you are to spend this night in my arms here in this room, it must be with Renée de Garac and not with Angèle Corton. It is thus that I would bid my dream adieu.'

C. S. Forester

THE MAN IN THE YELLOW RAFT
30p

'If Horatio Hornblower had engaged the enemy on an American destroyer during World War II . . . it would have been this kind of taut, vivid action – a salute to courage and endurance!

'His naval expertise is impressive . . . time and again this posthumous collection reminds us, with a pang, what an accomplished literary entertainer Forester became' – THE SUNDAY TIMES

GOLD FROM CRETE
35p

'Nine vivid tales of the Second World War building up to a tense and imaginative climax' – SUNDAY EXPRESS

'A brilliant fictional account of how an invasion in 1940 would have been smashed . . . Forester's story is one of nine that make up this posthumous collection by a master of narrative greatly missed' – EVENING STANDARD

Derek Robinson

GOSHAWK SQUADRON   35p

'You wouldn't know an enemy if he bit you on the arse'

Flying with Woolley is like living with a maniac. Brutal, callous and obscene, he moulds green young pilots into red-eyed, ruthless killers.

For the coming bloodbath, Goshawk Squadron with their patched-up planes must first learn to shoot the Boche in the back ... By 1918, chivalry had long been dead ...

'Uproarious, fast-moving and relentlessly cynical' – THE TIMES

'The most readable novel of the year ... totally authentic' – THE DAILY TELEGRAPH